# THE FAMILY REUNION

BOOKS BY KAREN KING

PSYCHOLOGICAL THRILLERS

*The Stranger in My Bed*

*The Perfect Stepmother*

*The Mother-in-Law*

ROMANTIC COMEDIES

*Snowy Nights at the Lonely Hearts Hotel*

*The Year of Starting Over*

*Single All the Way*

# THE FAMILY REUNION

KAREN KING

bookouture

Published by Bookouture in 2023

An imprint of Storyfire Ltd.
Carmelite House
50 Victoria Embankment
London EC4Y 0DZ

www.bookouture.com



ISBN: 978-1-80314-833-5
eBook ISBN: 978-1-80314-832-8

# 1

## 26TH OCTOBER

### *Mary*

Mary shivered and pulled her raincoat closer around her as an icy gust of wind blasted through her body. She was an idiot sitting out here in the rain, but she had been so desperate to get away from the others, to be out of the tension-filled atmosphere, that she hadn't cared. Thank goodness they were all going home today instead of tomorrow. She'd had quite enough of being cooped up with her warring family and longed for the peace and quiet of her home, and to leave her grown-up children to get on with their own lives. Never again would she suggest a family holiday. Oh, why hadn't she simply booked a nice restaurant for a family meal for her birthday instead of persuading everyone to come to this remote cottage in Dartmoor for a whole long weekend?

*Because you wanted your family to get on and thought that a break together would mend fences.*

Well, instead of bringing them all closer, this holiday had just exposed secrets. Secrets that had blown everyone's life apart. And shown Mary that she couldn't trust any of her children.

She closed her eyes, fighting back the tears. How she had yearned to find Hope over the years. And now she had, and brought her long-lost daughter back into the family fold, hoping to make up for the awful thing she had done, it had all gone dreadfully wrong. Her dreams of a united happy family were shattered.

And on top of that Mary had to face it: the thing she had dreaded for years was actually happening. She had early-onset dementia, like her mother had had before her. She was losing her mind. There was no other reasonable explanation for everything that had happened.

*Creak.*

She glanced nervously over at the bushes as they swayed in the wind. The garden was secure but it was getting dark and it was a big garden. She was out of sight of the cottage here.

*No one would hear me scream.*

She shivered as the words seared into her mind. The hairs prickled on the back of her neck as another creak echoed through the deserted garden. She told herself that it was only the wind blowing through the trees but even so, she felt uneasy and decided to go back inside and join the others. Maybe the atmosphere had settled down now. She stood up, buttoned her jacket and took a deep breath, bracing herself to re-join her fractured family. Then her ears pricked up as suddenly the gate creaked open. One of the others must have gone out for a stroll, also keen to get away from the strained atmosphere. She waited to see who it was as a figure stepped through the gate and the spotlight from the house shone on a man's face. 'Mary.'

She stared at him, puzzled. Who was he? How did he know her name? What was he doing here? She stiffened, her heart pounding. Had he followed her? What did he want?

The man raised his left hand to shield his eyes from the light and a scream rose up in Mary's throat, her heart thudding even faster. She would recognise that snake tattoo winding around his wrist, the head and tongue sliding down his hand, anywhere. She had seen it in her nightmares for years.

How had he found her? Every instinct told her to run but her feet wouldn't move, it was as if they were rooted to the spot. She stifled the scream, her hand flying over her mouth as she stared at him in terror, her eyes fixed on his face. Older now, but yes, the same eyes, the same easy smile. He'd hunted her down, just as she had feared he would. Icicles of fear shot up her spine.

*Run! Run!* Her mind urged her on but still her legs wouldn't move.

'Mary... at last.' His voice was soft as he started walking towards her. He'd always used a soft voice with her, she remembered. She'd thought he was gentle, kind, until she'd seen the other side of him. Seen what violence he was capable of.

'Get away!' she yelled, trembling with fear. 'Don't you dare come near me.'

'I know it's a shock, Mary, but...'

Somehow, she unlocked her legs, backed away from the menacing figure approaching her, turned and fled down the wet path, the scream finally bursting out, her lungs aching with the effort of gasping in air as she raced as fast as she could, fear giving wings to her feet. Hardly able to see through the rain, she bolted around the corner, running for her life towards the safety of the cottage. Surely someone would hear her screaming and come out to see what was happening?

'Mary!' The wind carried his voice and she ran even faster, the memory of the last time she had seen him seared in her mind. His booted foot going in for a final kick. The blood pouring everywhere.

He'd been taken into custody the next day and she had fled

before he was let out, but she had lived in fear all these years that he would come for her. And now he had found her.

She was at the back door now. Sobs retching in her chest, she reached out for the handle then froze as a hand clasped her shoulder and gripped it tight.

# 2

## SIX MONTHS AGO – APRIL

'And I'm delighted to say the Villager of the Year Award goes to Mary Hudson, for her spectacular fund-raising efforts this year, especially with the auction which raised the lump sum of...' Penelope paused for dramatic effect, moving her head so that her smile encompassed everyone in the large village hall. Beside her, the mayor beamed too. 'Five thousand, two hundred and fifty pounds.'

A loud round of applause and a few cheers resounded around the room. Joanne and Jason, standing each side of Mary, clapped ardently. 'Well done, Mum,' Jason whispered.

Mary gave her son a shaky smile. She wished Paul was here, standing by her today, squeezing her hand supportively, telling her how proud he was of her. She fingered the rose charm on the Pandora bracelet he'd bought her for Christmas. The last charm he would ever buy her. She missed him so much. Paul was always loving and supportive; Mary had been so grateful that he had come into her life, and she missed him every single day since he'd been taken from her. They had just celebrated their thirty-eighth anniversary when he had died suddenly from a burst aneurysm. Three long months had passed now and it was still hard to believe her beloved husband was gone. She blinked back the tears that were never far from her eyes as her daughter Joanne lightly touched her arm to get her attention. 'Mum, Penelope's calling you up on stage.'

Mary looked over and saw Penelope smiling at her. 'Could you come up to collect your award, Mary?'

Mary got out of her seat and walked over to the stage, a bright smile fixed on her face. She had been delighted to be nominated for the Villager of the Year award but hadn't expected to win. She didn't need an award; she was happy to raise funds for the Children's Hospital, where she'd worked for many years before she'd taken early retirement last year when Paul, who was ten years older than her, had retired from being a chartered surveyor. They had both planned on taking it easy, travelling, enjoying their retirement together. But Paul had been taken so unexpectedly.

Mary had kept in close contact with the hospital when she'd retired, volunteering one day a week and raising funds in various ways. Such as this auction. The money would be very useful for updating and refurnishing the family room, the much-needed respite area for the families of children in the wards. She hadn't wanted to let them down when Paul died, and organising the auction had given her something to get out of bed for in the morning, taking her mind off the devastating hole Paul's unexpected death had left in her heart and life.

She could feel everyone's eyes upon her as she stepped onto the stage, her family, friends, neighbours all clapping heartily. Joanne and Damien and their two children, Kelly and Connor, by their side. Jason and Alison with their two sons, Oliver and Nicholas. The two little boys were clapping eagerly whereas Kelly and Connor looked slightly embarrassed, as teenagers do. She was sure this wasn't the way they wanted to spend their Sunday afternoon.

'As you all know, Mary works tirelessly to raise funds for the

Children's Hospital. She is a credit to the village and an example to us all,' Penelope announced in her clear, well-enunciated voice. They were only in the village hall but Penelope was a commanding presence and always conducted herself as if she was in a grand theatre.

At this point the mayor stepped forward to pick up a medal resting on a cushion on the table in front of him. A camera flashed as he hung it ceremoniously around Mary's neck before kissing her briefly on the cheek. There was another loud round of applause. Mary smiled, and thanked him politely, managing to keep composed as she turned to face the audience. Villager of the Year. It was something the village had only started a couple of years ago and she felt privileged to be chosen for the award when so many other residents also helped raise money for charity.

If only Paul was still here, he would have been beaming with pride, clapping enthusiastically. And tonight they would have gone out for a special meal at their favourite restaurant to celebrate.

A young girl walked on stage and presented Mary with a beautiful bunch of flowers. As Mary took them from her, the camera flashed again and everyone shouted 'Speech', so Mary took a deep breath. 'Thank you all so much for this award, and the flowers,' she said, her voice wobbling a little. 'And for your support in helping me raise such a wonderful amount for the Children's Hospital.' She swept her gaze around the room. 'I could never have done it without your generosity.'

More applause as she left the stage to re-join Joanne and Jason. Jason gave her a big hug. 'Very well done, Mum. We're so proud of you,' he said. 'And so would Dad be.'

That meant more to her than anything, much more than the award, the flowers. Her family was the most important thing in her life.

Ceremony over with, the buffet was served and everyone

mingled and chatted. Mary sipped her wine slowly and looked around. She was proud of her family. Joanne, always impeccably dressed, was a PA, and Jason was a partner in a thriving IT consultancy company. They both lived a comfortable lifestyle but always had time for others.

A respectable family.

She had done well for herself. Her hard work and determination had paid off.

She took a sip of her cava as she recalled how once it had seemed as if she had lost everything but somehow she had clawed her way out of the abyss.

*You don't deserve it. You're a fraud.*

The thoughts flashed across her mind, unwanted but not totally unexpected. Whenever she managed to succeed at something, earned praise and recognition, the guilt was there, whispering into her ear.

*No one would respect you if they knew your dark secret.*

# 3

'Mary! How lovely to see you out and about. And congratulations, my lovely, for winning the award. So well deserved.'

Mary turned around, a smile already forming on her lips. 'Hello, Stella.'

'Ralph and I have been very worried about you. Paul's death was a big shock to us all, and we know it must be hard for you without him. You were such a devoted couple.' Stella's face brimmed with sympathy. 'Paul was so well-liked and respected.'

Mary nodded, swallowing back the lump that was forming in her throat.

'Don't be a stranger, dear, pop in any time you want some company,' Stella told her, patting her hand. 'We are always delighted to see you.'

She knew that Stella meant it. She and Ralph were old friends of Mary's. Ralph and Paul had been to university together and kept in touch ever since. 'I will,' she promised.

'In fact, we're having a dinner party next month – why don't you come?' asked Stella.

'Thank you but...' She faltered. She wasn't quite ready to socialise yet, not without Paul.

'Too soon? I understand,' Stella said sympathetically. 'You'll join me for a coffee in the café tomorrow, won't you? It would be so good to catch up.'

'Oh go on, Mum. It will do you good,' Joanne urged, catching the tail end of the conversation. Her daughter was right, Mary acknowledged. She had dreaded coming today, but knew she couldn't let everyone down, and it had done her good. She needed to get on with her life.

'I'd love to,' she replied. She'd missed Stella, she felt she could talk to her about anything. Well, almost anything.

'Are you sure you don't want to come back for a while? Maybe stay overnight?' Jason asked as Mary went to leave.

'You're very welcome,' Alison assured her.

'We've invited Mum back to ours too,' Joanne cut in.

When Paul had first died, Mary hadn't been able to face being in the house without him, so she had stopped at both Joanne's and Jason's for a while, taking Bailey, her beloved parakeet, in his cage – but it was too busy, too quarrelsome at Joanne's. Kelly and Connor were always arguing, doors slamming. And she could sense the tension between Joanne and Damien, much as they both tried to hide it. And Jason and Alison had their hands full with Nicholas and Oliver being so young, that Mary felt in the way. She preferred the peace and quiet of her own home even if it did seem empty without Paul.

'Thank you, both of you, but I'm looking forward to going home, putting my feet up and watching a film,' she said. 'I'll see you on Wednesday, Alison.' Wednesdays and Fridays were the days she looked after Nicholas.

'Okay, thanks, Mary,' Alison replied pleasantly.

'If you're sure...' Joanne looked disappointed. 'At least let us take you home, you don't want to carry those flowers and the award home.'

It was only a short walk, but yes, she would be glad of the lift. 'Thank you,' Mary agreed.

Joanne dropped her off at the door. 'Phone me if you need anything,' she said, waiting until Mary opened the door and went inside before waving, then driving off again.

'Hello, hello,' Bailey chirped, hopping about on the perch as soon as she pushed open the door of the lounge. Mary immediately walked over to the cage. 'Hello, Bailey.' She unlatched the cage and the little bird flew out onto her shoulder, cheeping happily.

She was so grateful of the little parakeet's company, a bit of life around the house. Paul had given him to her, along with the cage, three birthdays ago. She'd named him Bailey because the first thing he'd done when she had opened his cage was fly out and dip his beak in Paul's glass of Baileys on the coffee table. They had both soon grown very fond of the cute parakeet, and to Mary's delight he had learnt quite a few phrases. Bailey had now flown over to the armchair that Paul used to sit in and was hopping along the back, chattering. He used to take it in turns to perch on the arms of their chairs, or on both their shoulders, nibbling at their earlobes. Now he had to make do with just her.

The house seemed so empty without Paul. He had been a quiet man, spending his spare time reading, listening to the radio or doing a bit of gardening but he had been a comforting presence in the house, always greeting Mary with a smile, a kiss on the cheek and a hot drink whenever she came home. Or a glass of wine if it was a special occasion, like today. She closed her eyes and stood there for a moment, imagining him hugging her, telling her how proud he was, then taking out the bottle of wine he'd have put in the fridge to chill earlier, opening it, pouring them both a glass. Raising it and saying proudly, 'To you, my darling.'

*Oh Paul, why did you have to die?*

Mary put the bouquet of flowers down on the coffee table

and Bailey immediately flew down to investigate. She walked over to the sideboard and picked up the photograph of Paul in the silver frame, taken a few months before he died. She swallowed a lump in her throat as the much-loved face in the photograph stared back at her. The once-fair hair now silver but still thick, even though Paul had been almost seventy, the still-handsome face rather weathered with fine age lines around the blue eyes and mouth. Paul had been a good, kind man, but also one who was very aware of appearances, of his social standing, which was why Mary had always been terrified of him finding out her past, convinced that he would be appalled and it would destroy their marriage. She loved him too much to risk losing him, then cruelly and unexpectedly he'd been taken from her. His sudden death from a burst aneurysm three months previously had taken everyone by surprise, especially Mary. Paul had complained of a headache and a stiff neck but apart from that had been his normal, cheerful self. The following morning he'd been sick and said the headache was getting worse. Then he'd slumped in his chair before her frightened eyes and she was frantically dialling an ambulance. Paul had died before he even reached hospital. Joanne and Jason had been devastated, as had Mary's grandchildren. Mary felt as if her heart had been ripped out and her body was just a shell going through the motions each day. Paul was the love of her life. They had been together since she was twenty, meeting when he had come into the hospital where Mary was working as a nursing assistant, to visit his niece, Yvonne. Mary had been struck by his kindness, his laugh, his good looks. Paul said that the first thing he had noticed about Mary was the sadness in her eyes.

Paul often visited Yvonne, and always stopped to talk to Mary if she was on duty. When Yvonne was discharged, Paul asked Mary for a date. She had been about to refuse – she never dated, preferring to keep men at arm's length since Robbie – but there was something about Paul, something that told her she could trust him, that made her want to find out more about him, so she'd accepted. They had dated for two years before they married and Joanne had come along three years later. As she had held her little daughter in her arms, tears had flowed down Mary's cheeks, and she'd sworn that no one would ever harm her little girl. She would protect her precious baby with her life. It was the same when she had Jason two years later.

Paul was a good husband and father and they were happy together. They'd got engaged in the Eighties; no one back then expected their partner to have never had another lover by their twenties, so all Paul asked her was if she'd ever been engaged before, and she'd said she hadn't, which was the truth. 'I have, but my fiancée went off with someone else,' he confessed. 'I had to tell you, I don't want there to be secrets between us.'

'You don't have to tell me anything. The past is the past,' she'd replied. She didn't want him to unburden his secrets to her because she had no intention of telling him hers.

Mary had taken a break from working until Joanne and Jason started school and then had returned to work, later qualifying as a nurse.

This large, detached house was full of memories of the years they had spent together, raising their two children, entertaining their friends. Paul's clothes still hung in his wardrobe, his photos were everywhere. And every night Mary listened to the last answerphone message he'd left on her phone. 'On my way home now, darling. See you soon. Love you.' She was grateful that she'd been too busy preparing their dinner to answer the phone that day, as it meant that now she had a permanent memory of his voice. He'd left the message a couple of days before he died but although she usually deleted the messages once she'd heard them, this time she hadn't. It was as if she'd subconsciously known that it was the last message Paul would ever leave her. After he died, that answerphone message – being able to play it and hear Paul's clear, calm voice telling her that he loved her – had been a lifesaver for Mary.

In the long, dark days after Paul's death, Mary had wanted to hide away, bury herself in the comfort of their family home. Joanne and Jason had persuaded her to get on with her life, to continue her charity work. 'Dad wouldn't want you to grieve like this, Mum,' Jason had told her.

Joanne had suggested she sell the house and move in with them. A real daddy's girl, she was still struggling with Paul's death, but Mary wanted to keep her independence. She loved her children and grandchildren but she didn't want to live with them. Family life was too noisy for her now, she liked to go home to her own house and potter about.

'Promise me you'll go out this week,' Jason had said when he found her sobbing at home a couple of weeks after Paul had died. 'Meet your friends for a coffee, have a walk around the shops. Just get out of the house.' She could see the anxiety in his eyes, blue like Paul's had been.

She'd nodded. 'I will.' Jason was right, it was time she lived her life again. She had a loving family, good friends, and lived in a gorgeous village on the outskirts of Solihull. She was lucky. Especially when she remembered how her life could have been. Paul had gone and she would miss him forever but somehow she had to carry on. It was what he would have wanted. So she had gone back to her volunteering, arranging the auction that had raised so much money.

Alison, Jason's wife, was lovely. She had popped in this morning to do Mary's makeup and hair for this afternoon. When she'd suggested a few weeks ago that Mary look after three-year-old Nicholas a couple of days a week while she worked to give her something to focus on, Mary had readily agreed. She enjoyed spending time with her little grandson, even if it was exhausting trying to keep up with him. Nicholas was full of joyful energy. The day whizzed by when she looked after him and she was so tired when she went to bed that she fell straight to sleep without her sleeping pills.

Mary looked at the photo again, Paul's eyes shining tenderly out at her, then placed it back down on the sideboard and went to put the flowers in water.

Later, when she got into bed, she reached for her phone and replayed Paul's last message, tears welling in her eyes. She knew that her grief over Paul would never disappear but it was time to live her life again. It had been good to be out in the community today, and it had made her realise that it was time to do something she hadn't dared do while Paul was alive. She hadn't been brave enough to take the chance, to risk ruining the wonderful life they all had. But now Paul had gone she had nothing to lose.

It was time to face her past.

# 4

Mary woke the next morning to the sun dancing through the half-open curtains and shining on the framed photo of Paul she kept on the cabinet by her side of the bed. It was as if he was smiling at her, telling her to embrace the day. She reached out and picked up the photo, her heart breaking again as her eyes rested on the face she had woken up to for thirty-eight years. She missed him terribly.

She had to look forward, though, and get on with her life. She would be sixty this birthday, which was no age; she had years ahead of her. People started new careers at sixty – or went back to old ones. She could do that, go back to nursing. It was something to think about. But first she had to deal with her past. She got out of bed and went straight down into the kitchen to make a cup of tea. After flicking the kettle on, she went into the lounge and took the cover off Bailey's cage. 'Hello,' he chirped, fluffing up his wings, delighted to see her.

'Morning, Bailey,' she said, a smile already springing to her lips at the little bird's antics. She knew that he wanted to come out of his cage but she had things to do first. She gave him a treat then went back into the kitchen, grabbing a cup out of the cupboard and popping a tea bag into it as the kettle came to the boil. Tea made, she took a screwdriver from the drawer by the sink and went back into the bedroom. Taking a sip of the tea, she put the cup down on the bedside cabinet then knelt down and unscrewed the plinth at the bottom of the wardrobe and took out the small, battered biscuit tin. She carried it over to the bed, sat down and opened it up, the tears flowing down her cheeks as the memories came flooding back. Her precious baby, her firstborn. If only she had been able to keep her. Hope she'd called her little daughter – the only thing she could give her. Hope for a better life. Hope that someone would love and look after her because she, her mother, couldn't.

Forty-five years had passed; Hope might not even be alive. Mary's heart sank at the thought. *Be positive*, she told herself. There was every chance that Hope was still alive. And she was going to find her.

She carefully looked at the mementos in the tin one by one: the small envelope, yellowed now, containing the lock of dark hair tied with a white ribbon; the black and white Polaroid image of the baby with her tuft of dark hair fading but still visible, the white flannel she had washed her baby with, and finally a large envelope containing some newspaper cuttings, a black and white photo of herself when she was pregnant and another photo that she never wanted to look at again but couldn't bring herself to destroy.

Paul had never known about this part of her past. No one did. The pain of having to give up her baby had been almost too much to bear so she had buried it, closing the door on that part of her life, but every now and again the door had opened, whenever she passed a baby in the early years, every 21st November – Hope's birthday – when Joanne was born, then Jason, and her grandchildren. There were times when the longing to find her first daughter had overwhelmed her and she had almost confessed all to Paul, but she had been too scared of his reaction, of losing him. Now Paul had gone, and while Joanne and Jason might be shocked and disapprove, Mary knew she had to find Hope. To reunite her family.

She fetched her iPad and, sipping her tea, did an internet search on 'finding lost families'. She found several websites, and was astounded at how many people were looking for lost family members. Many of them had simply lost touch over the years, some had been adopted as babies, but others were foundlings, abandoned with no knowledge of their background. Like Hope. Some of the stories were heart-breaking. It was sad yet comforting in a way that she wasn't the only person who hadn't been able to look after their baby. She had loved Hope so much, she hoped that when she finally found her daughter she could assure her of that.

She spent the morning browsing the websites, and leaving a message on a few boards, hoping that if Hope was looking for her she would see them and respond.

After a couple of rounds of toast – giving Bailey the corner of the crust as he loved to chew on it – and a shower, she set off to meet Stella.

They had a coffee and a slice of Victoria sponge while they chatted. Stella was genuinely interested in how Mary was feeling and she felt a little guilty that she had shut her friend out the last couple of months. 'Absolutely no need to apologise, you've been grieving,' Stella reassured her when Mary apologised for not being in touch, or returning her many texts and calls. 'Do remember that I'm always here for you, though. Any time, day or night.'

'I know. Thank you. I'm coming through it now,' Mary told her. It was good to see her friend, and to be out again. For a moment she was tempted to tell Stella about Hope but she decided against it, knowing how much Stella liked to gossip. She'd wait until she found Hope before she told anyone.

She checked the message boards when she returned, hoping

for a reply, but there was nothing. Well, it had only been a few hours. She felt more at peace now she'd taken that step.

---

The week passed by, then another and another, with still no response to her messages. Mary's hopes were dashed as each day passed. It occurred to her that Hope might not have seen the messages, that perhaps she didn't even know about the message boards, but then surely that meant she wasn't searching for her mother. If Hope was still alive it seemed that she didn't want to be found. She hoped that was because she was happy in her life, had loving adoptive parents and a family of her own and wasn't interested in finding the mother who hadn't wanted her.

Except that Mary had wanted her. She had wanted her very much.

There were other things she could do to find Hope, tracing services you could pay for, but Mary had decided against that. If Hope didn't want to be found then didn't she owe it to her to leave her alone and allow her to live her life? She had no idea how disrupting it would be for Hope to have her birth mother burst into her life. No, she would leave the messages on the board hoping that if one day Hope wanted to find her, she would see them. If not, then she simply had to accept that she had given up her right to have any part in her firstborn's life, and at least she had tried to find her.

She had resigned herself to this when one day at the end of May she received a message.

> *I think you're my mum. I was abandoned in a telephone box in Birmingham in 1977 wrapped in a lemon blanket and with a note saying 'I'm Hope, please look after me'.*

Mary read it three times, hardly believing the words she saw. The writer had also described all the items Mary had left with baby Hope and even named the shopping centre where Mary had left her. There could be no mistake.

She had found her daughter.

# 5

The thought of meeting Hope occupied Mary's mind all day. She had never forgiven herself for giving her baby away, despite reminding herself that she had been young, alone, and her strict father would have thrown her out. Her mother had died three years earlier and it was amazing how easily Mary had slipped into her shoes, cleaning the house, cooking the meals, while trying to keep up with her schoolwork. She had felt so exhausted, so alone. Her father never noticed her, apart from to shout or lash out when she did something wrong such as messing up a meal or not cleaning up properly. He worked long hours and was tired when he finally got home, eating his meal in silence while he watched the TV. Mary felt lonely and unloved until she met Robbie. He'd turned up one week with a bunch of his biker mates at the café she worked at on Saturdays to earn some money to buy the essentials she needed and didn't want to ask her father for. She'd been fascinated by them, all dressed in black leather biker jackets, adorned with fringes and studs, the girls wearing jeans or short skirts with black-lined eyes and pale makeup. They'd all been so loud, so carefree, so unconventional. How she'd wished she had a gang of friends like them, that she had the freedom to dress and act how she wanted. Her father was so strict. He had a fit if she wore a dress that showed her knees, or a smidgen of lipstick. He had always been prone to violent rages and Mary was scared to disobey him, especially now her mother wasn't there to talk him down.

Her eyes strayed to a tall youth, long raven-black hair resting on his shoulders, knee-high black leather boots, his black leather jacket open to reveal a black T-shirt with a skull and crossbones on the front. He was leaning over, talking to a gorgeous girl with wavy chestnut hair when suddenly, as if sensing Mary's stare, he looked up and his dark brown eyes met hers. She was transfixed. The intensity of his gaze held her captive, she couldn't move. Then he smiled, a slow smile, and returned back to his conversation with the other girl.

The next Saturday they came in again and the guy strolled over to the counter and ordered a can of Coke. As he handed Mary the money, she noticed the snake tattoo winding around his wrist, the head and tongue sliding down his hand. Fascinated, she couldn't tear her eyes away until she realised that he was talking to her. 'Want to come for a spin on my bike when you've finished your shift?' he asked casually.

Hardly believing that someone like him could be interested in her, she replied, 'Sure, I'll be finished at five,' as nonchalantly as she could.

At five o'clock, he came back alone, ordered another Coke and waited for her. She got on the back of his bike without even asking where they were going and they sped off into the night. He kissed her that night, so passionately that she felt herself melt in his arms and eagerly agreed to see him again.

After that they'd seen each other most evenings, when Mary's dad was at work, and soon she was one of the gang. Robbie's girl. He said he loved her, and she gave in far too quickly to his demands for sex because she loved him too and didn't want to lose him to one of the other girls who were happy to 'put out' as he called it. A few months later, she realised that she was pregnant. She didn't want to face it at first, the consequences if her father found out were terrifying. She had never told Robbie where she lived, they always met at a local shopping precinct.

One night, she set out to meet him, determined to tell him about the baby. It was his baby too and he loved her. They would work something out.

She closed her eyes tightly now to block out the memory of that night. She had buried it so deep that even now she couldn't bear to remember it.

A few days later she had read in the local newspaper that Robbie had been sent to prison for two years for stealing and crashing a car. He should have got life, *would* have got life if anyone had known the dreadful thing she knew he had really done but she was too scared to tell anyone. Terrified, she had stayed in her house apart from going to the local shops, hiding her pregnancy with baggy winter clothes until the day she gave birth alone. And abandoned her baby.

Then she'd tried to put it all behind her and get on with her life, training to be a nurse, wanting in a way to 'give back', to atone for abandoning her baby by helping others.

But now she'd found Hope. And surely her daughter would want to know who her father was?

She would tell her that they had loved each other but he died, Mary decided. There was no need for her to go into more detail than that, for her to know the monster her father was.

# 6

## FOUR MONTHS AGO – MID JUNE

Mary took out her phone and swiped to the photo of Cathy – as Hope was now called – that her long-lost daughter had sent, scanning her face for any likeness to herself or Robbie. She had dark hair and brown eyes like him, and a small, upturned nose like Mary. She'd often wondered if Hope's eyes had remained blue or turned brown like Robbie's.

It seemed so strange to see this photo of an adult woman and know it was Hope. Her memory of her daughter was as a tiny baby, and here she was old enough to have children, maybe even grandchildren of her own. All that growing up Mary had missed out on, possibly more family who she had never met.

She'd sent Hope – Cathy, she corrected herself, she was Cathy now – a photo of herself too. She wondered what Cathy had thought of it. Was she as eager to see her birth mother as Mary was to see her? She had signed up to the message boards, though, Mary reminded herself, which meant she had wanted to find her mother but that could be because she was full of anger at how she had been abandoned and wanted to tell Mary what she thought of her. Cathy had arranged a DNA test to prove that they were mother and daughter before they met up.

They had both sent a sample of their hair in an envelope to the test centre and the results had confirmed it, but Mary already knew that Cathy was her daughter. The details she'd provided of her birth, the yellow blanket, the note, all proved it.

She swallowed, feeling nauseous as the memory of that night resurged. Whatever Cathy's reaction was she had to face it, try to explain to her how frightened and alone sixteen-year-old Mary had been back then and pray that her daughter would understand, and forgive her, even though Mary had never forgiven herself.

She hadn't felt this nervous since her wedding day to Paul, when she'd been convinced that something would happen to prevent him from turning up, that she wouldn't be allowed to experience such happiness. Happiness was for other people, not her. She wished Paul was here with her now, he had always known the words to make her feel better. Except that Paul hadn't known about her abandoned daughter, had he? At first she didn't tell him because it was too awful for her to face up to. She buried it for years, compartmentalising it in a box labelled 'past' and never opening it. No one knew her terrible secret and she wanted to keep it that way. As the years passed it became even harder to have the conversation – she didn't want to upset their happy, stable marriage – but it also became more difficult to push Hope to the back of her mind. When she gave birth to Joanne and looked at her little face, she remembered Hope's eyes looking at her and the intense love she'd felt for her. The knowledge that she'd let her first baby down so badly had made the tears spill down her cheeks, and once she started crying she couldn't stop. The midwife said that mothers were often emotional after giving birth. Paul had been so kind and hugged her tight.

The same thing happened when she had given birth to Jason. Every progress they both made, their first smile, their first step, Mary tortured herself with how she had missed all this with Hope. Her only comfort was that she had seen a newspaper report that Hope had been adopted, there were no more details, but at least she knew that her baby was probably being brought up by a loving couple who couldn't have children of their own and would love and look after her. Something Mary hadn't been able to do. Somehow, she managed to soldier on, even though it felt like a part of her heart had been ripped out. As Joanne and Jason got older, and had children of their own, the longing to find Hope grew stronger and stronger, but she still didn't dare act on it. She couldn't bear to see the disappointment in Paul's eyes when she told him her dark secret, maybe even risking losing him if he felt that he couldn't cope with the dreadful thing that she'd done. She was worried about Joanne and Jason's reaction too, but today she wasn't going to think about that. Today was about meeting Hope. Or rather, Cathy.

They'd arranged to meet in a café in town. It seemed friendlier, less intimidating than a restaurant. Mary fretted about what to wear, finally selecting white linen trousers and a summer print top, wanting to look casual but smart.

The café was fairly empty when she walked in. She glanced around, but there was no sign of Cathy. She ordered herself a coffee and sat down at a table near the door, so she wouldn't miss her coming in. Five minutes passed, then ten. She'd been deliberately early but couldn't help worrying that maybe Cathy had changed her mind and decided not to come after all. She sipped her coffee slowly, trying to make it last, trying to ease the worries swimming around in her mind. Then, as she drained that last drop, the door swung open and Cathy walked in. She was tall as Robbie had been, her long legs clad in jeans and black leather boots. Just like her father had worn the first time she'd seen him, except Cathy wasn't wearing a leather jacket, but a white T-shirt, her long dark hair spilling over the shoulders. Again it hit Mary how grown up she was, her little baby gone forever. And how different to her other children, Joanne and Jason, who had both inherited Mary and Paul's blonde hair and blue eyes. Cathy turned to look around and her eyes found Mary's, deep brown eyes like Robbie's. Mary's breath caught in her throat as they stared at each other for a moment. Her daughter. Her firstborn. She was overwhelmed by emotion. She took a deep breath and stood up to greet Cathy as she strode over to the table. She longed to run towards her daughter, to embrace her, but Cathy looked guarded, distant.

'Hello, Mary,' Cathy said.

Mary could feel the tears brimming in her eyes and took a moment to compose herself before smiling. 'Hope.' She saw the frown cross her face and instantly realised her mistake. 'Sorry. I mean Cathy. It's just that I'm used to thinking of you as Hope.' Her mouth suddenly dry with fear, she swallowed then smiled. 'It's so good to see you. Thank you for coming. Shall we sit down?'

Cathy nodded briefly, then pulled out the chair opposite and sat down.

'I can't tell you how much it means to me to see you.' Mary reached out and touched her hand. She couldn't help herself. She wanted to check that she was real, her baby girl, all grown up, sitting opposite her. Cathy hesitated for a moment and Mary thought that she was going to snatch her hand away but she left it there. 'You must have lots of questions,' Mary said tentatively.

'Only two,' Cathy replied curtly, levelling her gaze at her. 'Tell me why it took you so long to try to find me. And why you gave me away in the first place.'

'I didn't want to give you up.' Mary's eyes were brimming with tears as they rested on Cathy's impassive face. Would her dear, lost daughter ever forgive her? 'I loved you from the moment I saw you but I knew that I couldn't keep you.'

She waited until the waiter brought the coffee Cathy ordered, then haltingly she related the whole story to her.

# 7

## NOVEMBER 1977

Mary clutched her stomach, almost bent over double with the pain. She didn't know what to do. The pains had been getting stronger and stronger which must mean that the baby was coming. She was terrified. She was all alone, her dad was at work and she didn't dare call him and tell him what was happening. He'd be furious. He'd disown her. She screamed as another pain tore through her. She knew nothing about having a baby but somehow she had to bring her child into the world.

*Please God help me.*

She grimaced; the pains were relentless now. If only her mum was still alive. She would have been disappointed in Mary, but she would have helped her. If her mum was still here she might never have been driven to seek love in Robbie's arms at all.

'I'll love you forever. I'll look after you,' Robbie had promised.

It was a big fat horrible lie.

She could feel the sweat on her forehead. She gulped deep breaths, trying to calm herself down. She cast her mind back to the films she'd watched with scenes of a woman giving birth.

They never went into much detail, of course, but she remembered the screaming, the midwife telling them to take deep breaths, and to push. That's how Mary felt, that she wanted to push. How long before the baby would come out? What the hell should she do?

Another wave of pain seared through her. She took deep breaths, trying to breathe her way through it as it said in the book she'd sneaked a look at in the library last week. It also said that she would need something to cut the baby's cord when it was born and something to tie it with, so she'd bought a pair of thick shoelaces in readiness. Almost bent double with pain, she clutched her stomach, and shuffled to the kitchen. She lit the gas hob to re-boil the kettle, crying as another wave of pain scorched through her, then took a pair of scissors out of the drawer and a cup out of the cupboard. It seemed to take ages for the kettle to whistle but finally it did and she removed the top, pouring the boiling water into the cup then placing the scissors, blades down into the scalding water. Another contraction. Tears filled her eyes. She couldn't believe this was happening. She'd been in denial for so long, ever since that awful night...

She yelped as another pain ripped through her, clutching the work surface for support. The pains had begun just after her dad left for work that morning. She had known instantly that the baby was on the way so had taken a clean towel out of the airing cupboard to wrap the baby in, and put it in the navy shopping bag she'd had hidden under her bed for ages, containing the soft yellow blanket, the shoelaces and the thick plastic tablecloth she'd bought from a jumble sale a few weeks ago. She wished the towel was softer and the blanket a new one but there was no money to spare for new towels or baby blankets. It would have to do. She should have taken a bigger towel to lie on too but at that point, she couldn't manage to walk up the stairs again. She glanced at the clock. It had only been two hours since she took the last paracetamols but she really needed more pain relief. She wished she had waited a little longer before taking them. She hadn't realised how bad the pain would get. How could women keep having babies when they had to cope with so much pain? She took a clean tea towel out of the drawer and rolled it up so that she could put it between her teeth to bite on, something else she'd seen in a film, hoping this would stop her screaming. She didn't think any of the neighbours were in. Everyone should be at work, but even so she didn't want to risk it. She couldn't let anyone know what was happening.

Another pain shot through her and she felt a strong urge to push. Her legs were buckling underneath her. The baby wasn't going to wait much longer. She took the plastic tablecloth and shoelaces out of the bag and laid them down on the kitchen floor as another contraction built. Then she gripped the handle of the cup of boiling water containing the scissors and carefully put it down on the floor by the edge of the tablecloth. She was shaking now. She couldn't believe this was happening but somehow she had to get through it.

*Keep calm. Breathe. It will be okay.*

She managed to lie down then put the rolled-up tea towel between her teeth and bit down hard on it, praying for the God she didn't believe in but hoped existed to help her. Then another pain flooded through her and she felt an uncontrollable urge to push hard...

Mary felt like she was being torn apart as the baby shot out. She heard it cry and tears of relief poured down her cheeks. Thank God! Her baby was alive. Her heart was racing but she took deep breaths, trying to keep calm, remembering that she still had to deliver the placenta then cut the cord and tie it. She gently lifted the baby onto her tummy, smiling when she saw that it was a little girl. Love consumed her as she looked at the baby's tiny blood-smeared face, eyes squeezed shut, fists clenched, screaming angrily as if she was furious that Mary had brought her into this cruel world knowing that she couldn't keep her.

And she desperately wanted to keep her. So very very much that she thought her heart would break.

She pushed the grief away. She had to concentrate. The book said that pressing the stomach should ease the placenta out so that's what she did. More pain and her baby was crying so loud. This was worse than she had ever dreamt possible.

The placenta was out. She couldn't bear to look at the horrible mess, she didn't know what to do with it. And now she had to cut the cord. The thought terrified her but she knew it had to be done.

*Keep the baby higher than the cord and don't cut it too short, then you'll be okay*, she reminded herself as she tied one shoelace around the placenta a few inches from the baby and the other lace a little further down, then picked up the scissors. Keeping them steady, she cut the cord. Then she held her baby against her chest. Her beautiful daughter. Her eyes were open now, cornflower blue and fixed on Mary's face. Oh God, she loved her so much. How could she give her up? She couldn't bear it. She kissed her on the forehead. 'I'm so sorry, darling. Really I am,' she whispered. 'I wish I could keep you.'

The baby felt cold, even though Mary had put the electric fire on, so she placed her carefully on a clean part of the tablecloth and reached for the towel. She needed to wash her. Somehow she found the strength to get up and clean her baby with the bowl of lukewarm water and flannel, then wrapped her in a towel. Next, she washed herself, putting on the clean underclothes and sanitary towel she had ready and waiting. She looked at the clock. Her father wouldn't be home for another two hours. She had time to hold her baby for a while.

She carried the baby into the lounge, and placed her on the sofa where she would be safe while she quickly cleaned up. It had been a good idea to use the plastic tablecloth; there was no mess on the floor. No sign that a new life had just been started here. She wrapped the tablecloth around the placenta and, after putting it in a carrier bag, took it out to the dustbin, burying it amongst the rubbish so it wasn't visible. The dustbin men would come tomorrow so it would be gone then. She hurried back inside, washed her hands and went back to her baby, taking the towel off her and wrapping her tiny body in the lemon blanket. She sat down and cuddled her tight.

'I love you, little girl,' she told her, tears flowing down her cheeks. 'I love you so much. I wish I could keep you.'

The baby's blue eyes were fixed on Mary's face as if she understood every word. She was so beautiful. So perfect. And so defenceless. Mary wanted to keep her so much her heart ached but she knew it was impossible. Her dad didn't know about Robbie. If he had he would have forbidden her to see him but she wouldn't have listened. She was bowled over by eighteen-year-old Robbie, had fallen hopelessly in love with him.

She held the baby tight. 'I'm sorry I can't keep you. I hope you have a lovely life. I hope you get adopted by parents who really love you. I hope...' Her voice trailed off as she looked down at the baby's sweet little face. She wanted to give her a name. It was the least she could do. 'Hope,' she whispered to her. 'I'm going to call you Hope.' She kissed her forehead and cried because she desperately wanted to keep her. 'I pray that your name brings you luck and that you have a good life, full of hope and love,' she told her.

She looked at the clock and saw that an hour had gone already. Hope was whimpering now, her fist to her mouth. She was hungry. Instinctively, Mary put the baby to her breast and Hope suckled. She smiled at her beloved baby, tears flowing down her face, and nursed her for a few precious minutes. Then she placed her down on the sofa again and went to fetch her bag. She took out the dummy she'd bought – white so it would be okay for either sex – unwrapped it then went over to the kettle to put boiling water over it, remembering that everything had to be sterilised. When it had cooled down, Mary put the dummy in Hope's tiny rosebud mouth and the baby sucked on it eagerly. She picked up her Polaroid camera from the coffee table where she'd placed it earlier, along with a white postcard and a black biro, and took a photo of Hope, wanting a permanent memory of her baby girl. She waited eagerly for the photo to pop out. When it did, she held it carefully by the corners and placed it on the table to dry, then picked up the black pen and wrote neatly on the postcard in capitals. 'Please look after Hope because I can't.'

She washed the tears from her face and tidied her hair in case she bumped into someone, then placed Hope, still wrapped in the blanket and sucking the dummy, into the shopping bag with the postcard, and placed the now-dry photo in her pocket.

'Please don't cry,' she whispered to Hope. After pulling on her coat and slipping her feet into her shoes, Mary let herself out of the back door, holding the bag close as she walked up the back garden, out of the gate and down the street. It was dark and quiet. She turned the corner to the bus stop, relieved to see the bus approaching. She knew where she was leaving Hope. She'd been thinking about it for weeks. Her baby would soon be found there. Mary couldn't bear to think of Hope being all alone, cold and hungry.

Three stops and she was off the bus. She walked slowly down the street. There were a few people about and she didn't want to look suspicious. She knew that the press would report about Hope, that the authorities would try to find her mother so Mary had to fade into the background and not do anything that could draw attention to herself, make anyone remember her.

At last she was at the shopping centre, and to her relief the telephone box was empty. She opened the door and stepped inside, then put the bag down and picked up the receiver, memorising the number on the dial as she pretended that she was making a telephone call. She looked around constantly. It was quiet, but there were a few people walking around. She wanted to take Hope out of the bag and give her a last kiss but didn't dare so she whispered, 'I love you, Hope,' then she walked out, leaving the bag containing her baby inside. She walked over to the other phone box nearby and dialled the number she had just memorised. She watched, willing someone to come past and answer the phone. It was cold. Even though Hope was wrapped up in the bag, she would freeze if she was left for long.

Mary's heart skipped a beat as a lady walked over to the phone box and opened the door. She held her breath as the lady walked inside, picked up the receiver then dropped it as she looked down at the bag. Mary crossed her fingers; maybe Hope had cried and alerted her. The lady picked up the bag and opened it, a look of shock on her face and Mary breathed a sigh of relief. Her baby was safe now. Tears flowed down her cheeks and she wiped them away with her sleeve. She couldn't let anyone see her cry. She couldn't let anyone guess the dreadful thing she'd done. Pulling herself together, she caught the bus home, getting back in time to wash her face and get a meal cooking for her father.

But later, when she was in bed that night, she buried her head in her pillow, clutching the white flannel that she'd washed the baby with in her hands and let the tears come, for the baby who had been hers for such a short time and who she would never see again, and for herself, for the terrible thing she had been forced to do. Her heart was breaking and it felt like it would never mend.

# 8

As Cathy listened, Mary noticed, with relief, that the expression on her face softened.

'Didn't you ever think of me again once you'd dumped me?'

Mary flinched at the question. 'Always. I know it seems like I heartlessly abandoned you but I left you in a safe place where I knew you would soon be discovered. And I waited and watched nearby until you were,' she reminded her. 'I was so young, so scared. So desperate.' She looked imploringly at Cathy. 'I hope you can forgive me. I really did – do – love you very much. I was desperate to find out what had happened after the lady had found you. I searched the newspapers for stories about you.' She opened her handbag and took out a brown envelope, taking out several yellowed newspaper clippings and putting them on the table in front of us. 'See, I kept all these. I was so anxious to know whether you had someone to care for you, a loving home. All I wanted was for you to be happy, to have a good life. To have parents that loved you.'

Cathy picked up one of the clippings and read it. 'Newborn baby girl abandoned in telephone box' it shouted, there was a grainy black and white photo of a woman holding a baby wrapped in a blanket. Mary looked at the photo and swallowed back the lump in her throat. Would Cathy ever believe that she hadn't wanted to give her up but that she'd had no option?

'I still have that blanket and the dummy,' Cathy whispered. 'It made me think that perhaps you did care for me a little as you'd wrapped me up to try and keep me warm and you gave me a dummy to comfort me.'

'You kept them?' Mary again fought back the urge to wrap her arms around her daughter at this news. Cathy seemed to be softening a little but she wasn't sure that she was ready for a hug yet. 'I loved you so much. And I longed to keep you but I knew that I couldn't. I cleaned you up and fed and cuddled you, hanging on to every precious moment I had with you. It broke my heart to let you go but...' Mary took a moment to compose herself before continuing. 'I kept a lock of your hair, look. And took a photograph of you.' She passed the envelope with the lock of hair, and the faded Polaroid photo over to Cathy and saw her daughter's face soften. She'd kept them in the biscuit tin, along with the newspaper cuttings, now placed in the bottom of her wardrobe as she no longer had to hide it from Paul. She'd been hoping that one day she would meet her lost daughter and could show it to her, let her know that she had loved her and had wanted a permanent memory of her.

'I was so happy when I read that you'd been adopted. I knew then that I'd done the right thing, you would be loved and cherished, would have a happy life.' She fixed her eyes worriedly on Cathy's face. 'You have had a happy life, haven't you?'

Mary saw a flicker of something – hurt? – cross her face. Oh, God. She raised her hand to her mouth. Had Cathy been unhappy? But Cathy was nodding. 'My adoptive parents were very kind to me,' she said.

Relief washed over Mary. 'Oh thank goodness for that. It's all I wanted for you.'

'What about my father?' Cathy asked. 'Did you ever tell him about me?'

Robbie. Mary picked up her coffee as her mind went back to the lad she'd fallen head over heels for. She took a long sip before shaking her head. 'He was eighteen, older than me. We loved each other, but... he died. A motorbike accident.' Her hand shook, rattling the cup on the saucer, as she came out with the lie but she knew that it was better, safer, than the truth. Even now she could remember vividly how horrified she had been when she had realised what Robbie was really like and that she would have to deal with the pregnancy alone.

They were both silent for a while, sipping their coffee then Cathy asked, 'Do you at least have a photo of him?' she asked.

Mary had guessed she would ask that and had wondered whether to bring the photo of her and Robbie with her but had decided against it. She didn't want Cathy to be able to find out anything about her father, to learn what he had done.

'No I haven't. Sorry. We didn't take many photos back then.'

'What did he look like?' she asked.

An image of Robbie flashed into her mind, long legs astride his motorbike, his dark hair flopping across his eyes and curling at the nape of his neck, the zip of his leather jacket open to reveal a black T-shirt with a skull on the front, knee-high black leather boots, the snake tattoo winding around his wrist and onto his hand. He looked wild. Why hadn't she seen that then? Or maybe it was the wildness that had attracted her, when life with her dad was so empty and controlled. Another image flashed across her mind, his face that night... She screwed her eyes tight.

'Mary?'

She opened her eyes and shook her head. 'Dark hair and brown eyes, like you.' She hoped that's where the likeness stopped, that Cathy didn't have Robbie's temperament. 'He was tall, good-looking. A bit cocky.' She smiled ruefully. 'Typical eighteen-year-old, I guess.'

Cathy's eyes never left her face, as if she was drinking in every word. Mary couldn't – wouldn't – tell her what her father was really like. 'Do you have a photo of you back then?'

'I have one of me when I was pregnant with you.'

Cathy's eyes lit up. 'Really?'

Mary took out the small black and white photo she'd slipped into her purse that morning, and placed it on the table in front of Cathy. She looked so young, her long blonde hair spilling onto her shoulders. Cathy picked it up and studied it. 'You were just a child. Did my dad die before I was born?'

Mary swallowed and nodded. Another lie. But a necessary one.

'Tell me what you remember about him. Please.'

'He was part of a local motorbike gang.' She screwed up the napkin in her hand. 'I told you my dad was terribly strict, and Robbie and his gang, they seemed so free, they did whatever they wanted. I felt like I belonged somewhere when I was with them.'

'Do you think you would have got married if he hadn't died?'

'I don't know. I never got the chance to tell him about you. And I would have needed my dad's permission. He would never have agreed. He would probably have sent me to some mother and baby home to have you adopted.' Maybe that would have been better, who knew? 'I moved away afterwards, tried to put it behind me, told myself you were better off without me. I started training to be a nurse, living in the nurses' hostel. I wanted to give back, I guess, to the nurses who helped look after you when the woman who found you took you to hospital.'

'So what then? You got married? Had more children?'

'Yes, a few years later, I married Paul. We met when he came to hospital to visit his niece and we hit it off right away.

We have two children, Joanne and Jason. They are grown up now with children of their own. Joanne is thirty-five and Jason is thirty.' It felt important that Cathy knew she had waited quite a long time before she had any more children. That she hadn't just abandoned her then gone off to have another child which she had decided to keep.

She watched, guilt eating into her as Cathy ran her finger around the coffee cup. What was she thinking? It sounded so callous, so cruel that she had abandoned her firstborn then gone on to have two more children, children she had kept, loved, cared for. 'I really am very sorry. I would have kept you if there had been a way but I was so young... and my father.' She fought to control her emotions. She would not cry; that would just look like she was trying to manipulate the situation. 'I'm so glad it all worked out for you. I've tortured myself for years about abandoning you, wondered what sort of life you had.' Mary sat back in her chair and took a good look at her beautiful daughter all grown up but still her baby. 'Now you must tell me more about yourself. Do you have children?'

Cathy took a moment to reply and when she finally did it sounded as if the word was being forced out of her. 'No.'

She offered no explanation and Mary's head swam with questions. Was it by choice? Had being abandoned at birth scarred her so much that she didn't want children of her own? She had kind adoptive parents, though; she'd had a good life, she reminded herself. Maybe she couldn't have children. Or had never met the right person. Much as she wanted answers, Mary didn't feel that she had the right to ask the questions. It would be so tragic if Cathy couldn't have children, when Mary had had her at such a young age and callously abandoned her.

Not callously. Forced to. It had been heart-breaking and she had been terrified.

'I really am so sorry. I would have kept you if I could,' she repeated. 'I hope you can find it in your heart to forgive me.'

Cathy's eyes held a myriad of emotions but she nodded slowly. 'I can see that it was a difficult situation.' Then she asked the question that Mary had known would come and didn't really know how to answer. 'But why now? I've been wanting to find you for years. Why have you only recently searched for me?'

She had to be as honest as she could. It was the very least her daughter deserved. 'I never told my husband Paul about you. I never told anyone,' she admitted. 'It was such a shameful thing back then, to have a baby at barely sixteen, and then to abandon you how I did.' She rested her head in her hands for a moment as the memories flooded back. For years afterwards she'd been terrified that someone would find out what she'd done, that she would be punished for it. She looked up to see Cathy watching her thoughtfully. 'The longer I left it the harder it became. I was scared that Paul would leave me when he found out what a terrible thing I'd done. He was a kind man, but he was so... respectable. I wasn't sure if he would have understood or forgiven me. A few months after he died, I started trying to find you.'

Cathy looked Mary in the face, her expression inscrutable and there was a glint of steel in her dark brown eyes.

'So I was your dark, guilty secret?'

# 9

That hurt but she was right. 'I'm afraid so. I know how awful that sounds but I promise you that I never forgot you. Never a day went by when I didn't think of you, or regret what I'd had to do.'

She didn't want to look at Cathy, sure that she would see resentment and scorn in her eyes but she forced herself to and was surprised to see that the strange look had gone and now there was only compassion in Cathy's eyes.

'I understand why you did what you did,' Cathy said softly. 'I'm glad you tried to find me as soon as you could.' She tucked a loose lock of hair behind her ears. 'I am guessing that you haven't told your other children about me?'

'Not yet,' Mary admitted, feeling that she had failed her all over again. 'But I'm going to tell them. I want them to meet you. If you want to meet them, that is?'

Cathy nodded. 'I'd love that. I can't believe that I've got a brother and sister.'

'Your adoptive parents didn't have any more children then?' Mary asked. There were so many questions she wanted to ask

Cathy about her childhood. 'Did you know that you were adopted?'

'Yes. They always said that I was special because they chose me. They loved me dearly. Unfortunately they died some years ago but they would be very pleased that we've found each other at last.' She paused. 'And no, they didn't adopt any more children. Do you have any photos of my sister and brother?'

'I've got some on my phone. Do you want to see photos of when they were small or recent ones?'

'How they are now. Please,' Cathy added.

Mary picked up her phone and swiped to the photo gallery, selecting a photo of Joanne and her family in the summer. It suddenly hit her how different she looked from Cathy, with her blonde, well-cut hair and upmarket clothes. Cathy's clothes were obviously chain store as was her handbag. It was hard to believe that they were related.

She turned the phone around to show Cathy. 'That's Joanne with her husband Damien, and her two children, Kelly and Connor.'

Cathy peered closely at the photo. 'Is that your house or hers?'

'Mine. We had a picnic in the garden in the summer holidays.' She turned the phone around and swiped to a photo of Jason with his family. 'And that's my son, Jason, with his wife, Alison, and their two sons, Oliver and Nicholas.'

Cathy studied the photos, especially the one of Jason, Alison and the boys. What was she thinking? That she'd been robbed of being part of the family too? Or that they looked so different to her? 'I'm sorry I couldn't keep you,' Mary repeated. 'But you had a good life, a loving home, didn't you?'

Cathy lifted her eyes from the phone screen, her expression inscrutable, then her mouth broke into a smile. 'Yes, I did. I was very happy.'

'And now? Do you live nearby? Where do you work?' She

didn't want to shower Cathy with questions, but she hardly knew anything about her.

'I live the other side of Birmingham and I work in a local supermarket,' Cathy replied. 'I expect your other children have far grander jobs.'

Another stab of guilt. Tears sprang to Mary's eyes. 'I can't apologise enough for letting you down. We've both missed out on so much.' She took a tissue out of her handbag and wiped her eyes with it. 'I know it was my fault, you don't have to remind me of that. But I always wished I could have made a different choice and kept you.'

'It's okay. I understand,' Cathy replied. 'I'm glad we've met and talked it over. I feel like I've got answers now.'

'So am I.' Mary leaned forward. 'Can we meet again soon? There's so much I want to know about you. I've missed such a large part of your life,' she asked. 'Perhaps you could come to my house next time, meet Joanne and Jason? Or is it too soon?'

Cathy seemed to consider this. 'Could we get to know each other more first? I'd love it if we could spend some time, just the two of us. We've missed so many years...'

Mary nodded eagerly. 'That would be wonderful.' There was nothing she wanted more than to spend time with her lost daughter. 'Could you bring me some photos of yourself when you were younger? I would love to see them. Every birthday I tried to imagine what you looked like. What age you started crawling, walking, talking. All the precious moments I missed out on.'

'I'd like that,' Cathy agreed.

So they arranged to meet again for lunch on Friday, Mary was only looking after Nicholas for a couple of hours that morning. 'May I hug you?' Mary asked tentatively as they both got up to leave.

After a moment's hesitation, Cathy nodded and Mary

wrapped her arms around her and hugged her tight, her heart filled with happiness as Cathy returned the hug.

---

'I met Hope, Paul. I finally met her.' Mary picked up Paul's framed photo from the dresser and sat down on the sofa gazing at it, wishing that Paul was sitting beside her and she could tell him all about it. Except that if Paul was still alive she would never have found Hope – Cathy – would she?

'What would you have thought, Paul? Would you have forgiven me?'

It was only now, as her granddaughter Kelly was almost the age she'd been when she had Hope, that Mary was starting to forgive herself. She'd been a frightened child with no one to turn to. She'd panicked. And once the deed was done there was no going back. 'She's strikingly pretty,' Mary continued. 'She has dark hair and brown eyes like Robbie and a small, upturned nose like me.' She wondered what Robbie was doing now. Hopefully he really was dead, like she had told Cathy. He deserved to be dead for what he had done. She closed her eyes and took deep, calming breaths. It was all a long time ago. She'd been just a kid, fifteen when she met him, sixteen when she gave birth to Hope. He was three years older. Nowadays society had changed and he could be charged for rape. The words flashed into her mind unexpectedly and they shocked her. She stopped to consider them for a moment. Robbie had never forced her. He'd pressured her, though, taken advantage of her vulnerability, of the knowledge that she had adored him. He had known that he was her first lover, he should have looked after her, made sure that he didn't make her pregnant. But then Robbie had never really cared about anyone. The last time she had seen him, he'd made that crystal clear.

Anyway, the past was past, all she could do now was move

forward. That's what she'd told herself when she'd read that Hope had been adopted. She'd resolved to put it all behind her and make a new life for herself. Now Paul had gone she had to do the same, make another new life for herself, one without him. At least this time she wasn't completely alone. She had Joanne and Jason, and Cathy. She had to try and make it up to her eldest daughter for all the years she'd missed out on, and bring her into the family when she was ready. She wanted to tell Joanne and Jason right now but Cathy had asked if they could spend time getting to know each other without distractions first and how could she refuse? She owed her some undivided attention. The other two had had all her love and attention all their lives.

The front door opening jolted Mary out of her thoughts. 'Mum! Are you there?' Joanne had insisted on having a key when Paul died, saying she was worried about Mary being on her own. 'You're not getting any younger, Mum. What if you're ill or have a fall? No one will be able to get in to help you,' she'd said. Jason had also tried to get her to have a doorbell camera installed, so that it came up on her phone – and his – who was at the door but she'd refused because it felt like she was being spied on. They'd had a CCTV camera installed years ago. That and the spyhole and chain on the door protected her enough. It was a safe neighbourhood, she reminded them. She had always felt secure there.

'In here!' Mary called.

'Where have you been? I popped in this morning but you were out,' Joanne said, a delighted expression on her face. 'I'm so pleased you're getting out and about again.' She looked at the photo Mary was holding. 'I know it's hard, Mum. I still miss Dad too.' She swallowed, her eyes misting over. Joanne had been so close to Paul and his death had hit her badly. It had hit Jason too, but he had coped better than Joanne did. But then father and son had clashed sometimes, as was often the way.

'I know you do, darling.' Mary stood up. 'It's lovely to see you. Did you pop in for anything special or just to check in on me?'

Joann walked over and kissed Mary on the cheek. 'I was wondering if you wanted to come over on Friday evening and have dinner with us? I can pick you up about four?'

Mary hesitated, it was a lovely idea but she was meeting Cathy for lunch then and didn't want to have to rush away. 'Thank you, darling, that would be wonderful but I'm going shopping in the afternoon so will come to you about six, if that's all right.'

'Perfect,' Joanne beamed. 'Would you like to stop the night?'

'It's very kind of you but honestly I'm fine at home on my own now,' Mary replied.

After a quick chat Joanne was off out again, calling 'See you Friday' as she pulled the front door shut behind her. Mary was glad Joanne hadn't questioned her more about where she'd been. She didn't want to lie but couldn't tell her about Cathy just yet. She would soon though. She couldn't wait to have all her family together but until then she was going to enjoy the time she spent with her precious lost daughter. She had found Hope at last and this time she was never going to let her go.

# 10

'How's Nicholas been?' Alison asked when she arrived to pick him up on Friday lunchtime. She was half an hour late, and Mary was all ready to go out. Nicholas's bag was packed and he was drinking some juice. Alison glanced curiously at him then at Mary. 'Are you going out?'

'He's been as good as gold but he's tired now. He'll probably fall asleep as soon as you get home,' Mary replied as she rummaged through her handbag. 'Yes, I'm off shopping with a friend, when I can find my keys that is!'

'Oh Mary, you're always misplacing something,' Alison said with a smile. 'They're over there by the kettle.'

'Oh, yes I remember now, I went to my car earlier to get something out of the boot.' Alison was right, she was really distracted lately. It drove Joanne and Damien mad but Alison and Jason were quite good-humoured about it. She grabbed the keys. 'I'm sorry, I don't mean to be rude but I must dash.'

Alison looked a little disappointed that they weren't having their normal cuppa and a chat. 'Oh, okay, sorry I was a bit late.' She held out her hand to Nicholas. 'Come on, Nicky, Nanny has to go out.'

'Bye, darling.' Mary gave Nicholas a kiss on the cheek and followed them out, locking the door behind her.

Alison waved then ushered Nicholas into her car and drove off, with Mary setting off straight after them. She and Cathy were meeting in a café in Birmingham city centre so that Cathy could take the train as her car was in for repair. Mary decided to leave her car in the station car park and travel by train too, not wanting to tackle the busy city traffic.

Cathy was waiting when she arrived at the café, and to her surprise and pleasure, immediately greeted Mary with a hug. She seemed delighted to see her, the frosty edge Mary had noticed before when they met had thankfully gone. She'd brought a handful of photos of herself when she was younger, from a toddler to about seven, as Mary had asked, as well as a photo of her with her adoptive parents. They looked a lovely couple. Mary was so happy it had worked out for her.

'I wish I could have met them and thanked them for looking after you, for loving you and giving you a wonderful home,' she told Cathy.

'I know. I wish I could have met my biological dad, but at least we have each other,' Cathy replied. She leaned across the table and placed her hand on Mary's. 'I'm so glad about that.'

'So am I,' Mary told her.

They spent a wonderful afternoon together, linking arms as they wandered around the shops and when Cathy stopped to admire a gorgeous trouser suit, Mary insisted on buying it for her, and some shoes and a bag to go with it.

'It's very kind of you, but you mustn't spend all your money on me,' Cathy said as Mary asked her to choose a necklace too. But her face lit up so much when she spotted a diamond pendant that Mary couldn't resist.

'Let me spoil you a bit,' Mary told her. 'We've got years to make up for.'

Cathy's face broke into a huge smile and she hugged Mary. 'I'm so happy that we found each other.'

'So am I,' replied Mary, delighted by Cathy's response.

---

'Hello, Mary, you look well,' Damien said, kissing her on the cheek when she arrived at his and Joanne's house just before six.

'I feel well.' Mary's nose twitched as the smell of chocolate fudge cake floated out from the kitchen. 'Has Joanne been baking?' she asked in surprise. Joanne was usually far too busy to bake.

'No, it's Connor. He's developed a love of cooking, would you believe? Wait until you taste it, he made us a chocolate cake last week and it was divine.' Damien pinched the fingers and thumb of his right hand, kissed them and then tossed them dramatically away from his lips in the familiar chef's gesture. 'Mind you, the kitchen looks like a bomb's hit it after he's been cooking in there.'

Mary grinned, pleased that Connor had chosen a hobby he could share with the family. He spent far too much time holed up in his room playing computer games. As for Kelly, she was never off her phone.

*I wish I could tell Joanne about her sister*, Mary thought as she stepped inside. She was bursting to share the news with someone, although she was nervous how her family would take it. Cathy was right, though, it was best to spend time getting to know each other first. Then Mary could break the news to the rest of the family.

It was a pleasant evening. The chocolate fudge cake was delicious and Connor blushed as they all praised him, even

Kelly. Mary couldn't help thinking how Cathy had missed out on having a family, and blaming herself for that. Cathy must be so lonely on her own. If only she could make it up to her for all the years she had missed out on.

'Have you thought any more about downsizing, Mary?' Damien said as he poured them all a coffee from the coffee filter. 'I bet you're rattling around in that place now.' Both Joanne and Jason had been trying to persuade her to sell the family home and buy something smaller ever since Paul died. Mary knew they were right, the place was too big for her on her own, but she couldn't face the move. The house held so many memories, all the years she and Paul had lived there, brought up the children. And it would be such an upheaval.

'You can move in with us, if you don't want to live on your own,' Joanne offered again. Jason had offered the same. 'You won't be a nuisance to us, I promise.'

'Of course you won't, you'd be very welcome,' Damien said. 'We could even build a granny flat on the side of the house if you wanted your own space.'

Granny flat! She wasn't old enough for that yet! And kind as it was for them to offer, she had no intention of living with any of her children. She wanted her own life.

'Please don't worry, I am fine living on my own. And I will think about downsizing soon,' she promised. She didn't want to be selfish. Moving to a smaller property not only made sense but meant she could release some capital and help Joanne and Jason out. She knew that that they could both do with some extra money. It was always a struggle when you had a family.

She could help Cathy too, she realised. It would be one way to pay her back for all the years she hadn't been in her life.

# 11

'You found the house then. I was half-expecting a call from you for more directions,' Mary said, opening the door with a smile when Cathy arrived on Monday morning. She'd phoned Mary yesterday to say that she had the next day off work and had sorted out some photos to show her. 'If you don't mind me coming to your house,' she'd added.

'I'd love that,' Mary had said enthusiastically.

'Google found it no problem,' Cathy told her now. 'It's a beautiful house.'

'Thank you, we've been really happy here and I'm reluctant to move even though it's much too big for me,' Mary said, stepping back to let Cathy in. 'Go left into the kitchen,' she said. 'We can chat while I finish preparing lunch.'

'Oh you shouldn't have gone to so much trouble. I don't expect you to feed me,' Cathy told her.

'It's no problem. It's nice to have company,' Mary told her. 'It's only chicken salad wraps.' She glanced at Cathy. 'If you're okay with that?'

Cathy nodded. 'It sounds delicious.' She followed Mary,

gazing around the luxury fitted kitchen in awe. 'Wow! This is amazing. I think my kitchen would fit into this twice at least.'

Mary felt a little awkward. She could see how it might look from Cathy's point of view. Although Cathy had assured her that she'd had a happy childhood, it was clear that it had been a far different one from Joanne and Jason. She had been reluctant to talk about herself much but Mary got the impression that Cathy didn't have much money at her disposal and wondered if she was struggling financially. The car she had arrived in – a blue Nissan – was quite old and when she'd taken her purse out of her bag to pay for the coffees at their first meeting, Mary had noticed that both the bag and purse had seen better days. That's why she'd insisted on buying Cathy some clothes the last time they'd met. She wanted to make it up to her for the years she hadn't been there, for not having the life that her other two children had.

'I'll put the kettle on, shall I?' Cathy asked cheerfully.

'Yes please, tea for me,' Mary replied. 'You'll find tea bags in the pot by the kettle.'

'You said that you were reluctant to move, but it sounds like you've been thinking about it?' Cathy remarked as she made a mug of tea for them both.

'Joanne and Jason think I should, they want me to move into a retirement home, a warden-controlled apartment. Well, actually they'd like me to move in with one of them but I don't intend to do either. I'm not that old and doddery yet.' She threw a smile at Cathy. 'They mean well, and they're right, the house is too big for me but I can't bring myself to sell it just yet.'

'Do you feel safe here all alone?' Cathy sounded concerned. 'You're quite set back from the road and the house does rather shout "money". Have there been many break-ins?'

'Not for a while. We have an alarm, as do all the houses along the road. It's a quiet neighbourhood and we've never had much trouble here.'

'Do you have CCTV?' Cathy stirred milk into the tea.

'We have cameras at the front and back. They're linked to my laptop although to be honest the wi-fi connection isn't good here and the system is often down. Jason's been trying to get me to have one of those doorbell alarm apps but I don't think that's necessary.' Mary finished doing the wraps. 'Shall we take this out into the garden? It's too nice a day to stay inside.'

'That's a lovely idea. Where do you keep your trays?' Cathy glanced around.

Mary opened a cupboard and took out a tray, placing the two plates on them. Cathy placed the mugs next to them and insisted on carrying the tray out into the garden.

They sat on the patio at the back and started looking through the photos that Cathy had brought with her. Mary picked up a black and white one of baby Cathy sitting up. She must have been about six months old. She felt a pang of regret and sadness.

Cathy reached out and placed her hand on Mary's. 'Hey, if it upsets you, we don't have to look at them.'

'I want to.' She could hear the quaver in her voice. 'I want to know all about your childhood and your life now. All these years there's been an empty space in my heart where you should have been. I can't tell you how sorry I am that I couldn't keep you.'

Cathy squeezed her hand and Mary raised her eyes to meet her daughter's. Compassion shone out of them. 'No need to say sorry. I understand. The past has gone, we need to look forward to the future now.'

Which was exactly what Mary wanted to do. She intended to spend as much time as she could getting to know this lovely woman.

'Look at me here!' Cathy held up a photo of a mischievous toddler. 'I reckon I look like you there.'

She did a little, with that dimple by her nose and the small smile playing on her lips.

There were a few photos of Cathy when she was older, one when she must have been in her early twenties. Her hair was swept up and she was wearing an evening dress, as if she was going somewhere special. 'This is beautiful,' Mary told her.

'Would you like it?' Cathy asked then looked anxious. 'You don't have to. I don't want to be pushy.'

'I would love it, thank you,' Mary told her.

'I printed out the photo you sent me of you and put it by my bed,' Cathy confessed. 'I wanted you to be the first thing I see when I wake up. I can't believe that I've finally found my mother.'

Mary saw the tears in her eyes and squeezed her hand. 'And I'll put this one in a frame too.'

Cathy grinned. 'Thanks. I would really feel like I belong if you did that. Do you have any photos of your grandchildren?' she asked. 'I'd love to see them, if you don't mind, that is. It would make me feel more at ease when I meet them.'

'Of course. Most of them are on my iPad, ' Mary told her. 'I'll go and get it. Shall we sit inside now? It is getting a bit chilly.'

Cathy picked up the tray. 'Lead the way.'

As they went into the lounge, Bailey squawked. 'Hello, hello.'

Cathy smiled in delight. 'Oh, you have a parakeet!'

She went over to the cage where Bailey was hopping about on his perch. 'Hello, hello,' he squawked.

'Aren't you gorgeous? Is it a he or she and what's its name?' she asked.

'A he, and he's called Bailey,' Mary said. 'Paul bought him for me as a birthday present. He's a godsend, he's such good company. I let him out in the evenings when I'm here alone and he flies around, then settles on my shoulder.'

'He's adorable.'

'He likes you, look how animated he is.' Mary looked delighted as the parakeet fluffed up its feathers and hopped around on the perch. 'Maybe you'd like to come around one evening, when he's out of his cage?'

'I'd love to. I'll bring supper with me and maybe we can watch a film together... if that's okay?' Cathy suggested.

Mary patted her hand. 'That sounds perfect. It would be good to have company in the evening; Joanne and Jason are busy with their families... and it's evenings when I miss Paul most – that and when I wake up in the morning.' Her eyes clouded over with sadness.

'Well, you've got me now. I'm happy to come around and keep you company whenever I can,' Cathy said, giving her a hug.

Mary hugged her tightly back. 'That would be wonderful.'

They embraced for a moment then sat down on the sofa. Mary got out her iPad, typed in her password, Bailey2019 – 'That's the year I got him,' she said – then clicked onto her photo gallery. Cathy seemed to really enjoy looking at the photos and Mary left her browsing while she went to the bathroom.

'You have a beautiful family,' Cathy said, glancing up when Mary came back down. 'I think I'm ready to meet my brother and sister now, if that's okay with you?'

Mary beamed. 'I'm delighted. I'll tell them this week and we can all have Sunday lunch together?' She glanced cautiously at Cathy. 'If you'd like to, that is.' She had organised the family Sunday lunch a couple of weeks ago so she knew that Joanne and Jason could make it.

'I'd love to.' Cathy looked nervous. 'I'm dying to meet everyone but I'm a bit scared that they will resent me,' she admitted. 'You seem to be such a close family and then I come along, an outsider.'

'Of course they won't resent you! And you're not an outsider! You're as much my child as they are. You're part of the family,' Mary reassured her.

Cathy's eyes clouded over, as they often did. Mary had sensed a sadness in her and wondered if it was because she couldn't have children. They'd not yet talked about why she was childless; asking felt too much like probing. She was enjoying getting to know Cathy, and willing to answer any questions she asked, but was careful not to pry into her private life. Cathy owed her nothing. 'But we don't have the same father, do we? And they know nothing about me. It will be a terrible shock for them.'

'At first, yes, but once they've digested the news that they have an older sister I'm sure that they will want to meet you and welcome you with open arms,' Mary told her. It was what she was hoping.

But whatever Joanne and Jason said, she was determined that they realise that Cathy was part of the family, and that they accept that as fact.

When Cathy had gone, Mary went over to the photo of Paul on the sideboard and picked it up. 'I'm so sorry I didn't tell you, Paul,' she said. Then her eyes caught another photo on the sideboard. It was the one Cathy had given her earlier, and was now placed over the top of a framed photo of Joanne. Cathy must have put it there when Mary went up to the toilet. She felt a lump in her throat as she realised how desperate her eldest daughter was to be part of the family, and how nervous she must have been of Mary's reaction to slip the photo there when she wasn't looking. Well, there were plenty of other photos of Joanne on the sideboard. She slid the glass out of the frame and replaced Joanne's photo with the one of Cathy. Then she stood the framed photos in order, Cathy, Joanne and Jason. Her three children, together at last.

# 12

## *Alison*

'Joanne's been summonsed to Mum's this evening as well,' Jason said, irritation spread all over his face. 'I don't know why she wants to see us both on a Tuesday evening! Surely it could wait until the weekend.'

He and Joanne didn't get on, never had. Apparently, Joanne had never forgiven him for coming along and spoiling her one-to-one relationship with her parents when she was five. Baby Jason had taken up a lot of their mum's time, a habit that continued to this day. Personally, Alison agreed with Joanne – Mary did spoil Jason. He only had to fix those big blue eyes on her and smile and she seemed ready to grant him anything. Which meant he'd never grown up. He never took responsibility for his actions, and got into mess after mess, then ran to Mary to get him out of it, and she always did, even if she had to go behind Paul's back to do it.

Whereas Joanne had been the apple of Paul's eye, a real daddy's girl. He had worshipped her, and she'd been devastated when he died. For weeks she hadn't been able to talk about her father without tears welling up in her eyes and threatening to fall down her always immaculately made-up cheeks.

'Do you want me to come with you?' she asked.

Jason shook his head. 'No, the way Mum's worded it, she wants it to be just me and Joanne.'

She was pleased he didn't want her there, she was sure that he was going to try and tap Mary for some more money. His business was in trouble. Again. He hadn't told her that, but his business partner Hugh kept Alison in the loop and had told her that things were getting dire and if they didn't sort it quick they would be bankrupt. Hugh was desperately trying to drum up more business, but Jason's solution was, as always, to run to Mummy. It was demeaning and Alison hated him doing it, especially when she was present. They were adults, they should be making their own way, looking after Mary instead of expecting Mary to look after them. She'd tried to tell Jason this last month when he'd gone for a handout but he had dismissed her concern. 'Mum can afford it – I'm not exactly seeing her short, am I? That house is too big for her and Dad left her well-cared for. Might as well have the money now while she's alive and I need it, rather than when she's dead.'

It was always 'I' with Jason. 'I want', 'I need', 'I'm going to'. He didn't know the meaning of the word 'we', had no idea how to share, take responsibility. Alison blamed Mary for that, she worshipped him. He could do no wrong in her eyes. If only she knew what her wonderful son was really like!

Whereas Hugh... Guilt flooded through her as she thought of how close she and Hugh had become. She hadn't set out to have an affair, neither of them had, but Hugh was so kind, so tender and supportive. She had been attracted to him instantly, and he said he'd felt the same way, but they had both resisted it. Then one night she and Jason had had a blazing row and he'd stormed out. Hugh had popped in to drop off some paperwork for Jason's meeting the next day, seen that Alison was upset and comforted her. He'd kissed her, and she'd kissed him back, and suddenly the attraction had been too strong to resist and they'd ended up in bed together, knowing that the boys were asleep and Jason would be out all night. He always stayed out when he was angry; sometimes Alison suspected that he caused a row so that he could storm off and disappear for the night. After that there had been no going back. Hugh had recently told her he loved her, and Alison loved him too, but while Hugh was single, Alison wasn't and they were both worried about the fallout if Jason discovered their affair.

'Okay, well, I've got a couple of clients to see to so could you pick up the kids from nursery and school seeing as you're working from home today?' Alison ran a mobile hair dressing service which brought in some much-needed extra income, and was something she could fit in around the boys, with Mary's help twice a week which saved a lot on nursery fees. It also got her out of the house and made Jason do a bit of parenting now and again. God knew what they'd have lived on without it. Jason's IT consultancy company had started off well, but had been hit by the pandemic a couple of years ago, and he lacked the staying-power to do the work needed to revive it. Without her income they would barely survive. Not like Joanne in her big house, her kids at private school, her stuffed-shirt husband, Damien, with his very well-paid job as a regional insurance consultant and Joanne's work as PA to a local businessman. Joanne was always lording it over them. Mary, though, was a dear. Alison really liked her and would be happy to have lunch with her any day, providing Joanne and Jason weren't there.

Jason pulled a face. 'When will you be back? I have to go to Mum's, remember,' he groaned.

'I'll be back by five,' she told him as she went out of the door.

She had a client to see to and then was meeting Hugh. She

had bought new underwear especially. Hugh liked her to wear satin and lace and was happy to provide the money for her to purchase them. The promise of what lay ahead made her stomach tighten. She knew that she was playing with fire, having an affair with Hugh, that she could lose everything, but she had fallen for him and he really cared about her. She couldn't remember the last time Jason had shown any real interest in her. They very occasionally had quickie sex on a Sunday morning when the kids were downstairs watching TV, but it was over in a few minutes and she didn't think it meant any more to Jason than it did to her. It was merely a habit they had got into. They didn't even kiss when they were doing it, let alone look into each other's eyes. Whereas Hugh couldn't get enough of her. She adored the way his eyes roamed over her body, that secret, suggestive smile on his lips. Hugh made her feel desired, alive. And she found out more from him about what was going on in the business than she did from Jason.

She wondered what Mary wanted to see Jason and Joanne about. Was she finally going to sell the house? It was a stunning home, six bedrooms, three bathrooms, a dining room, drawing room, large kitchen, huge gardens, situated at the end of a country lane, backing onto fields. Paul had been a chartered surveyor and they'd enjoyed a comfortable lifestyle and he'd made sure that he'd left Mary well-provided for. He'd left ten grand each for Joanne and Jason in his will, but everything else had gone to Mary. Jason hadn't been very happy at the time, he'd expected more, but as Alison had reminded him, Mary had worked too, putting money into the home, backing and supporting Paul. And she was his wife.

She just hoped that Jason didn't ask his mum for money in front of Joanne, that would be so humiliating.

She pulled up outside the small bungalow where her first client lived. Zoe Hall – she was housebound but a real character. Alison enjoyed doing her hair and chatting to her, Zoe was so upbeat.

She took her bag out of the back of the car and headed for the door. Hugh had booked them a hotel room for the afternoon. The thought made her heart beat faster.

# 13

## *Mary*

Mary paced the floor as she waited for Joanne and Jason to arrive. How would they react when she told them her dark secret, that forty-five years ago she had given away her precious firstborn child? Would they understand that she couldn't see any other way out at the time, and that this desperate act had haunted her all her life. How many times she had wished that she'd told someone, a teacher perhaps. She wouldn't have been able to keep Hope, her father would never have supported her, but at least formally giving her up for adoption wouldn't have been so awful as abandoning her. That seemed so cruel, so cold, as if she hadn't cared about her baby at all, which wasn't true. She had loved her so much. She had truly been in an impossible situation. And terrified after that last episode with Robbie.

She wrapped her arms around herself in a comforting hug as she looked around her luxurious home – a far cry from the cold, shabby terraced house she'd lived in with her father. She could hardly believe that she had been reunited with her precious daughter. And, amazingly, they had bonded straight away and Cathy had forgiven Mary almost as soon as she knew her story. Well, as much of it as Mary was prepared to tell her. Would Joanne and Jason forgive her too? Would Paul have done?

Bailey chirped as if he sensed her unease. She walked over to the cage to talk to him. 'It will be okay, won't it, Bailey?' He hopped over and perched right by the bars, bobbing his head up and down. 'Okay,' he repeated. 'Okay.' She smiled. Bailey never failed to cheer her up. She knew that he wanted to come out of the cage, and fly around as he was used to doing when she was in alone but Joanne always got irritated if Bailey flew on her head, and Jason never did remember to close doors. She didn't want to risk losing Bailey. He was so precious and one of her final links with Paul.

She turned as she heard the front door open. Both Joanne and Jason still had a key to the family home.

'Hi, Mum,' Jason called cheerily. He walked into the lounge, his hands in his pockets. 'Jo not here yet then?'

'She'll be along in a minute,' Mary said as Jason strode over and kissed her on the cheek.

'So what's the big news then? Have you decided to sell up?' he asked, flopping down on the sofa. Mary had deliberately sat on the chair so that Joanne and Jason could sit together, opposite her.

She was tempted to tell him. Jason was always so empathetic, he would understand. And it would be good to have his support if Joanne didn't take the news very well. But no, she would have to tell them together. She couldn't bear to tell the story twice.

Jason raised an eyebrow. 'Not the house then?' He leaned forward, forearms on his knees, hands outstretched, palms clasped together. 'Go on, you can tell me. I'll act surprised when you tell Jo,' he coaxed.

'I...'

'Hi, Mum!' Joanne's voice called from the hall.

Jason sighed and he sat back against the back of the sofa, bringing one foot up on his other leg. 'We're in here!' he called.

Joanne came in looking flustered. 'Sorry I'm a bit late, Kelly was acting up again.'

'Don't worry, Jason has only just arrived,' Mary replied. 'Look, can I get you both a drink? I'm going to make myself one.'

'Coffee for me,' Jason said.

'And me. I'll make it,' Joanne said, disappearing into the kitchen.

Mary wished that Joanne had let her make it, she needed the time to think about how she was going to say this. She'd been practising all morning but now Jason and Joanne were here she couldn't find the words.

Joanne returned a few minutes later holding a tray with three mugs of coffee. 'Here we are,' she said, putting it down on the coffee table.

'Thank you, dear.' Mary took the mug Joanne passed her.

'What is it, Mum? Your hand's shaking. Are you ill?' Joanne asked anxiously, sitting down on the edge of the sofa with her own mug and leaving Jason to get his.

'I...' Mary licked her lips and looked from one to the other.

'You are ill, aren't you?' Jason leaned forward again, his face pale. 'Is it your heart? Has the angina got worse?' Mary had had an angina attack just after Paul died and now had to carry a GTN spray with her.

'No. Look, this is a bit difficult. I'm not sure how you're going to take it.'

Joanne and Jason exchanged worried looks.

'You haven't met someone else, have you?' Joanne asked, her voice rising in panic.

'No, of course not!' Mary said quickly, shocked at the question. 'How could you think such a thing?'

'Then what is it, Mum? Spit it out. The tension is killing us!' Jason told her, reaching for his mug.

If only it was that easy. 'The thing is...' She paused and took a sip of her drink. 'Forty-five years ago I had a baby. A little girl.'

Jason's jaw dropped and Joanne almost spilt her coffee.

'You had a baby?' She could almost hear the cogs in Joanne's mind as she did the calculations. 'Oh God, you must have only been fifteen. Kelly's age!'

They both looked so appalled that Mary dreaded telling them the rest.

'I was. The baby was born just after my sixteenth birthday. Of course I couldn't keep her. My mum was dead and you know what your grandad was like.'

'So you had her adopted? And now she's found you and wants to get in touch?' Jason asked.

'Sort of.' She had to say it. 'Only I didn't have her adopted. I couldn't tell anyone I was pregnant. I was so scared of your grandad finding out. So I hid the pregnancy and gave birth at home alone. And when the baby was born I...' Her courage almost failed her. Both Jason and Joanne looked thunderstruck. 'I cleaned us both up then I abandoned her in a phone box in a shopping precinct.'

Both of their coffee mugs crashed to the floor at the same time.

# 14

'I'm sorry, I know it's a bit of a shock,' Mary said, bending down to scoop up the broken mugs and mop up the spilt coffee with tissue from the box on the coffee table. It gave her a chance to pull herself together and to avoid the horrified looks on both Joanne and Jason's faces.

'Did Dad know about this?' Jason found his voice first.

Mary shook her head. 'I never told him. I was so ashamed I didn't want to tell anyone. But I carried the guilt with me and when your father died, I knew that I would never rest until I found my missing daughter. So I went on a few tracing websites, and Cathy found me.'

'Are you sure it's her?' Jason asked. 'It could be anyone.'

'We did a DNA test. I am definitely her mother.'

'Have you actually met her yet?' Joanne asked sharply, suddenly finding her voice.

'The beginning of last month.'

Joanne looked shocked. 'And you're only just telling us?'

'We wanted to get to know each other a little first before introducing Cathy to you two.' Mary looked from Joanne to Jason.

'What happened to her? Was she adopted?' Joanne asked.

'Yes, she was. Life has been kind to her, thank goodness. She was adopted by a loving couple,' Mary replied.

'And what about the father?' This was from Jason.

'He was a local boy. He died in a motorbike accident before Hope – that's what I named Cathy – was born. I was terrified… and so alone,' she said, repeating the story she had told Cathy.

'That's so tragic,' Jason said sympathetically. 'You must have been really scared.' He stepped forward and gave Mary a hug. Tears sprang to her eyes. She knew that her darling boy would understand. 'And totally heartbroken to have to give your baby away.'

'Thank you, darling.' Mary dabbed her eyes with a tissue. 'I was. I thought I would never recover from it. I am so pleased that we are reunited again.'

'I'm so sorry that you went through that at such a young age.' Joanne's tone had softened now. 'I'm glad that you found each other. Where does Cathy live?'

'The other side of Birmingham,' Mary replied. 'I've asked Cathy to join us for lunch on Sunday so that she can meet you, and your families of course. I hope that's okay with you both.'

'Fine by me. I can't wait to meet my new big sister,' Jason said. He grinned at Joanne. 'And now you have a big sister too.'

Joanne looked at him in surprise, as if she hadn't thought about that. Jason seemed to have accepted the news better than Joanne had, but then Mary had expected that. Joanne hated change. And she had always loved being the eldest, pulling rank on Jason. She hoped that she wouldn't have a problem accepting Cathy.

'Fine by me too. Of course we'll welcome Cathy into the family, Mum. I'm so pleased that you've both found each other again.' She kissed Mary on the cheek. Then her eyes widened and she pulled away. 'I see that you have her photo up already.'

Jason followed her gaze to the three photos lined up on the sideboard and he grinned. 'Looks like you've been replaced, sis.'

# 15

*Alison*

'Is Mary okay? What did she want to talk to you about?' Alison asked when Jason returned later that evening.

Jason ignored her, walked to the drinks cupboard, took out a bottle of brandy, half filled a glass with it and took a long swig. Alison stared at him. Jason rarely drank. Not like Joanne, who always seemed to have a glass of wine in her hand. 'That bad?'

Jason coughed, wiped his mouth with the back of his hand and poured another glass of brandy, handing it to her. 'Yep.' He held out the glass. 'You might need a drink too.'

Thoughts spun around in Alison's mind. Was Mary ill? Had she decided to have a fresh start and move away from the area when she sold up? Or... had she found someone else?

'What is it?' she asked, holding the glass of amber liquid and bracing herself for whatever came next.

'Mum's got another daughter. An older daughter.'

'What?' It took a few seconds for the words to sink in. 'You mean she had another baby before Joanne? Did she have her adopted?'

'Worse than that.' Jason finished off the brandy. 'She had a baby when she was barely sixteen and she abandoned it. Left it in a shopping bag in a phone box.' Jason refilled his glass and sank down into the armchair. 'And now she's found her again and wants us to meet her.'

God, no wonder he was so shocked. Alison took a sip of her own brandy, wincing as it burnt the back of her throat. Wine was her occasional tipple, not spirits. She assessed what Jason had told her. It was so hard to imagine that kind, thoughtful, pillar of society Mary had given birth at such a young age and abandoned her child. 'Did Paul know?' she asked.

'No one knew. Not even her own father. Apparently she gave birth alone at home.' He shook his head, bewilderment written all over his face. 'Mum decided to find her when Dad died. Apparently, Mum and Cathy – as my lost sister is now called, although Mum named her Hope – have met and bonded so now she wants to welcome her into the family.'

He looked stunned and she could understand why. It must be such a shock to learn that his mother had another secret child, and in such awful circumstances too.

'I'm stunned so I can imagine how you feel,' she said. 'When does she want you to meet her?'

'Mum's invited her to join us for Sunday lunch.'

Alison hadn't expected that. 'So soon? And all of us together like that? Surely it would be best for you and Joanne to meet her first. It's such a big moment.'

Jason shook his head. 'It's a gathering of the clan to welcome the proverbial lost sheep.' He downed the rest of his brandy and slammed the glass down on the table. 'How are we going to explain this to Oliver and Nicholas?'

Alison studied him carefully, trying to gauge how upset he was. 'They're too young to bother about it much, we'll just tell them that Nanny had a baby years ago before she married Grandad.'

'And dumped it?'

'And had the baby adopted because she wasn't able to look after her.' They would have to gloss over it, concentrate on how wonderful it was that their nanny had found her long-lost baby again. Young children were pretty accepting. She didn't fancy being in Joanne's shoes, though, explaining it to her fifteen-year-old, Kelly, who was only a little younger than Mary must have been when she'd given birth.

'It's happened, Jason, and we have to deal with it,' she told him. Then she asked, 'How's Joanne taken it?'

He smirked. 'She's really rattled. She always lorded it over me because she was the eldest and now she's just the middle child. Mum's even got photos of the three of us on the sideboard, all lined up in a row, with Cathy first.' He grinned as if he found this amusing.

Although Joanne and Jason were outwardly polite to each other there had always been an undercurrent of rivalry between them and Alison knew that Joanne resented the fact that Mary doted on Jason. She wondered if Cathy's arrival would alter this.

'It's a shock, I know, but is it really that bad?' she asked. 'I bet your mum is delighted to have found her daughter at last. It's probably been eating away at her all these years, Jason. She must have felt so guilty.'

'The problem is...' Jason's eyes met hers. 'Does Mum feel so guilty that she'll give this Cathy a share of the money when she finally sells the house?'

# 16

## *Cathy*

Cathy turned off the engine and got out of the car, pleased to see that there were no other cars parked in the drive. She had deliberately arrived for Sunday lunch half an hour early, wanting to be there first, so that she could be standing side by side with Mary when Joanne and Jason arrived. 'I hope you don't mind that I'm a bit early? It didn't take me as long to get here as I'd thought, there's not so much traffic on a Sunday,' she said when Mary opened the door.

'Not at all. I'm not quite ready yet, though, I was about to set the table,' Mary said, leading the way into the hall.

They chatted away together, taking cutlery out of the drawers, table mats and serviettes out of the cupboard. They had just finished laying the table when the front door opened. 'Mum! We're here!' Joanne called.

'We're in the dining room!' Mary shouted. She grabbed Cathy's hand and they both turned to face the doorway as a tall, tanned woman with short blonde hair walked in, followed by a man then a teenage girl and boy. They looked even posher than in their photos, Cathy thought. She bet the kids went to private school. She felt a flash of annoyance as Joanne's eyes widened when they rested on her. She wasn't what Joanne had expected then. Well, the photo she'd given Mary was taken a few years ago and she'd been a lot younger and smarter than she was today, she admitted.

'Joanne, this is your sister, Cathy. Cathy, meet Joanne,' Mary said, her voice trembling a little.

*She's nervous*, Cathy realised. *She's worried what Joanne's reaction will be.* Joanne pasted a smile on her face but her eyes were cold. *She thinks she's better than me, well she's not, she's luckier, that's all – lucky that she wasn't the firstborn.* Cathy tilted her chin and looked Joanne straight in the eye. 'Pleased to meet you, little sis.'

Joanne bristled, her face flushing but her husband, Damien, smiled. He looked very public-school with his dark hair, smooth face and posh clothes and false smile. Cathy had met his type before, she bet he had a roving eye. And that Joanne knew and ignored it. 'Hello, Cathy, welcome to the family,' he said smoothly. Then he stepped forward and kissed her on the cheek.

'Thank you.'

Cathy glanced at the two children. A pretty but sulky-looking teenage girl, and a gangly, awkward-looking lad. Kelly and Connor, Mary had said they were called.

'Hello, kids,' she said easily. She could always relate to children more than she could to adults.

Connor flicked his fringe out of his eyes. 'Hi,' he mumbled.

Kelly looked at her curiously. 'Hello. Do you have children?'

'No, I don't,' Cathy replied. Kelly looked disappointed.

'Would anyone like a cup of tea or coffee? Jason and Alison will be here soon, I've just had a text from them to say they've been delayed a little,' Mary said.

'Coffee please,' Joanne said.

'Let me help you,' Cathy offered, not wanting to be left alone with this snooty woman. Joanne could barely disguise her contempt for her. She bet she hated it that their upstanding, respectable mother had such a sordid past.

She wondered what Jason's reaction would be.

Coffee done, Cathy sat down on the sofa beside Joanne, who carefully edged along a bit so that they weren't touching. 'Privileged' was the thought that crossed Cathy's mind as she looked at her and Damien, drinking coffee and making small talk in their posh voices. She bet neither of them had ever struggled a day in their life, never been cold or hungry. Never felt unloved.

She heard the front door open again then a male voice: 'Mum!'

Mary's face broke into a wide smile. 'Ah, here's Jason.'

Cathy kept her eyes fixed on the door as it opened and a fair-haired couple walked in, each holding the hand of a different young boy. Her brother and his wife. Jason had his head bent, talking to his son, trying to reassure him about something. Then he looked up and his eyes met Cathy's. She saw the shock of recognition in his eyes before he plastered a smile on his face. She'd thought he might have recognised her from her photo, even if it was taken a few years ago. She'd recognised him as soon as she'd seen his photograph.

'Hello, Cathy. Pleased to meet you.' His eyes held hers, daring her to show any sign that she knew him.

He needn't worry. She wouldn't tell his secret if he didn't tell hers.

# 17

*Alison*

Well, it had all seemed a little awkward at first, as was only to be expected, but now they were all chatting away, Alison thought in relief. She could see that Mary was nervous and desperate for everyone to get on. She'd probably been worrying for ages about what Jason and Joanne's reaction would be.

'You must tell us all about yourself, Cathy,' Joanne said with a big smile. 'Mum said that you were adopted very soon after... your birth. Where did you grow up?'

'Surrey,' replied Cathy. 'My adoptive parents were very kind to me. They were both dentists.'

Mary must have been pleased to learn that Cathy had had a happy childhood, Alison thought.

'And how do they feel about you finding your... birth mother?' Joanne continued.

'They both died some years ago but they would be pleased for me. I always knew that I was adopted. My parents said that I was extra special as they chose me.' Cathy didn't seem at all put out by Joanne's interrogation.

'I'm sorry to hear that, you must miss them,' Alison said sympathetically. 'Do you have a partner?' She had held back and allowed Joanne and Jason to do the talking at first but now she thought the atmosphere could do with lightening up a little. Cathy must have been nervous coming here, wondering what they would all think of her.

'No, I did marry but we divorced some years ago. I prefer to be on my own,' Cathy said with a small smile.

'Please excuse all the questions, Cathy, obviously we're all very curious about you,' Damien said, a friendly smile on his face. 'And we're delighted that you and Mary are reunited at last.'

Honestly, he was such a smooth operator, not many people saw beneath that affable exterior to the controlling and overbearing person Damien really was. Alison didn't know how Joanne put up with him. Mind you, living with Jason wasn't a walk in the park.

Mary beamed. 'And so am I. Now let's all sit down and have lunch,' she said. 'Everything's ready. Cathy came early to help me.'

Cathy immediately sat down to the right of Mary and Jason quickly sat on her left. Alison glanced over at Joanne and saw a scowl cross her face. She wouldn't like it that Cathy had come early to help and was now sitting next to Mary. She loved being the eldest, the one her mother always turned to for help. Although Jason was Mary's favourite, everyone knew that.

They chatted over dinner – roast beef with all the trimmings followed by lemon meringue pie, which Cathy had made – exchanging titbits from their lives, although Cathy did more listening than talking, Alison noticed. She seemed genuinely interested in Joanne and Jason.

Cathy insisted on stopping to help Mary clean up, pointing out that she didn't have to work until Monday afternoon and had no children to get off to school either so the others waved goodbye and left. But instead of going to their own house, Joanne and Damien followed Jason and Alison home so that they could all discuss the afternoon's events. Alison got their two boys off up to bed and Kelly and Connor were sent into the lounge to watch TV so the adults could talk in peace. Alison came down to find Damien holding court in the kitchen.

'Well, that was a bit awkward. I get that Mary is happy to find her long-lost daughter, but I'm not sure what I think of Cathy. She's a bit... rough.' Damien grimaced. 'That awful accent. And she's nothing like you and Jason, Jo. Although I guess that's probably only to be expected as you have different fathers. She does have a slight resemblance to Mary, though.'

He was right. The first thing that had struck Alison was how different Cathy was with her jet-black hair and dark brown eyes. Mary had fair hair and blue eyes, and so had Paul, Joanne and Jason too – although Joanne's hair was enhanced by regular hairdresser visits now and Jason was going a bit thin on top. Cathy was tall too, with a thin, sharp face whereas Joanne and Jason both had rather rounded faces. She could see a bit of Mary in her though with her small, upturned nose and thin lips. Her speech was different too, not just the Brummie accent, which was odd as she said that she grew up in Surrey – though she did live in Birmingham now so must have moved away when she was older and had left home – but also the way she pronounced her words. She'd obviously gone to the local comprehensive. She'd have thought that with Cathy's adoptive parents both being dentists, they would want her to go to a private school and get a good education.

'She's not very communicative, though, is she? She answered our questions as briefly as possible, we still hardly know anything about her,' Joanne pointed out.

'It must have been difficult for her, Jo, meeting you all for the first time. And, well...' Alison paused. 'I'm not being snobby but it's obvious that she's not got a lot of money. She probably felt a bit awkward.'

'I guess so,' Joanne agreed.

'She seems nice, though, and it's good to see Mary so happy. The past few months have been hard for her,' Alison added. She knew what it was like to be a newcomer in this family. She and Jason had been together eight years, married for six of them and she still felt like an outsider at times.

'It must be strange for you, Jo, not being the eldest anymore,' Damien said.

Jo flushed. Alison thought that was a bit of a cruel remark. Everyone knew how Joanne prided herself on being the one who looked after her parents, the one her mother had leaned on since Paul had died. Yet she and Mary weren't close; their personalities didn't really gel.

'It'll be a change for you to be bossed about by someone, whereas nothing's really changed for me. I'm still the youngest. The only boy. And the favourite,' Jason added. Alison could hear the tinge of amusement in his voice. He was enjoying seeing Joanne being usurped from her position.

'It must be a shock for Cathy too,' Alison cut in. 'Fancy meeting your mother for the first time at the age of forty-five. And to know that she's pretty affluent, and has two more children that she kept and looked after. That's got to hurt.'

'Is there any chance it could be a mistake that this Cathy really is Mum's long-lost daughter?' Jason asked. She could hear the hope in his voice. She bet he was thinking of having to share the money Mary had promised to give them when the house was sold. It was all about the money with Jason. Always had been.

'Afraid not, they matched on the DNA database,' Joanne told him.

'I guess we'll just have to accept it then,' Jason sighed.

'Seems like it. I'm just as upset as you are,' Joanne confided.

'I can't believe that Mum's kept this big secret from us all these years. And from Dad too. Would she ever have told us if Dad hadn't died, do you think? Or would she have gone to the grave taking her secret with her?'

'I wish she had. I don't want to play bloody happy families,' Jason grumbled.

'Neither do I but we're just going to have to go along with this. It's what Mum wants,' Joanne told him.

'I wonder what Paul would have made of it. Do you think it would have split them up?' Damien asked.

'I don't know. I think he would have been shocked but he would have accepted it. Dad idolised Mum, he always said that he couldn't believe his luck when she agreed to marry him. Mum should have told him. It was wrong to keep something as big as this from him,' Joanne said.

Jason shrugged. 'I don't see why. It all happened before he even knew Mum, and yes, she abandoned the baby but she was just a kid and scared stiff. And she did keep watch to make sure that the baby was found. I can understand her wanting to put it all behind her and get on with her life.'

Alison noted how he said 'the baby' as opposed to 'Cathy'. As if they were two different people. 'Paul did like to keep up appearances, though,' she ventured. Joanne and Jason, especially Joanne, adored their father but Alison had always thought her father-in-law was a bit of a snob. She reckoned Mary did too, otherwise she would have told him about her daughter and tried to find her. It was obvious that it was something that had troubled her for years otherwise she wouldn't have started the search as soon as Paul had died. She wondered what the teenage Mary had been like. It was tragic really that Cathy's father had died before she was born. Maybe he would have married Mary, and they could have kept Cathy and brought her up together. Mary's life would probably be a lot different to what it was now, though.

'Well, I have to admit that I wish she hadn't dug it all up now,' Jason admitted. 'Best to leave it buried after all these years.'

Looking at the scowl on his face, Alison wondered if he was worried about Cathy replacing him in Mary's affections as the favourite. Well, it would do him good if she did, he'd had his own way far too long. Alison was at the end of her tether with his devious and selfish ways.

'Let's see how it goes – they might be all over each other right now but they don't really have much in common, do they? Once the initial excitement of finding each other has calmed down they could well drift apart,' Damien pointed out.

'I hope so,' Joanne said. And Jason nodded his agreement.

# 18

## *Mary*

Mary had arranged to meet Stella for a coffee in the village café the next morning. Part of her wanted to tell Stella about finding Cathy, but she couldn't bring herself to, not yet. It had been so hard to confess everything to her family, she couldn't face going through it all again to her friend, and answering the inevitable questions. It had gone better than she'd expected, though; everyone seemed to get on and Cathy had messaged her once she got home last night to thank her for inviting her over and to say how much she enjoyed meeting everyone.

Mary had breakfast and tidied up a little then went out to her car, which was parked in the drive by the side of the house. She glanced quickly over it, as Paul had always insisted she do before getting in. 'Always check that you have no punctures, the lights are working and you have enough fuel,' he'd said. Then her gaze caught the flat back tyre and she groaned. A puncture! That was all she needed. She crouched down to have a closer look at the tyre. Goodness, there was a big nail in the sidewall of it. How had that happened? She guessed she must have driven over a nail on the way home, she was lucky it had held out until she got back. She checked all the other tyres, glad to see that they were okay then texted Jason to see if he could drop in on the way home from work to change the wheel for her before setting off to meet Stella. The café was only a quarter of an hour's walk and it was a nice day.

They had a lovely lunch and Stella insisted on giving Mary a lift home when she heard about her punctured tyre. 'Let me give you the number of our mechanic,' she said as she pulled up at the bottom of the drive of Mary's house. 'You'll be stuck without your car and you don't want to have to depend on your son all the time.' She opened the glove box and took out a business card, handing it to Mary. 'He's very reliable.'

Mary thanked her and took the card. 'See you soon.' As her friend drove off, it struck Mary just how isolated she was here, there weren't many amenities in the village and she'd hate to have to rely on the infrequent public transport. She had always adored this house, right from when she and Paul had first viewed it. Situated at the end of a long country lane on the outskirts of the village, a few minutes' walk from neighbouring properties, it had afforded the privacy they both wanted. She would be stranded without the car, though, and Stella was right, she didn't want to be calling Jason every time she had a problem.

As she walked down the drive to her car, she saw that it was jacked up and the back wheel missing. Jason must have dropped by to sort it out for her when she was out. He was so thoughtful, she thought gratefully as she let herself in.

---

Later, when Jason had returned and the wheel with the replacement tyre was back in place, Mary showed him the card with the number of the mobile mechanic. 'Stella recommended him, and it means I won't have to bother you again if something goes wrong. I hate to be a nuisance,' she said.

'You're not a nuisance, Mum. I'm always happy to help you,' he assured her. 'But...' He paused, suddenly looking serious. 'You know we're all worried about you being here by yourself. You're a bit out of the way here and, well, there's such a lot of crime in the area.'

'Is there? What do you mean? I haven't heard anything,' she asked, startled.

Jason nodded. 'I don't want to worry you, Mum, but times have changed and there's been a few burglaries. Big houses like yours in isolated positions are a magnet and the police are so under-staffed they don't even respond to burglaries anymore. And...' He raised his eyes to hers and she could see that the concern etched on his face. 'You really should keep your car in the garage at night. I'm sure that the punctured tyre was an accident but a car like that is a target for thieves. I've put it in the garage for you.'

Mary was stunned. She had never considered herself in danger. This was such a peaceful area. The thought that someone might steal her car or break into her house had never troubled her. She had CCTV and an alarm but the drive was open access.

'I wish you'd think about selling up and moving somewhere smaller, Mum. This house shouts money and if people know you live here alone...' He paused. 'It would be a lot a safer if you came to live with us, or move to a retirement apartment. Please say you'll think about it.'

'Oh darling, it would be such an upheaval,' Mary protested. She really didn't think she could face the stress of moving with all the sorting out and packing that entailed. Besides, she loved her home.

'I just want you to be safe, Mum. We all do,' Jason said.

She wanted to be safe too, Mary thought. She had never

been scared when Paul was here, but now she was starting to feel a bit uneasy, especially after what Jason had said. As she climbed into bed that night, she kissed his photograph, then replayed his answerphone message, wanting to hear his words of love. *Oh Paul, why did you have to leave me?*

# 19

'Cathy! Come in! This is really kind of you,' Mary said, beaming with pleasure when she opened the door to Cathy on Wednesday morning. 'I've got Nicholas for the whole day today so I'm glad of the company, and help.'

'It's a pleasure.' Cathy stepped into the house and followed her into the kitchen where Nicholas was sitting at the table colouring.

He looked up. 'Hello,' he said. He cocked his head to one side. 'Can I call you Auntie Cathy?' he asked.

'Of course you can.' Cathy knelt down to look at red and yellow splodges that he'd covered the sheet of paper with. 'That's very bright,' she said approvingly.

'Like red and yellow,' Nicholas replied, grinning up at her, a red splodge on his cheek and a yellow splodge on his nose.

He smiled. He was such an easy-going, polite little boy, he reminded Mary of Jason when he was growing up. Oliver was a little more difficult, inclined to sulk and be stubborn, so things had been easier once he started school. It would be the school holidays soon though and she would have both boys to look after so she intended to make sure she had a full schedule to keep them entertained, trips to the cinema, swimming pools, parks and playgrounds. When Oliver got frustrated he had terrible tantrums which she found difficult to cope with.

'Take a seat. Would you like a cup of tea or coffee?' she asked Cathy.

'Tea please. Let me make it.' She walked over to the kettle and switched it on. Then she glanced over at Nicholas with a smile. 'He seems very happy.'

Mary pulled out a chair and sat down by her grandson. 'He usually is very cheerful. It's a pleasure to look after him.'

'Hard work, though?' Cathy asked as she took two mugs off the mug rack. 'Do you want tea too?'

Mary nodded. 'Please.' She looked lovingly at Nicholas. 'Yes, it is a bit full on but I like to help out. And they're young for such a little time.'

'I know. I adore children.' Cathy paused and Mary sensed a sadness there. It seemed like she would have loved a child of her own. Why hadn't she had one? Was it because she couldn't have children or simply had never found the right partner?

Then Cathy continued, 'I often have Wednesdays off – Fridays sometimes too. I'd be quite happy to pop in for a couple of hours, give you a hand. You'll have both boys to look after from next week, won't you?'

'Yes I will. That's very kind of you. I'd really appreciate it if you're sure.' Mary watched as Cathy put a tea bag in each mug and poured boiling water over then added sugar and milk. She and her eldest daughter both liked their tea the same way.

Cathy carried the two mugs over to the table, put one in front of Mary then sat down beside her. 'You look a little tired. I guess you aren't sleeping well at the moment. Hardly surprising,' she said. 'Would you like me to take Nicholas in the garden to play for a while when we've finished our drink, give you chance to have a little rest?'

'That's so kind of you,' Mary said. 'My head is pounding a little.'

Cathy leaned over the table and placed her hand on Mary's. 'If you ever need any company or help, you only have to ask.'

'Thank you, that's really kind of you. But what about your work?'

'I work every other weekend, so have weekdays off then instead,' Cathy replied. 'And I often do late evening shifts too, so have daytimes free. I always offer to do the anti-social hours, as so many of the staff have families.' She leaned forward and looked at the picture that Nicholas was now colouring. 'You've done that really neatly,' she said admiringly.

Nicholas gave her a big grin. 'Nanny said not to go over the lines.'

'And you hardly have. Well done.'

Mary watched as Cathy chatted easily to Nicholas. She had a good way with children, knew how to talk to them without talking *down* to them.

'Nicholas and I were about to have lunch, would you like to join us?' she asked.

'That would be wonderful, thank you,' Cathy replied. 'I'll help you do it.'

They took lunch out in the garden and spent a lovely afternoon chatting while Nicholas played. Cathy asked a little more about her birth and Mary went up to get the flannel out of the tin, wanting to show her that she had loved her so much she had even kept the flannel she had cleaned her with.

Cathy looked really touched when Mary showed her the now-yellowing flannel. 'I can't believe you've kept this all these years.'

'I didn't wash it for ages,' Mary told her. 'I didn't want to wash away your smell, but eventually I had to.'

'That's so lovely to know. I'm so sorry for what you had to go through.' She reached over and squeezed Mary's hand.

Leaving Cathy to play with Nicholas, Mary put the flannel back in the tin, surprised to hear the upstairs bathroom chain flush as she came out of her bedroom, then the door opened and Cathy came out. 'Sorry, Nicholas wanted to use the loo downstairs, so I dashed up here. I hope that's okay,' she said.

'Of course,' Mary told her.

'What time is Alison picking up Nicholas?' she asked as they walked downstairs together. Peering out of the window, Mary saw that Nicholas was now on the swing, he must have gone straight out into the back garden.

'About four, after she's collected Oliver from school,' Mary told her. 'Although Jason might finish work early and collect him.'

'Not long then, so you'll be okay if I go now?' Cathy asked after checking her watch. It was three-thirty. 'I've got work this evening and there's a few things I need to do first.'

'Well, thank you for visiting. I hope we haven't tired you out,' Mary told her.

'Not at all. I've enjoyed every minute of it,' Cathy reassured her. 'I'll see you on Friday, same time?'

'Thank you. That's so kind of you,' Mary replied. She would be grateful for her help and it would give her and Cathy a chance to get to know each other better too. She'd lost so many years with her daughter, there was still such a lot that she didn't know about her.

# 20

Cathy returned on Friday, texting Mary to let her know she was on the way. Mary was relieved when she heard the bell ring. She and Nicholas had been playing Hungry Hippos for half an hour now and she was getting tired of it. It would be lovely to have some adult company. And Cathy had been so good with Nicholas on Wednesday.

'I'm so glad to see you,' Mary said as she opened the door. 'We're playing Hungry Hippos, Nicholas is winning but the game is taking forever and I'm dying for a cuppa.'

'Let me make you one – or would you prefer me to take your place in the game?' Cathy offered as she stepped inside.

'Oh, take my place in the game, please!' Mary said, glad to be handing over to Cathy. 'I'll go and put the kettle on.'

Cathy took off her coat as she followed Mary into the lounge. 'Hello, Nicholas.' She held out her arms.

'Auntie Cathy!' Nicholas's face broke into a grin. He scrambled off the chair and ran over for a hug. Mary watched happily as he wrapped his arms around Cathy and she returned the hug.

'Auntie Cathy is going to take over from me while I make a cup of tea. Is that okay?' Mary asked.

'Course.' Nicholas grabbed Cathy's hand and led her over to the table. 'Nanny is yellow and red.' He leaned closer. 'She's not doing very well.'

Cathy grinned and winked at Mary, as if she'd guessed that Mary was trying to lose so that the game would be finished earlier. 'Well, let me see if I can do a bit better,' she said. 'Shall we put the game on the floor? It will be easier.'

Nicholas grabbed the board and placed it down on the carpet. Cathy got down beside him. 'You can go first.'

When Mary returned with a tray containing two mugs of tea, a beaker of juice and a plate of biscuits, Cathy and Nicholas were sprawled out on the carpet playing, and Nicholas was squealing with laughter as his hippo snatched the Golden Ball. 'I've won again! I'm the champion!'

'You certainly are.' Cathy ruffled his hair. 'Shall we take a break now and have a snack?'

Nicholas scrambled to his feet. 'I'll wash my hands,' he said.

'He's a lovely little boy,' Cathy said as she got up and sat down at the table where Mary had just put down the tray.

'He is. I enjoy looking after him, it's just a bit exhausting at my age. I'm grateful for you popping in.' She smiled at Cathy.

'It's a pleasure.'

Nicholas joined them at the table and eagerly drank his juice.

'Shall we have a bit of quiet time now?' Cathy suggested when they had finished their drinks. 'Nanny is looking a little tired. How about we snuggle up and watch a cartoon on the TV?' She glanced at Mary. 'Is that okay?'

Mary nodded gratefully. She really was tired. She wasn't sleeping well lately. 'It's a splendid idea.' She lifted the top of the pouffe and took out a bright blanket. 'This is Nicholas's cuddle blanket.'

Cathy took it from her. 'Settle yourself down, Nicholas, and I'll put this over you while Nanny puts on the TV,' she said. Nicholas happily lay down on a cushion and Cathy covered him with the blanket, sitting down beside him. Mary pressed the remote and the TV flicked into life. She selected the cartoon channel and sat down in the armchair. Within a few minutes she could feel her eyes closing. When she woke up a little while later, Nicholas was sleeping and there was no sign of Cathy. Maybe she'd gone to get a drink, Mary thought, getting to her feet. She needed the toilet. As she walked out of the door, she saw Cathy in the hall.

'Have you had a nice rest?' she asked. 'I was about to make a cuppa and wake you up. I have to go soon.'

'Thank you, that would be appreciated. I just need the loo.'

Cathy smiled. 'That's where I've been. I'll go and put the kettle on.'

They had a cup of tea then Cathy left, promising to drop by over the weekend. A little while later, Jason came for Nicholas.

'Are you okay, Mum? Nothing else happened?' he asked.

'No, thank goodness,' Mary told him. 'Will you stop for a drink?' she asked, suddenly reluctant to be alone in an empty house after it had been so full all day.

'Sure. Is it okay if I borrow Dad's printer? Mine's decided to stop working and I've got some files I need to print out this evening.'

'Of course. Keep it. I don't use it and Dad would want you to have it.'

'Thanks. I'll pop up and get it.' Jason headed up the stairs for Paul's study while Mary turned to Nicholas.

'Would you like some milk and biscuits?'

The little boy nodded and they both went into the kitchen. When Jason came down with the printer, they all sat chatting for a while.

'Come over this weekend, Mum. You know that you're welcome anytime. Don't sit here by yourself,' he said.

'I'm fine, honestly. I'm just going to relax this evening,' she assured him.

After they left, she settled down to watch the TV for a bit, letting Bailey out of the cage so he could stretch his wings. It had been good to have Cathy's company today, she'd really enjoyed it.

She was tired, so decided not to go to bed too late. She made herself a cup of hot chocolate, said goodnight to Bailey, who had now gone back in his cage, and covered him up, then carried the hot chocolate upstairs to bed. She pushed open the bedroom door and went flying, spilling hot chocolate everywhere. Groaning, she sat up, rubbing her leg, and looked around to see what she'd tripped on. Her wardrobe door was open and a handbag had fallen out. She must have knocked it out when she was putting the tin back earlier. She really had to be more careful. She could have broken her leg or hip.

# 21

Mary was so tired she fell asleep as soon as her head touched the pillow, only to be woken a couple of hours later by loud banging. She switched on the bedside lamp and sat up, listening intently, had she been dreaming? No, there it was again. Something was definitely banging.

She slid out of bed, pulled on her dressing gown and reached for the phone, then crept over to the window and pulled the curtain aside at the end, peering out into the dark. It was all quiet now. She turned to go back to bed, jumping in alarm as another bang resonated through the silent house. What was it? She paused, straining her ears to locate it, sure it was coming from inside the house. Had someone broken in? She panicked, clutching her phone. Should she call the police?

*The house is locked, no one can get in, not without setting off the alarm,* she told herself as she tiptoed out of the bedroom and listened at the top of the stairs.

The next bang was so loud she trembled and had to grip the banister for support. It sounded as if it was coming from the room next door. The spare bedroom. She selected the number for the police, her finger hovering over the call button ready to press it if she needed to as she carefully walked over to the bedroom and pushed open the door – gasping in alarm when she saw the blind blowing in the breeze. The window was wide open! Her terrified gaze darted around the room. Had someone climbed in? Were they hiding from her? Her heart thudding, she swallowed back a scream and held up the phone in one hand, her finger on the call button as she hit the switch on the wall with her other hand, flooding the room with light. She almost collapsed in relief when she saw that the room was empty. She must have left the window open herself. She walked over to the window and closed it firmly. She really was getting forgetful.

# 22

*Alison*

'How did you hurt your arm?' Alison asked, noticing the big blue bruise on the top of Nicholas's arm as she pulled off his messy T-shirt.

'Auntie Cathy did it. It was an accident,' he said, rubbing the bruise.

'Auntie Cathy?' Alison frowned. 'When?' They hadn't seen Cathy since Sunday... unless she'd come around to see her mother one of the days in the week when Nicholas was there. Her mother-in-law hadn't mentioned it, though.

'Today,' Nicholas said matter-of-factly.

So Cathy had been to visit Mary when she was looking after Nicholas. Why hadn't Mary mentioned it when Jason went to pick him up?

'How did she do it? Did Nanny see?' Alison demanded. It was a nasty-looking bruise. One that looked like it had been caused by a thump or a fall.

Nicholas shrugged. 'Nanny was asleep. Auntie Cathy was in Nanny's bedroom playing hide and seek.'

Alison frowned. Cathy should know better than to play hide and seek in Mary's bedroom. The boys were never allowed upstairs in any of the rooms. 'And how did she hurt your arm?'

Nicholas shook his head. 'It was an accident. She banged it on the door when she was hiding.'

Alison crouched down so that she was eye level with Nicholas. 'What door?'

Nicholas looked awkward. 'The wardrobe door.'

How could a wardrobe door cause a bruise like that? The trouble was Nicholas's concentration and vocabulary wasn't that brilliant. She tried to question Nicholas further but all he said was that Cathy had been hiding in the wardrobe and he'd found her. She guessed maybe that Cathy had pushed the door open to jump out and it had caught Nicholas's arm. Well, she shouldn't have been playing hide and seek in Mary's bedroom, and especially not in her wardrobe. Had it been an excuse to snoop? She'd have to talk to Jason later.

As it was, Jason was working late so Alison didn't get a chance to talk to him until the next morning.

'Did you know that Cathy was at your mum's yesterday?' she asked when he came out of the shower, drying his hair.

Jason paused, towel in hand. 'Cathy? Are you sure? Why?' he asked. She couldn't figure out whether he was surprised or worried.

'I've no idea but Nicholas has a big bruise on his arm and he said that "Auntie Cathy" did it yesterday. He said she was playing hide and seek with him and hid in your mum's wardrobe when your mum was asleep.'

Jason sat down on the bed, his hair still wet and sticking up. 'How bad is the bruise? Surely you don't think she did it on purpose?'

'He said she banged it on the door so it sounds as if it was accidental.' Alison folded her arms. 'The point is, what was

Cathy doing in Mary's bedroom? And why hasn't your mum mentioned that she's been visiting her?'

'I guess she never thought.' Jason looked worried. 'Do you think Cathy is up to something? That's she's trying to worm her way in with Mum?'

Alison considered this. She could understand that Mary and Cathy had lots of lost time to make up for and wanted to get to know each other more but she wasn't happy with Cathy spending time with Nicholas without their knowledge or permission. Especially now that Nicholas had a bruise, which Cathy apparently hadn't even mentioned. 'I don't know,' she said finally. 'I'm going to talk to your mum about it on Wednesday when I take Nicholas over. I don't want anything like this happening again. And I think she needs to be warned that Cathy might be snooping.'

'Maybe I should be the one to have a word with Mum,' Jason said.

Alison shook her head. 'It might sound as if you're trying to badmouth Cathy because you're jealous. It's best if I speak to Mary, I can focus on my concerns for Nicholas.'

Jason nodded. 'Okay.' He looked at his hair in the mirror and grimaced. 'I'd better put some gel on this, I look like a bloody hedgehog.' He dipped his fingers in a tub of gel and rubbed it into his hair. 'I'll be back at lunchtime.'

She hated it when Jason worked on a weekend, but he'd been quite upbeat just lately so maybe business was picking up. She hoped so. Actually, she'd go and see Mary this morning, she decided. Show her the bruise on Nicholas's arm. It could have faded by Wednesday and she wanted to make sure that it didn't happen again.

---

Mary's face broke into a big smile when she opened the door. 'Hello, dear. This is a nice surprise. I wasn't expecting you,' she said. 'Do come in.'

'We're not disturbing you, are we?' Alison asked as she and the boys followed Mary into the kitchen.

'Not at all, I'm not going out until after lunch. It's always lovely to see you. Do sit down. Would you all like a drink?'

'Thanks, that would be great.' Alison took two tablets out of her bag and handed them to the boys. 'Sit down and play quietly while I talk to your nan,' she said.

'Is anything wrong?' Mary asked, giving her a worried look.

'I don't want to cause trouble, but...' Alison twiddled a strand of her hair around her finger, wondering how to phrase it. She didn't want to make it sound like she was accusing Cathy of anything untoward. 'Well, I noticed a big bruise on Nicholas's arm when he was changing yesterday and he said that he did it when he and Cathy played hide and seek in your bedroom.'

'I don't understand...' Mary looked puzzled. 'Cathy did pop in yesterday but I'm not aware of them playing hide and seek in my bedroom.'

'Nicholas said that you had fallen asleep on the sofa.' She tried not to make her tone sound accusing, although she was angry. She'd left Nicholas in Mary's care, she had no right to leave him unsupervised with Cathy – they barely knew her.

'Let me show Nanny your bruise,' she said, walking over to the little boy and pulling up the sleeve of his jumper to show Mary.

Mary looked shocked. 'Goodness, that *is* a nasty bruise.' She knelt down and looked at Nicholas's arm. 'So you were playing hide and seek in my bedroom?'

Nicholas nodded, looking a bit worried. 'Auntie Cathy started it.'

'And what did you knock your arm on?'

'The wardrobe door. Auntie Cathy jumped out.'

'It's a bit of a liberty if you ask me,' Alison said. 'I'd have a word with Cathy.'

'I'm sure she meant no harm. She was just trying to entertain Nicholas while I had a rest.'

'It's worrying that you feel asleep too, Mary. Is it too much for you to look after the boys? It will be both of them now that school has broken up. Are you sure you can manage?' When Mary had agreed to look after the boys a couple of days a week in the holidays, saying it gave her something to fill her days, Alison had been pleased as it gave them the chance to see her regularly so could keep an eye on her. Also it saved them money. But maybe it wasn't a good idea.

'It absolutely is not. I'd just had a bad night. It won't happen again,' Mary said firmly.

'Okay but can you please have a word with Cathy? Tell her to be more careful. I don't want Nicholas to get hurt again.'

'Of course I will. I'm sure she hadn't realised that he had hurt himself otherwise she would have mentioned it,' Mary said. She handed Alison a mug of coffee then took a tin of biscuits out of the cupboard and placed them on the table.

'You might want to suggest that they don't play hide and seek in your bedroom again, anyway. It is a bit of a cheek,' Alison pointed out as she took a chocolate biscuit out of the tin. She had thought Cathy was okay but this seemed a bit off, as if she was snooping. And surely Nicholas would have cried out when he knocked his arm? Why hadn't Cathy mentioned it?

Unless Nicholas had spotted Cathy snooping and she had tried to get him out of the bedroom before Mary awoke and caught her, accidentally knocking it?

Another idea sneaked itself into her mind. Or she had hurt Nicholas to warn him not to tell on her?

She shook the idea from her mind. That was ridiculous. Wasn't it?

# 23

## *Cathy*

Cathy selected the photo gallery on her phone and looked again at the photo of the man who must be Robbie. She'd found it in Mary's tin in the wardrobe yesterday. When she'd seen Mary put the baby flannel into the tin and then place the tin in the wardrobe, she'd been bursting with curiosity about what else was in there so had sneaked a look when Mary was asleep. She'd found a strip of two black-and-white head-and-shoulder shots of a teenage Mary (she recognised her from the photo Mary had showed her of when she was pregnant) and an older dark-haired lad, wearing a leather jacket, the sort taken in a photo booth. The lad had jet-black hair, piercing brown eyes and an angular face with attitude written all over it. They both looked impossibly young. Especially Mary. When she'd turned the photo over she'd seen the words 'Me and Robbie' written on the back. Also in the box she'd found a newspaper article about Robbie being sent to prison for car theft.

Mary had lied, Cathy thought furiously. She'd told her that Robbie had died in a motorbike accident before Cathy was born. Had Mary made that up because she was ashamed that she'd fallen pregnant so young to someone she hardly knew and who'd turned out to be a criminal? Cathy had taken out her phone, and snapped photos of both the article and the photograph. She was putting the tin back in the wardrobe when Nicholas came in and found her so she had to pretend that she was playing hide and seek and had been hiding in the wardrobe. He'd wanted to hide too, it had taken her a job to get him out of the room.

She stared at the image of teenage Mary and Robbie. Robbie might still be alive and if he was, she wanted to find him too. Someone out there would know him.

# 24

*Alison*

'What do you think of Cathy?' Joanne asked as she and Alison sat down with their cups of coffee and sandwich later that afternoon. She'd messaged Alison and asked her to meet her for a chat, and Alison had immediately guessed what it was about. So had Jason, and he had agreed to watch the boys so that Joanne and Alison could both talk in peace. Obviously he'd want to know everything Joanne had said when Alison returned home.

Alison tore the corner of the sugar sachet and poured it into her coffee, stirring it slowly. 'She seems okay but...' She told Joanne about Nicholas's bruise. 'I know kids get bruises, especially when they're playing. And he seems to adore Cathy.' She looked up at Joanne. 'But she should have mentioned it.'

'Yes she should. And what was she doing in Mum's bedroom in the first place?' Joanne asked. She took a small container of sweeteners out of her bag and emptied two into her coffee. 'I don't think I trust her. It's all a bit too convenient, isn't it, her finding Mum a few months after Dad died? His death was announced in the papers and a quick google would provide the information that he was well-off. I think she's turned up, playing dutiful daughter because she knows Mum has money and wants a handout.'

'Maybe but she really is Mary's daughter, there's no doubt about that. They had a DNA test,' Alison pointed out. 'Jason even got Mary to show him the letter with the results.'

'Did he?' Joanne looked thoughtful. 'So he doesn't trust her either?'

'He calls her Cathy Cuckoo,' Alison admitted. 'He thinks she's worming her way into Mary's good books so that she can tap her for some money.'

'Damien thinks the same too, so we all seem to be on the same page. It's very worrying. Especially as Mum seems to spend all her spare time with Cathy now, and she feels so guilty about abandoning her that I think she'd do anything to make it up to her.' She brushed a strand of hair behind her ear. 'Mum's so vulnerable now she's on her own.'

Alison pondered this over. 'All we can do is try and keep an eye on the situation, but as I said to Jason, Mary is an adult, and compos mentis. She can do what she wants with her time – and her money.'

Joanne scowled. 'I'm not prepared to sit back and let Cathy rip my mother off just because Mum feels guilty for something she did as a teenager.' She shook her head. 'Actually, I still can't believe the whole sordid story. I feel like my mother isn't the woman I thought she was.'

'It was a long time ago and she was in a bad place. We've all done things we regret,' Alison told her as she tucked into her sandwich, although she did agree with Jason and Joanne, there was something about Cathy that she couldn't put her finger on.

'Okay, so she might be Mum's long-lost daughter but that doesn't mean she's a nice person,' Joanne said. 'She's had a completely different upbringing to us. We know nothing about her. And it seems a bit off for her to come to the house to help Mum look after Nicholas. She's really getting her feet under the table.'

Joanne had a point, Alison thought. She'd been a bit narked that Mary hadn't told her Cathy had come around, and Nicholas was already calling her Auntie Cathy. 'Jason is suspicious too and is keeping an eye on things. You know how close he is to Mary, he'll find out if Cathy is trying to exploit her.'

'I'm close to her too,' Joanne retorted.

Damn, she'd hit a nerve. 'I know you are, Jo. It's just she turns to Jason as the man of the family now Paul has gone.' She gathered her bag. 'Well, I must get going, I've left Jason with the kids.'

'I'll get this, I invited you,' Joanne said when the waiter brought the bill. She took a bank card out of her purse and handed it to him.

'Thank you,' Alison said with a smile. 'My treat next time.'

'I'm afraid your card has been declined, madam. Do you have another one?'

'I don't understand it, there should be plenty of money on there. Damien's just got paid.' Joanne looked really embarrassed.

'Please let me pay,' Alison said.

'It's fine, I have cash.' Joanne dug into her purse and took out a couple of notes.

She looked angry and worried, Alison thought. She wondered if Damien was gambling again. He'd got them in such a mess last time, almost losing their home, the children about to be pulled out of private schools. Joanne had been on the brink of leaving him but Paul had stepped in. Surely Damien wouldn't risk losing his home and breaking up the family again?

As they both walked out of the restaurant, Joanne glanced over the road and clutched Alison's arm. 'Well, speak of the devils. And don't they look cosy? Three guesses who's paid for all those clothes.'

Alison followed her gaze and saw Mary and Cathy walking along the street, arm in arm, chatting away easily together, designer shopping bags dangling from their free arms. What were they doing here? Cathy said she lived the other side of town and it wasn't her mother-in-law's usual shopping haunt. Mary hadn't mentioned this morning that she was meeting Cathy later.

'Should we call out to say hello?' Alison asked, but Mary and Cathy had already disappeared around the corner.

'I'm not chasing after them. Let's see if Mum mentions it,' Joanne said. 'Anyway, I've got to get off. See you soon, Alison.'

---

Alison told Jason about it as soon as she got home, knowing that Joanne would probably phone him later anyway. 'Joanne was really put out. She thinks that it's very suspicious, Cathy doesn't look as if she has enough money for all those clothes and she said Mary is being secretive. She thinks the same as you, that Cathy is after Mary's money.'

He raised his eyebrows. 'Does she? It's not like me and Jo to agree on something.' He frowned. 'I get that Mum wants to make up for lost time, and spend as much time as she can with Cathy, but I think we need to keep a close eye on her. Mum's not herself at the moment.'

'That's exactly what Jo said,' Alison told him. 'Have the kids had their tea?'

'No, they had lunch late so I thought I'd better wait 'til you got home.' He got up and reached for his jacket. 'I've got to go now, a meeting with a new client.'

'On a Saturday evening?' Alison asked.

'You have to be prepared to work any time if you want to

succeed,' Jason told her, kissing her quickly on the forehead. 'See you later. Don't wait up, I'll be late back.'

Another Saturday night alone for her then, Alison thought, annoyed. It was typical of Jason to leave all the childcare to her again and without even a word of apology or thanks. She took her phone out of her pocket and texted Hugh.

# 25

## *Mary*

It had been such an enjoyable day yesterday. Mary loved treating Cathy, she was so appreciative for everything. Mary had mentioned the bruise on Nicholas's arm to her and Cathy had immediately looked horrified. 'I'm so sorry. I had no idea he'd hurt himself. He wanted to play hide and seek and I agreed but I couldn't find him anywhere, then I saw your bedroom door open. I pushed the door wide open and heard him shout. He'd been hiding behind the door! It must have hit his arm. I'm so sorry, I should have checked.'

Nicholas had said Cathy had been hiding in the wardrobe, but Mary knew the little boy often got mixed up. 'I knew it must be something like that. I'll explain to Alison.'

'Should I? I feel terrible,' Cathy had offered. 'I did tell Nicholas that he shouldn't be hiding in your bedroom but I didn't scold him, I promise. I was kind but firm.' She looked really troubled. 'I hope Alison isn't upset.'

'Don't worry, she'll understand,' Mary had told her.

After the shopping trip Mary had mentioned that she was

going to tackle the front garden the next day so Cathy offered to come over and help. She arrived soon after Mary had finished breakfast and they immediately got started tidying the flower beds.

'I could do with some more pretty plants,' Mary said when they'd finished. 'It's looking a bit bare.'

'Let's go to the garden centre and get some, they're usually open until two on Sundays. We can go in my car – the boot is already messy,' Cathy suggested.

So they both cleaned up and headed over to the garden centre, returning with a boxful of plants a couple of hours later. They had just finished putting them in the garden when Jason arrived.

'Hello, you two seem busy,' he said, thrusting his hands in his pockets as he surveyed the colourful flower beds.

'The garden was looking so sad, Cathy offered to help me tidy it up,' Mary told him, standing up and brushing her hands on her jeans. 'Did you want something or have you just popped in for a chat?'

'I wanted to check on you, make sure you're okay. I worry about you being here all alone.'

'I'm fine,' Mary assured him, thinking it best not to confess that she'd scared herself stiff the other night when she'd left the window open in the spare bedroom and had heard the blind blowing. 'We're stopping for a break now so why don't you join us?'

'Sure, I could do with a cool drink,' he replied.

Cathy stood up and wiped her forehead. 'I'll go and get a jug of orange juice and some glasses, but first Jason, can I explain about Nicholas's bruise?' She repeated what she'd told Mary. 'The door must have banged against his arm. I had no idea it was bruised or I would have mentioned it.'

Jason nodded. 'It was a surprise to find out that you were helping Mum look after Nicholas. She didn't mention it.'

'I didn't get a chance. You and Alison are so busy, we hardly get a chance to talk,' Mary told him. 'That isn't a criticism. I know how hectic life is with young children.'

'Mary didn't know I was coming on Wednesday. I popped in to see if she needed any help, I know how demanding young children can be. Then I offered to come over on Friday too.' Cathy folded her arms. 'I was going to help her this week as she is looking after both boys but if that's a problem—?' She raised an eyebrow questioningly.

For a moment, she and Jason locked gazes, almost as if they were challenging each other. Mary watched them, confused at the undercurrent that seemed to be between them, but then Jason shrugged. 'Not at all. I'll let Alison know.' He turned to Mary. 'Actually, I'll pass on the refreshments, Mum. I only dropped by to check you were okay but as you have Cathy for company I'll leave you to it.' He kissed her on the cheek and walked back over to his car. Mary watched him, puzzled. She hoped he wasn't upset.

'Well, I don't think Jason's pleased that I'm here,' Cathy said. 'I get the impression that he and Joanne resent me a little.'

'I'm sure they don't. He's probably a bit stressed over work,' Mary told her. 'Take no notice of him.'

'Oh I won't. It's you I come to see.' Cathy linked her arm through Mary's and they walked back into the house.

They spent another hour or so chatting then Cathy went home. 'I'll see you on Wednesday,' she said.

---

The fresh air and gardening had tired Mary out and she slept well that night, not waking until gone eight the next morning. She went downstairs to uncover Bailey, who was chirping happily, then went out the front to admire the new flower beds. But as she stepped outside she gasped in horror. The beautiful, colourful flowers they had planted yesterday were all dead. They lay flattened and broken, as if someone had trampled all over them.

Mary clutched her chest as she stared at the broken stems and crushed flowers. Someone had done this deliberately. Someone had come into the garden while she was sleeping and trampled on her flowers. Why?

She took a few deep breaths to calm herself then telephoned Jason to tell him what had happened. 'Have you checked the CCTV, Mum?' he asked. 'It covers the whole drive so should show you the culprit.'

Of course, she hadn't thought of that.

'I'll come round when I can take a break from work, but try not to worry. It'll probably be kids. They get their kicks out of doing things like this.'

'But why now? We've never had trouble before.'

'I don't know but stuff like this is on the increase. And maybe word has got around that you're living by yourself. I wish you'd move in with us for a bit until you sell the house and get something smaller. I don't want to worry you, Mum, but I'm not sure you're safe there.'

*Neither am I*, Mary thought, as she ended the call. She fetched her laptop, booted it up and clicked on the CCTV app. There was no recording. The wi-fi must have failed again.

The phone rang again. Jason. 'Did the CCTV show anything?' he asked.

'Nothing at all. The wi-fi must have gone off again,' she told him.

'Oh no. You really should keep an eye on it, Mum.'

'I didn't notice. I haven't been on the laptop for ages,' she told him. They were always losing the signal to the wi-fi but it didn't really bother her as she rarely used her laptop and had unlimited data on her phone and iPad, although sometimes her mobile signal was bad too.

. . .

Jason came around a little while later, and checked out Mary's CCTV app on the laptop – as if he didn't trust her to do it correctly, Mary thought irritably. 'It hasn't recorded anything for weeks, Mum,' he exclaimed. 'I'd better check the wi-fi router.'

He went into the lounge where the router was kept behind the TV. 'For goodness' sake, Mum. You've switched it off. No wonder it doesn't work!' he said, clearly exasperated.

'I did not switch it off!' she protested.

Jason sighed. 'It's definitely been turned off, Mum. It had to have been you, you're the only one here.' He ran his hand through his hair. 'I've put it back on again now. Let me check the laptop and make sure the CCTV is working.'

He clicked back on the app then shook his head. 'It says the software needs updating too. You're running on an old system but the trouble is the new system isn't compatible with your laptop so you're going to get glitches.'

She hated modern technology, always updating systems. Why couldn't they leave things how they were?

'So what do I do?'

'I'll update it for now and we can hope but we need to get you more reliable CCTV. You've had this for years. Please, come and stay with us for a few days, Mum, just until we get you a new CCTV sorted out,' he said. 'I don't like you being here on your own with this going on.'

Mary shook her head. Tempting as it was, she knew that she couldn't let fear drive her out.

'I'll be fine, I promise,' she said.

Jason looked up from the laptop a little while later. 'Right, I've updated it. Now don't touch the router!' he told her. 'I'll sort you out another system as soon as I've got a bit of time to spare.'

. . .

Jason obviously told Joanne because she came over that evening and tried to persuade Mary to go back with her too. 'I don't think you're safe here, Mum,' she said.

'Of course I am. It was just kids messing around,' Mary told her, hoping that she sounded braver than she felt.

'I wish you'd think about selling up and moving somewhere smaller, Mum. This house shouts money and if people know you live here alone, you're an easy target,' Joanne said. 'It would be a lot safer if you came to live with us, or moved into a retirement apartment.'

Which was exactly what Jason had said to her when her car tyre was punctured. After seeing Joanne off, Mary poured herself a small sherry and sat down, deep in thought. Had someone got it in for her? Was she in danger? Or was it a random act? And who had switched the router off? She knew she hadn't. She never touched the router.

Unless... A thought wormed into her mind. Her mother had always done things then forgotten about it. Ordering things, giving things away, putting food in the oven and forgetting about it, hiding her purse in the washing machine. She'd gotten early-onset dementia in her forties and they hadn't realised what was happening until a neighbour found her wandering the streets late one night, looking for her dog which had died many years ago. Mary had always feared that she would get it too. Had the stress of Paul's sudden death triggered it?

# 26

Alison called on Tuesday to say that she had no appointments for the next day so the boys could stay home with her. Much as she loved her grandsons, Mary was relieved. She phoned to let Cathy know. 'You don't think it's because of me, do you?' Cathy asked. 'I'm sure Alison still blames me.'

'Of course she doesn't, Alison is very understanding,' Mary reassured her. Then she paused. 'Look, why don't you come around this evening instead – if you aren't working, that is? Bring the old school reports and workbooks you promised to show me. I'll rustle up something to eat for us.'

'I'd love that. But only if you allow me to bring dinner. I don't want you slaving away in the kitchen,' Cathy insisted.

She really was such a kind, thoughtful woman. Mary felt blessed to have found her.

Cathy arrived at dead on six, a big smile on her face and a supermarket shopping bag in her hand.

'Right on time,' Mary said, her heart lifting at the sight of her. She glanced at the bag. 'Are you preparing tea here?'

'No, it's all done, ready to heat up,' Cathy said, following Mary into the house and along the hall to the kitchen. She put the bag down on the kitchen table. 'Cottage pie, steamed vegetables followed by some of the walnut cake I made yesterday.' She beamed, taking a plastic container out of her bag and opening the lid to show Mary two pieces of walnut cake. 'See, a slice each.' She smiled.

'Wonderful. Walnut cake is my favourite,' Mary told her.

'I know.'

It touched her that Cathy had remembered and thought to bring her a slice. 'I'll put the oven on then, shall I?'

'No, you sit yourself down, Mum. Let me spoil you for a change,' Cathy told her.

Mary's eyes shot to Cathy's face at the word 'Mum'. Cathy had never called her Mum before; in fact, she avoided calling Mary anything if she could help it. Her heart skipped a beat as she stared at her daughter.

'I hope it's okay to call you that. Only...' Her voice quivered a bit. 'You are my mum and you feel like it in here.' She balled her fist and pressed it to her chest. Tears sprang to Mary's eyes.

'Of course it is, darling girl,' she whispered and then they were both hugging each other. She was so grateful that she'd had the chance to meet her long-lost daughter and put things right between them.

'What a soppy pair we are,' Cathy said, pulling away with a grin and looking a little awkward.

Mary grinned back and wiped her eyes with the back of her hand. 'I'd better get this oven on.'

'No I insist!' Cathy was switching on the oven before Mary could stop her. 'Sorry but I simply can't sit here and let you do everything,' she said with an apologetic smile.

After they'd put the cottage pie in the oven to warm up, they went into the lounge and Cathy walked straight over to the cage where Bailey was hopping up and down on his perch. She always made a beeline for Bailey whenever she arrived. 'Hello, hello,' he chirped.

'Hello, Bailey. You're a happy little chappie today,' she said. Mary loved how Cathy took time to talk to Bailey. Jason and Joanne always ignored him.

'Has he been out today?' she asked.

'No, I'll let him out later, after supper. He'll only be a nuisance while we're eating. He's so cheeky he always tries to sneak some food from my plate.'

Cathy laughed. 'Greedy Bailey.' She turned to Mary. 'Why don't we eat on a tray on our laps in here? It would be much cosier.'

Mary was happy to agree. She often ate her dinner on a tray in front of the TV in the lounge since Paul had died, hating sitting at the dining table by herself.

'That was a delicious meal, thank you,' Mary said as she devoured the last forkful of cottage pie.

'You're welcome. It's nice to have someone to cook for,' Cathy said with a smile.

It sounded like Cathy was as lonely as she was, Mary thought as she went to get up and take her tray into the kitchen, but Cathy took the tray from her. 'You sit there. I'll put these in the dishwasher and get the walnut cake.'

Cathy really was helpful, and a pleasure to be around. And she did it in a genuine, caring way, not in the bossy, tutting way that Joanne did everything. She seemed to enjoy helping while Joanne didn't even try to hide the fact that she was busy and Mary felt an inconvenience.

Bailey started squawking loudly again. 'You'll have to wait, cheeky, we haven't had dessert yet,' Cathy told him and, as if he understood her, the little bird shut up.

As soon as they'd finished the walnut cake, Mary went over

to let Bailey out of the cage. He was chirping insistently. 'I'm not sure whether he will come out with you here, I only usually let him out when I'm alone,' she told Cathy.

'Oh, I think he's used to me by now.' She smiled. 'But don't worry, I won't take offence if he decides he doesn't want to come out.'

Mary opened the cage door and put her hand in, pointer finger stretched out. Bailey hopped onto it and chirped happily then flapped his wings and flew around the room. He settled on top of the curtains and peered down at them.

'If we take no notice of him and carry on with what we're doing he'll fly down onto the back of the sofa,' Mary said. 'Now did you bring those photos and school reports?'

'I did.' Cathy opened her handbag and pulled out a brown envelope.

'Shall we have a glass of wine while we're looking at them?' Mary suggested. 'I know that you're driving but if you only have a small one. Or a sherry, perhaps?'

'A small glass of wine would be good, thanks, Mum,' Cathy said.

'Will merlot be okay or do you prefer white?' she asked.

'Merlot is perfect,' Cathy said, taking some photos out of the envelope and spreading them out on the coffee table.

Mary poured them both small glasses and then went over to sit by her daughter.

Bailey squawked and flew down to join them, hopping along the table. Cathy laughed as he danced along in front of them, chirping, 'What you doing? What you doing?'

'Now don't you go pooping on those photos,' Mary scolded him.

'Oh don't worry, I can soon clean them up if he does,' Cathy said. She held out her finger in front of Bailey. 'Hello, cheeky.'

Bailey hopped onto her finger then flew up onto her head.

'Oh dear, he does love to do that. I hope he doesn't poop on your head,' Mary said, worriedly.

'It's fine, even if he does, it will wash out,' Cathy reassured her. 'I'm honoured that he likes me enough to come to me.'

She was so relaxed it was refreshing, Mary thought. Joanne would go mad if Bailey messed in her hair. And Jason always found him irritating. Cathy, on the other hand, seemed to love the little bird as much as she did.

She took a sip of her wine and relaxed as they sat back down to look through the rest of the photos, then read the reports. *Cathy is a very clever girl but she does like to chat*, one said. Mary grinned. 'One of my teachers said that about me. I was always talking.' Until her mother died and her world fell apart.

'Another thing we have in common. Chatty Cathy they called me,' she said with a grin. She got up. 'I must go the loo, then I'm afraid it's time for me to go, it's getting late.'

Mary glanced at the clock as Cathy left the room. Ten-thirty already. Where had the time gone? It had been such an enjoyable evening, it had flown by.

Suddenly she heard a thump and the shatter of breaking glass then a brick came hurtling through the front window, landing in front of her. Mary screamed and jumped to her feet, staring at the shards of broken glass and the brick. Panic-stricken, she turned to look at the lounge door as she heard the sound of the front door opening. Someone was coming in! Her chest tightened and she sank back onto the sofa, gasping for breath.

# 27

'Mum!' Cathy came running in. 'Mum! Are you okay?'

'It's my angina!' Mary gasped, clutching her chest. 'My spray... my bag.' Agitated, she pointed to her bag.

Cathy's gaze darted around the room, spotting the bag down by the side of the sofa. She grabbed it, shook out the contents onto the coffee table and handed Mary the GTN spray, who took it gratefully and sprayed a couple of times under her tongue. Then she leaned her head back and closed her eyes. Cathy sat down beside her. 'Are you okay now?'

Mary nodded.

'What happened? I heard a noise outside when I went to the loo so thought I'd check what was going on. Then you screamed...'

Mary opened her eyes weakly, gazing in horror at the broken glass on the carpet in front of them. 'Did you see who did it?' She swallowed. 'When I heard the front door open I thought they were coming in...' she stammered.

Cathy wrapped her arms around her to comfort her. 'That was me. So sorry that I scared you. I'm afraid that I didn't see anyone. It's so dark.'

Mary was shaking. 'I don't understand. Why would someone put a brick through my window?' She was still really shaken up. If Cathy hadn't been there she would have had a heart attack, she was sure of it.

'I don't know. Kids passing by in the street maybe,' Cathy replied.

'Kids!' Mary exclaimed. 'That's what Jason said. Who *are* these kids who are suddenly terrorising me, trampling on my plants and putting a brick through my window?'

'Oh Mum, I'm sure they're not targeting you personally. It's just you're the big house at the end of the lane, and your open drive is so accessible.' Cathy gave her another hug. 'Look, let me clean up this mess and put something over the window. I'll phone the police, although I'm sure that they won't do anything tonight. And we'll contact your insurance company tomorrow and get it fixed. Meanwhile why don't I stay over for tonight. You'll feel better with someone else here.'

Mary nodded. She no longer felt safe in her home. 'Please. I always keep one of the spare bedrooms made up, and there's toiletries in the bathroom.' She reached out and touched Cathy's arm. 'Thank goodness you were with me when this happened.'

'I'm glad I was here too. I dread to think what would have happened if you'd been alone. I had no idea you had heart trouble.' Cathy patted her hand. 'Now stay there while I phone the police and get this cleaned up. I don't want you cutting your feet.'

The police said that they'd send someone as soon as possible but it wouldn't be until the next morning so Cathy cleaned up the broken glass then found a piece of board from Paul's study to put across the window. Finally, she made Mary a cup of herbal tea, taking it into her bedroom.

'Goodnight, Mum,' she said softly, kissing her on the forehead.

'Goodnight, darling.' Mary drank the tea then settled down to try and sleep, feeling safer knowing that Cathy was in the next room although she couldn't help being nervous about what would happen next.

---

'Mum! It's me, Joanne!'

Joanne's voice shouting up the stairs woke Mary with a jolt. She glanced at the clock. Ten past nine. Goodness, she'd slept like a log. What did Joanne want? She must have popped in before work. Pulling on her dressing gown, Mary slipped her feet into her slippers and opened the bedroom door. 'I'm coming, dear.'

There was no sound from Cathy's room so Mary headed down the stairs. Joanne was pacing around in the kitchen. She glanced pointedly at the two empty wine glasses on the side. 'I see that Cathy stayed overnight. Her car is in the drive,' she added as Mary came in.

'Yes she did. Lovely to see you, darling. Is it your day off?' Mary grabbed two cups out of the cupboard and placed them by the kettle. 'Do you have time for a cup of tea?'

'No thanks, I have to be in work for eleven.' She frowned as she saw that her mother was wearing her nightclothes. 'Were you still asleep? Is Cathy still in bed?'

'Oh yes, we had such a lovely evening, chatting and catching up last night and...' She swallowed before continuing, 'Then someone put a brick through the lounge window. Cathy didn't want to leave me on my own after that so she offered to stay over.'

'Brick through the window?' Joanne repeated in horror. Her gaze went to the front lounge window and rested on the board Cathy had hastily fixed there. 'Oh my God, I can't believe I didn't notice that! When did this happen? Why didn't you tell me?'

'It was very late, I didn't want to worry you. Cathy was here so I was fine, she boarded up the window and called the police. They're coming around later.'

'Oh Mum!' Joanne hugged her. 'You must have been so scared. I'm glad that Cathy was with you...' She frowned. 'She does seem to be here a lot. Doesn't she ever work?'

'She works different shifts, dear. And she has no family... except us,' Mary added. Surely Joanne wasn't jealous that she and Cathy were spending so much time together? They had a lot to catch up on.

'Oh hi, Joanne, good to see you so early.' Cathy walked in, rubbing her hair with a towel. 'Did Mum tell you about the drama last night?'

Joanne stared at her, stunned. Mary guessed that it was because Cathy had called her Mum. 'Er... yes... it's dreadful,' she stammered.

'I've made you a cuppa.' Mary held out the mug of tea.

'Thanks, Mum. I'll go and get dressed before the police arrive.' Cathy took the mug, nodded at Joanne and disappeared upstairs again.

Joanne pulled herself together. 'Do you want me to stay until the police arrive too? I can call someone to sort the window out for you.'

'No thank you, darling, Cathy isn't in work until later and she was here at the time it happened so she's staying and will help me. But I do appreciate the offer.' Then she remembered that Joanne had dropped by unexpectedly. 'Did you come for anything in particular, or just to see me?'

'I wondered if you wanted to come to dinner tonight? You could maybe stay over too, you must be shook up after what happened.'

Mary added milk to her own tea and stirred it. 'Thank you, dear, but could we make it tomorrow please? I have such a lot to sort out today and I've no idea when the police will come, and I also need to contact the insurance to sort out getting the window fixed.'

'That will be sorted by this afternoon though so why don't I pick you up when I finish work? I don't like you being alone here overnight, especially after this.'

Cathy came back into the room in time to hear the tail end of the conversation. 'I'll stay with Mum tonight,' she said. 'I can come after work. I'm on afternoon shifts this week.'

'That's really kind of you; I would appreciate the company,' Mary said gratefully.

Joanne looked a little put out but she merely nodded. 'All right, Mum. I'd better go then, I'll be late for work.' She picked up her bag. 'We'll see you tomorrow about six. Lasagne and salad okay?'

'That would be wonderful. And thank you for asking me. I do appreciate it,' Mary told her as she saw her out.

The police arrived mid-morning and took a statement from them both but said it was highly unlikely they'd be able to do anything.

'Things like this are happening all the time,' the policeman told them. 'Unless you have an idea who it is, we can't really do anything.'

'I don't feel safe here anymore. I'm going to sell the house,' Mary said when the police had gone.

'Are you sure? I don't like to think of some mindless yobs driving you out,' Cathy said. 'I could stay over a couple of nights a week, if that would make you feel safer?'

'That's really kind of you, and I would appreciate that. I am a bit unnerved, but that isn't the only reason I want to sell up.

I've realised that Joanne and Jason are right, this house is far too big for me. It's time I moved into something smaller and cosier.'

'I think that's wise. Then you'll have some funds to take it easy, enjoy yourself. Go on a few holidays, or a cruise perhaps. I've always fancied going on a cruise,' Cathy said almost wistfully.

'Then you must come with me. We'll go on one as soon as I sell the house.'

Cathy looked horrified. 'Oh no! I wasn't hinting. Please don't think that.'

Mary shook her head. 'Of course I don't, but I would love the company. And...' Her gaze met Cathy's. 'When I sell the house I'm going to give you, Joanne and Jason an equal share of the money left over, once I've bought my new home. There should be at least seventy thousand each, I'd have thought.'

Cathy looked dumbstruck. 'Seventy thousand! That's more than I earn in a couple of years. I couldn't possibly take that much money off you. I couldn't take any money off you.' She shook her head vehemently. What a refreshingly unmaterialistic person she was. Mary knew that Joanne and Jason wouldn't have any qualms about taking their share from her.

'I insist. You are my daughter and from now on will be treated the same as my other children.'

Cathy looked stunned and quite tearful. 'You really are a generous woman. I hope Joanne and Jason realise how lucky they are.'

'I'm the lucky one to have you all in my life,' Mary replied. 'I'm getting on in years now. Paul's death has taught me that no one can take life for granted, and I want to make the most of the years I have left, and help my children enjoy their lives too.'

# 28

'If you're sure that you want to move, why don't we go online and see what's available?' Cathy asked. 'What sort of property do you want?'

Mary had already been thinking about that. 'I fancy living in something small and cosy, a cottage perhaps. I don't want to move far, though. I'd like to stay close to the village,' she said.

'I'll do a quick internet search.' Cathy took out her phone and jabbed a few keys. 'Look, there's a couple of cottages available in the village.'

Mary squinted as she tried to read the details on the screen. 'Let me get my iPad, I'll be able to see better,' she said, going over to the sideboard and taking her iPad out of the drawer.

'The estate agent is called Country Properties,' Cathy told her.

Mary typed in 'Country Properties' and the website flashed onto her screen. She soon found the cottages. They both looked nice but they were semi-detached and she wasn't sure about that, having being used to privacy all these years.

'You never know, it might make you feel safer having neighbours,' Cathy said as if she'd read her mind. 'Shall I book an appointment to see them? We could go and have a look tomorrow morning, if you want, before I go to work.'

'I'd love to, if you're sure you don't mind coming with me.' Mary didn't want to mention it to Joanne and Jason yet, knowing they would insist on coming with her and taking over.

'Of course not. But let's take a look at some other estate agents' websites too – there's no rush. It's best to check out some alternative properties as well. It's a big decision,' Cathy advised. 'You might like a little bungalow. Or an apartment.'

So they spent an hour or so browsing a few websites and Cathy made some appointments for viewings then she had to leave for work. 'I'll be back about nine tonight,' she promised.

The insurance company sent someone to fix the window, and both Jason and Joanne phoned to ask Mary if she was okay and once again both tried to persuade her to move in with them, but she told them not to worry; the window had been fixed and it seemed that it had been kids again so she felt quite safe.

Cathy came back around after work and they had another pleasant evening chatting and sharing memories.

'Goodnight, Mum,' Cathy said as they both went up to bed, after checking that everything was safely locked up.

'Goodnight, Cathy.'

When Mary lay down to sleep that night, she felt the happiest she had done for a long time. She pressed the answerphone on her phone to hear Paul's message, as she always did, wanting to hear those words 'I love you' before she went to sleep. 'I wish you could have met Cathy, Paul,' she whispered. 'I should have looked for her sooner. You were a kind man. You would have understood.'

It was no good harping back to the past, though. As Cathy said, they needed to look forward to the future and she was so happy that her firstborn daughter was part of it.

---

Cathy had booked appointments to look around two cottages, three bungalows and a new luxury apartment block so it was going to be a busy morning. 'How about I take you in my car?' she suggested. 'You can relax and enjoy being the passenger.'

Mary was glad to not drive. She still felt a bit jittery after everything that had happened and was relieved that Cathy was accompanying her – she could do with another opinion. She didn't want to make a mistake. She was dreading moving. The thought of getting rid of stuff, of packing and relocating was really daunting but Cathy had promised to help as much as she could.

The two cottages they viewed were very pretty but as Cathy pointed out, they needed some refurbishment and the stone walls meant that they would be cold in the winter. 'You could do with something easy care, Mum,' she said, linking her arm with Mary's. 'You need to be able to relax now, not worry about doing repairs to your house or keeping warm. And there might come a time when you don't want to climb up and down stairs.'

She was right, Mary thought. They went to see the bungalows next, but Mary didn't like the location, they were too near the high street and traffic. Finally, they went to look at the new apartment block. Mary preferred older properties with character but she was impressed with the location and the apartments really did look luxurious. There was a communal garden too. 'It's lovely but I'm not sure that an apartment is for me,' Mary said. 'I would feel safer, but I'd miss my garden. I think a bungalow would be best.'

'I agree, I think a bungalow would be perfect for you. We can keep looking, properties come up on the market all the time,' Cathy reassured her. 'Take your time, enjoy house hunting. I know that you want to move but there's no rush, is there?'

Mary didn't like to say that she was scared to stay in the house by herself. She didn't want Cathy to feel obliged to stay every night, she had her own home and worked on the other side of town. She'd be all right, she told herself. Her property had been damaged but there had been no personal threat to her. As the police said, it must just be kids, running riot; it was the school holidays so they were probably bored. Not that that was any excuse.

---

'Well, I've got some news,' she told Joanne and Damien as they tucked into their dinner later. 'I'm planning on putting the house on the market, and I'm meeting the estate agent to discuss it next week.'

'You are? That's fantastic, Mum.' Joanne looked delighted. 'That sprawling house is too much for you on your own and the area does seem to be getting a bit rough now. Do you want me to come and view some apartments with you?'

'No thank you, darling.' Mary helped herself to some more salad and a slice of garlic bread. 'I've decided I would prefer a little two-bedroom bungalow instead. Cathy and I looked at a couple today. They weren't quite what I wanted, but we're going to look at some more next week.'

'You and Cathy!' Mary saw the look Joanne shot at Damien.

'A bungalow sounds great, at least you'll be on the level,' he said.

Joanne glared at him. 'Surely an apartment is safer, Mum, and easier to keep clean. Plus there would be no garden for you to look after.'

'I want a garden. I like sitting outside in the summer. If I get a bungalow then the garden will be manageable.'

'When are you going to look at properties next? I'll come with you after work,' Joanne offered quickly.

'There's no need, darling. I know how busy you are and Cathy is quite happy to accompany me,' Mary said, reaching for another slice of garlic bread. 'This really is delicious. Did you make it yourself?'

Mary tried not to notice the scowl on Joanne's face. It was obvious that she was feeling a bit pushed out by Cathy, as was Jason, but Cathy listened to her and had bothered to ask her what kind of home she wanted. She wasn't trying to push her into a retirement apartment like Joanne and Jason. It was as if they thought she was past it now. Well, they were wrong. She had a life to live and was going to live it.

# 29

## *Alison*

Jason was speaking on the phone when Alison walked into the kitchen the next morning and it was obvious by the expression on his face that he was annoyed. She heard Joanne's shrill tones and guessed that something had happened with Cathy. Honestly, Joanne and Jason never seemed to be off the phone to each other since Cathy came on the scene.

'Well, that's a good thing, right? We want her to sell the house, don't we?'

Alison pricked up her ears and glanced over at Jason. It sounded like Mary had finally agreed to sell up.

'Yes but don't you find it a bit suspicious that Cathy has only been on the scene a few weeks and she's got Mum to agree to selling up, whereas we've been trying for ages?' Joanne's voice boomed from the phone.

Jason held it further from his ear. 'I guess all the stuff with the car tyre and the trampled flowers and now the broken window have made her nervous.'

'Maybe, but I think Cathy is talking Mum into this because

she wants a share of her money. She never seems to leave Mum's side. She's stayed over twice this week. I wouldn't put it past her to move in under the pretence of looking after Mum.'

Alison sighed. She didn't have time to listen to the rest of the conversation, she had the boys to get ready. She was dropping them both off at Mary's today and, going by what Joanne was saying, Cathy was likely to be there. She knew that Mary could probably do with the help, but was still upset about how Nicholas had bruised his arm. It wasn't like him to play hide and seek in Mary's bedroom. She only had two appointments this morning so realistically she could collect the boys at lunchtime but Hugh had promised to take her out for lunch, followed by an afternoon at a posh hotel. And she really needed some time with Hugh.

---

However, when Alison arrived at Mary's there was no sign of Cathy's car.

Nicholas looked disappointed. 'Where's Auntie Cathy?' he asked when Mary let them in.

'She's working this morning so she's coming along later,' Mary told him.

'Well, I hope she doesn't decide to play hide and seek with Nicholas again. It was quite a nasty bruise.'

'I'm sure she won't. And to be honest I am grateful for Cathy's help with the boys. I love them both but they can be a little exhausting. And I'm sure that Joanne has told Jason that I'm selling the house and downsizing? Cathy is helping me look for properties.'

'That's very kind of her, but make sure she doesn't talk you into buying anything you don't want.' Alison paused, choosing her words carefully. 'I think Jason and Joanne would like a bit of input too.'

Mary looked exasperated. 'Look, I realise that Joanne and Jason might be feeling a little left out at the moment, and that it will take them some time to get used to having an older sister but right now I'm very grateful for Cathy's support and company. You're all wonderful and I know you all care about me, but you have such busy lives.'

Alison felt bad. It was only natural that Mary would be feeling nervous after everything that had happened. She'd be terrified if someone put a brick through her window. And it was good of her to look after Nicholas and Oliver, especially in the circumstances. 'I know, and I'm glad that you have company. But remember that you're welcome to stay over at ours any time.' She stooped down and kissed Nicholas then Oliver. 'Be good for Nanny, please,' she said.

'Is Auntie Cathy coming soon?' Nicholas asked.

'Yes, she'll be here after lunch,' Mary told him.

'Hooray.' His face broke into a huge grin.

'Can we go and talk to Bailey?' Oliver asked.

'Yes, of course,' Alison told him. Bailey's cage was too high up for Nicholas and Oliver to reach but they loved talking to him.

'Thanks so much for looking after them. I'll be back by five. Why don't you pop over tomorrow and I'll treat you to a trim and deep condition?' Alison said.

'I'd love that. Thank you, dear,' Mary said. 'Now come on, boys, we've got some painting to do.'

# 30

*Cathy*

Cathy read the message several times.

> *I know him. His name is Robbie Hart. And he's not dead. He's very much alive. Why are you looking for him?*

She'd found the man who Mary said was her father. And he was alive. Mary had lied about that. Was it because she had been given the wrong information, or a deliberate lie because she didn't want Cathy to meet her father? The newspaper article had said that Robbie had been imprisoned for stealing cars so perhaps Mary hadn't wanted to admit that Cathy's father was a criminal. He had only been eighteen, though, maybe he had changed. Mary didn't seem the sort of person not to give someone a chance. She sent a message back:

> *He's my dad. I was abandoned at birth.*

> *Wow! Do you want me to find out if he wants to meet you?*

*Yes please.*

She sent that reply without hesitation. She suspected that Mary was hiding something about Robbie and she wanted to know what it was. She wanted to know everything about him. Not that she would mention any of this to Mary. She intended to keep her cards close to her chest until she knew everything there was to know. Mary trusted her and that was the way she wanted to keep it.

# 31

## *Alison*

Alison was surprised to see Jason sitting in the garden talking to Mary and Cathy while the boys played on the swing and slide when she arrived to pick them up later. Hugh had said Jason had a meeting this evening – had it been cancelled? If so, why hadn't Jason messaged her to say he was picking up the boys? It would have saved her a journey. She waved and made her way over to the table. 'This is a surprise, I thought you said you were working this evening,' she said.

Jason shrugged. 'I was but the meeting got postponed. I phoned Mum to see if the boys were still here and when she said they were I thought I'd better pick them up. I didn't want to put on her by leaving them too long.' He looked at her accusingly. 'I didn't expect you to be back so late.'

'I didn't mean to be, one of my appointments ran a bit over...'

'Don't worry, it isn't a problem, I've had Cathy here with me. She is so good with the boys,' Mary said hastily. 'Would you like some lemonade, Alison? Cathy made it herself.'

'Thank you but I think we should go, it's getting late. I really am grateful for you looking after them.'

'Of course. I'll go and get their things.' Mary got up and disappeared into the house.

'Did you come straight from work?' Alison asked Cathy.

'Yes, I enjoy spending time with Mum, and helping her with the boys.' She glanced at Alison. 'I'm sorry about Nicholas's bruised arm; as I told Jason, I had no idea he'd hurt himself – he never said. I guess he must have bumped it when he was hiding.'

Alison studied her thoughtfully. 'It's not like Nicholas to play hide and seek in Mum's bedroom,' she said pointedly.

Cathy smiled sweetly. 'Oh I'm sure he didn't mean any harm. Children get a bit carried away sometimes and Mary probably left the door open. She does sometimes.'

Suddenly, Mary came hurrying out, looking really agitated. 'Bailey's gone!' she gasped, clutching her chest as she tried to get her breath. 'The cage door is open and there's no sign of him. He's gone!'

'Mary, sit down. You'll have a heart attack. Where's your GTN spray?' Alison asked as she helped Mary onto a chair.

Cathy jumped up. 'Her handbag is in the kitchen, I'll go and get it.' She ran into the house, returning a few moments later with Mary's bag.

'Here, Mum, shall I get the spray out for you?' she asked, anxiously.

'I'm okay, dear, honestly,' Mary reassured her as she took the handbag from her, her breathing more regular now. 'I don't need the spray. It was just a shock. That little bird means so much to me.'

'He's probably not gone far. I'll see if I can find him,' Cathy offered. 'He could be perched on top of the curtains, or a cupboard.'

Mary gave her a grateful look. 'Thank you, dear. And

remember to keep the doors closed just in case he is in the house.'

'Is Nanny all right?' Oliver and Nicholas had noticed that something was wrong and come over to see. They both looked worriedly at Mary.

'Bailey is missing. He's flown out of his cage,' Alison told them.

Both boys opened their eyes wide. 'Is he lost?' asked Oliver.

'I hope not,' Mary replied.

Cathy came back out into the garden a little later. 'I'm sorry, Mum, there's no sign of him,' she said.

'I don't understand. Who opened the cage? It must have been one of the boys,' Mary said.

'It wasn't us!' Oliver protested.

'Of course it wasn't!' Alison said quickly. 'And the cage is too high for the boys, they couldn't reach the door,' she pointed out.

'They could if they stood on the pouffe. They're always hanging around the cage.'

Alison spun around to face Cathy. 'They wouldn't do that!'

Cathy ignored her and sat down next to Mary. 'I'm sure they didn't mean any harm, Mum. They probably just wanted to talk to Bailey,' she said soothingly.

'It wasn't my sons!' Alison protested firmly. 'They know not to open the cage.'

Cathy's eyes met hers. A shiver ran through Alison as she was sure she saw triumph in them. 'Well, who else did it?' she challenged, putting her arm around Mary's shoulders. 'Don't worry, Mum. Bailey might return when he's hungry. Leave the back door and the cage door open so he can fly back in. He's probably gone to stretch his wings.'

'Oh I hope so. I love that little bird.' Mary dabbed her eyes. 'I think that it might have been Oliver. He's always begging me to let Bailey out so he can fly around.'

'It wasn't me! Honest,' Oliver protested tearfully.

'And not me!' said Nicholas.

Alison looked from one to the other. Were they lying?

'Someone let Bailey out,' Jason said, standing up and looking earnestly at the two boys. 'We know you didn't mean him to fly away, you probably just wanted to talk to him. Please tell us who it was.'

Both boys tearfully denied it again.

Alison was sure they were telling the truth. But then if it wasn't one of the boys, who was it?

# 32

## *Mary*

They all scoured the garden, shouting Bailey's name, and left his favourite food out for him just inside the back door but to no avail. It seemed that Mary's beloved parakeet had flown off for good. Jason and Alison finally left with the boys, who were so distressed Mary couldn't bear to scold them. They were only young and she knew that they loved the little bird and were just as upset as she was that he had gone. She should have kept an eye on her grandsons more, instead of sitting out in the sun chatting to Cathy.

Cathy stayed late, obviously reluctant to leave Mary alone. When she had finally gone, Mary went over to the open cage, overwhelmed by sadness. Bailey had been the main thing that had kept her going in the dark days when Paul had died. Talking to the little bird, having it fly around in the evenings, perching on the chair arm beside her had made her feel less alone. Bailey had been something to get up for in the morning and was company in the evening. Now her precious pet had gone for good and the house seemed so quiet and empty. Everything seemed to be going wrong just lately. It was one misfortune after another.

Jason telephoned later that evening, apologising again, and offered to get her a replacement parakeet, she thanked him gratefully but declined. Bailey had his own special personality. No other bird could replace him.

---

Cathy called by the next morning. 'I'm due in work in a couple of hours but I had to see how you were,' she said. 'I've been worried about you. I know how much Bailey meant to you.'

Mary was glad to see her. 'I miss him so much. It was my own fault, though, I should have watched the boys more closely.'

'You can't watch kids all the time,' Cathy said soothingly. 'I bet they feel terrible about it now. They probably just wanted Bailey to fly onto their hand, like he does with you.'

That's what Mary had thought. She related how Jason had offered to buy her another parakeet. 'It wouldn't be the same, though,' she said sadly. 'We had such a bond.' She wiped her eyes. 'And Paul bought him for me.' She almost sobbed.

'I know the boys didn't mean any harm but I do think that Alison should make them admit it and apologise,' Cathy said. 'For their own good as well as yours.'

'I guess she feels really bad and doesn't want to think that her children are to blame,' Mary said sadly. Then she voiced the thought that had been troubling her. 'Unless it was me. What if I hadn't shut the cage properly? I can be a bit forgetful.' She'd been forgetting a lot of things just lately. What if it was her fault that her beloved bird had gone?

'I'm sure that you shut the cage, you always do.' Cathy reached out and squeezed Mary's hand. 'But even if you hadn't fastened the catch properly, the door wouldn't just spring open even if Bailey pushed it – someone would have had to open it.'

'I guess you're right,' Mary said.

'Look, I know this is none of my business but...' Cathy looked reluctant to continue, Mary guessed she still felt an outsider and that was sad because she'd been so helpful.

'Of course it is, you're part of the family too.'

'Well, I was thinking. The boys are smashing kids but they are a handful and now you're thinking of moving house you'll have such a lot to do.' She looked awkward. 'Now I feel like I'm badmouthing your family. I don't mean to, but I can see how tired and upset you are and you've had so much to deal with just lately. It's hard work looking after two young children two full days a week.' She paused. 'But perhaps Alison can't afford the childcare and of course you want to help.'

Mary considered Cathy's word. She loved the boys but had to admit that looking after them both was exhausting – and took up a large chunk of her week. 'Alison suggested it as she thought looking after Nicholas would take my mind off things and give me a bit of company when Paul died, but you're right, it is a lot for me. Look what happened today. I hate to let Alison down, though. And Nicholas starts nursery school in September so I'm sure I can manage for a few more weeks.'

'Then I'll come over as much as I can and help you,' Cathy offered. 'And I can stay over on weekends if you want.'

'That's so kind of you.' Mary couldn't believe how easily Cathy had slotted into her life. She had only known her daughter a couple of months but already couldn't imagine life without her.

'And I know you don't want another bird but maybe you might like a little dog when you move?' Cathy suggested. 'Not a puppy, they are so disruptive and take time to train, but what about an older dog? It would be good company for you, probably make you feel safer too, and give you an excuse to get out for a walk each day.'

That did make sense. Mary had always loved dogs, but when their English setter had died a few years ago, she and Paul had decided that they wanted to travel a lot so hadn't replaced him. Now she was on her own, and about to move, it seemed the ideal time to get another dog. 'I think that's a very good idea,' she told Cathy. She raised her mug. 'New daughter, new home, new dog.'

Cathy clinked her mug with Mary's. 'New beginnings.'

They caught each other's eyes and smiled. Finding Cathy had changed her life, Mary thought. She'd been sad and lonely before but now she felt hope again. She was making plans for the future. It was a wonderful feeling.

# 33

*Alison*

'The boys are really upset over Bailey but they insist that they didn't touch the cage,' Alison said to Jason later that evening when the boys were tucked up in bed. The more she thought about it the more annoyed she became. Mary had looked after the boys with no problems until Cathy came along, then suddenly Nicholas was playing hide and seek in Mary's bedroom and coming home with a bruise and both her sons were being accused of losing Bailey. 'And I believe them. They know how much Mary adores him. They wouldn't let him out.'

Jason looked irritated. 'Mum's really upset too!' he snapped. 'I don't know who else it could have been. Unless you think it's Cathy? Or me?'

'I wouldn't put it past Cathy,' Alison retorted, hands on her hips. 'She doesn't like Mary looking after Nicholas, she wants to have your mum all to herself. And I don't trust her. I don't believe her story that Nicholas went into your mum's bedroom to play hide and seek. Nicholas would never go in Mary's room, he knows he's not allowed.'

'He's three, Ali. It's the sort of thing three-year-olds do,' Jason told her.

Alison scowled at him. Why was bloody Jason so ready to believe Cathy over his own sons? She was sure that Nicholas and Oliver were telling the truth. She'd talked to Joanne about it and Joanne had said she thought Mary herself might have left the cage open. Apparently, she'd been getting really forgetful and Joanne and Damien were really worried about her. She told Jason as much. 'I hate to say this but I think that it's probably best if Mary doesn't look after the boys. Not after this.'

'You're overreacting, as usual. Mum's upset over Bailey, yes, but she adores the boys. She won't hold a grudge against them.'

'I'm more worried about her not being capable of looking after them properly. It's a lot for her to keep an eye on two energetic children, especially through the summer holidays. Joanne said it worries her too, Mary is so absent-minded since Paul died. What if she leaves the front door open and Nicholas runs out? There's no gate on the drive and it leads straight onto the road.'

Jason frowned. 'Look, I know Mum does seem distracted just lately but saying she can't look after the kids is a bit drastic. Besides, we can't afford to pay more childcare fees,' he pointed out.

'I'll have to not book any appointments for Wednesdays and Fridays and look after them myself.'

Jason didn't look very pleased. 'We're already struggling financially, how are we going to manage if you take on less work? Can't you take the boys with you?'

'What? Take a five-year-old and a three-year-old with me while I cut or dye clients' hair? Even if they behave themselves, which would be a miracle, it doesn't look very professional. I tell you what, why don't you try taking them to work with you? They're your children too.' She sighed. 'Look, this isn't something I want to do.' It would mean less opportunity to spend time with Hugh too for a start, she thought. 'But the boys' safety must come first and I don't think they're safe with your mum at the moment. And it isn't good for Mary's health either. Look how upset she was today.'

Jason raked his hand through his hair. 'I guess you're right. She's getting on a bit now. And she's got lots to do seeing as she's finally selling the house. You know how stressful that is.' He sighed. 'Maybe you could look for a local childminder? That would be cheaper than nursery, wouldn't it?'

'No chance now the holidays have started – they'll be fully booked. We'll just have to cope between us,' Alison told him. 'At least Nicholas goes to the nursery at the school in September so there will be no more childminding fees in term-time then.'

'I blame Cathy for this. Mum was okay until she came into our lives,' Jason grumbled. 'Now Mum's so obsessed with her perishing long-lost daughter she doesn't have time for anything else.'

'I know, there's something about Cathy I don't trust. But then I guess if you haven't known your mum for most of your life and suddenly find her again you would want to spend all your spare time with her, wouldn't you? And Cathy has been really helpful. It was a good job she was staying over the other evening when that brick was put through the window; I think Mary might have had a heart attack if she'd been on her own.'

Alison saw a flicker of something cross Jason's face but then it was gone. 'Maybe, but she's got too much influence on Mum. Don't worry, though, I've got her number. I'm keeping an eye on her.'

He walked out of the room, leaving Alison wondering what he meant.

# 34

## *Mary*

Cathy dropped in on Tuesday to tell Mary she'd seen a new development in a neighbouring village and there were still a couple of bungalow plots available. 'Would you like to take a look? I can drive you over there now,' she offered. 'It's called Meadow Farm.'

Mary immediately agreed, glad to have a distraction. She'd been upset all weekend about losing Bailey and then Jason had popped in on Sunday and told her that he and Alison thought looking after the boys was too much for her. Although Mary had been thinking that herself, she was still hurt that they'd made the decision not to leave her grandchildren in her care. As if she wasn't to be trusted. Another sign that they thought she was getting old and forgetful.

Maybe she was.

'Go and get yourself ready then and we'll get going,' Cathy said.

Mary felt more cheerful already. It was such a blessing that

Cathy had come into her life, she always cheered her up. Just an hour later, they were walking around one of the show homes.

'What do you think?' Cathy asked as they looked around. 'It's spacious, isn't it? And you can choose your own décor and fittings.'

'I love it, it's perfect,' Mary said. The bungalow was a decent size, with two bedrooms, one of them an ensuite, and there were two plots left. One in a corner of the development with a large drive and the other more central. They would both be ready for Christmas. And it would be lovely to move into a brand new home. After a bit of deliberation, she decided that she preferred the bungalow in the corner. In front of the row of bungalows was a pretty, grassed area with flower beds. The shops were only a short walk if she didn't feel like driving, and the small, easy-to-care-for back garden caught the sun in the afternoon. She could picture herself out there, reading, or drinking coffee and chatting with Stella. She would be comfortable here.

'Do you like it? Are you sure?' Cathy asked. 'You don't have to make a decision right now – although this is the last one of this size and will probably be snapped up soon.'

Mary nodded. 'It's ideal. A perfect home for me.' She made up her mind on the spot. She was going to buy it. She reached out and squeezed her daughter's hand. 'Thank you so much for all your support. I don't know what I'd have done without you. You've been a rock to me.'

'You're very welcome.' Cathy's face lit up. She looked so beautiful when she smiled. Most of the time, her eyes had a sadness to them and Mary wondered if her life had been as good as she insisted it was – but she wasn't brave enough to ask. She couldn't bear the guilt if it hadn't been. 'I'm so glad we found each other at last,' Cathy added.

'You and me both,' Mary told her. She couldn't imagine her life without Cathy in it now. Joanne and Jason were so busy with their families and work, whereas Cathy, like Mary, was all alone. It was almost as if they had been meant to find each other. 'Now I'm going to put a deposit down on this bungalow before someone else snaps it up then treat us both to lunch. If you have time, that is?'

'Plenty of time, I'm working lates. And thank you, lunch would be marvellous.'

Mary felt elated as Cathy drove them into the town. Paul's death had left a devastating hole in her life that meeting Cathy had helped fill. He would approve of Cathy, she was sure he would, and he would certainly approve of the bungalow. He would want Mary to get on with her life, to live it to the full. She felt tears spring to her eyes and was pleased that she wasn't driving. Oh Paul, if only he had lived longer. If only she'd been brave enough to confess to him about Cathy. He might have been surprised at first, but he would have accepted it, helped Mary find her. He was a good man. She should have trusted him.

They were eating dessert in the restaurant when Mary suddenly felt someone place a hand on her shoulder and heard Daphne's strident voice boom, 'Mary, what a surprise! And who's your friend?'

Her heart stilled for a moment as she saw Daphne eyeing Cathy, obviously waiting to be introduced. Mary had put off telling her friends about her long-lost daughter, wanting to keep it in the family for a while, knowing that the village tongues would soon start wagging. She could feel the tension in the air. Cathy was wondering how she was going to introduce her, she realised. Well, let the tongues wag, the time had come to admit her past. She straightened her back, fixed a big smile on her face and looked up at Daphne. 'Daphne, darling. Do meet Cathy, my eldest daughter. Cathy, this is my good friend Daphne. She lives in the village too.'

'Eldest daughter?' Daphne looked confused as Cathy nodded.

'Pleased to meet you, Mum's mentioned you a few times.' It was a lie, Mary hadn't, but she was grateful for Cathy saying that she had.

'But...' Daphne looked from Cathy to Mary.

'I had Cathy when I was very young and she was adopted. We've only just found each other again,' Mary explained.

Cathy put her hand lovingly on Mary's arm. 'It's been so wonderful to get to know each other.'

Daphne looked shocked and taken aback. 'Goodness, Mary, you are a dark horse! How old were you when you had Cathy then? You look as if you could be sisters, not mother and daughter.'

'I'm very grateful to Mum for allowing me to be adopted by a wonderful family instead of struggling as a single parent,' Cathy told her, ignoring Daphne's questions.

Cathy was protecting her, her mother. Mary's heart went out to her. Her marvellous, loyal, loving daughter. She refused to be ashamed of her. The past was gone. 'I've thought of you every day and it's made me so happy that we've found each other.' She met Daphne's stunned gaze. 'Would you like to join us for coffee?'

'Er no, thank you. I must dash. Delighted to meet you, Cathy,' she said and almost scurried off.

'She's off to spread the gossip, no doubt,' Mary said ruefully. She smiled at Cathy. 'Well, I'm too old to worry about that now. Having you in my life is far more important than what any narrow-minded people think.'

'It must have been so hard back then. Nowadays no one bats an eyelid if you have a child before you get married, no matter what age you are. And there's financial help too.'

'It was. I was terrified and alone...' The desperation of holding her newborn baby in her arms and knowing she couldn't keep her would never leave her. Or the fear when she had realised that Robbie wasn't who she thought he was and she was on her own.

'We have each other now, and that's what matters,' Cathy told her. 'Would you like me to come over on Friday and help you with the decluttering? I've got some boxes I can bring. We can take what you don't want to the charity shop. If that's okay with you.'

'Perfect. I'll do us lunch,' Mary told her. 'Now let me get the bill.'

'Are you sure? I'm happy to pay my half,' Cathy said. 'I'd love to treat you but money is a little tight at the moment.'

'Nonsense, I wouldn't accept.' Mary opened the zip compartment in her purse where she kept her notes. It was empty.

'Is something wrong?' Cathy asked.

'I took a few hundred out of the cash machine yesterday.' Mary frowned as she searched through her purse.

'Did you remember to pick up the notes? You've had a lot going on and it's easy to get distracted,' Cathy said. 'Once I was behind a lady and she took out her card then walked off leaving her money there. Luckily, I spotted it and ran after her.'

Mary hesitated. Did she take the cash from the machine? She'd been very flustered yesterday. 'I think I did.'

'Please let me get this.' Cathy reached for her handbag.

'I wouldn't dream of it. It's not a problem. I'll use my card,' Mary told her. Thank goodness that was still in her purse. She really was getting forgetful.

She pushed the worry from her mind. As Cathy said, she'd been through a lot this past year so it was no wonder she got distracted sometimes. Thank goodness she hadn't been with Joanne, if she got to hear of it, she'd be all for putting her in a home!

# 35

Mary could hardly believe that it was Friday already. The week had sped by and though she had to admit that she'd been hurt when Jason had told her that he and Alison had decided that looking after the boys was too much for her, it was actually a relief. She had barely had time for anything this week. She'd called Stella on Tuesday evening to tell her about Cathy, knowing that Daphne would have wasted no time spreading the news and Stella had been very understanding. 'You poor darling, what a terrible time that must have been for you but how wonderful that you've found each other now. You must introduce me to Cathy. I'd love to meet her.' So Mary had promised she would.

Mary had also had the house valued ready to put it on the market, there was no rush as the bungalow wouldn't be completed for a few months but the estate agent said he would put the feelers out. The rest of the week had been busy with tidying things up, ready for the photographs and for prospective buyers to look around. She would need to have a good sort out for the move, scaling down from a large house into a two-bedroomed bungalow was a daunting task, Mary realised. The loft was still full of things from Jason and Joanne's childhood, as well as Paul's things. The garage, the study, the shed in the garden were full of his own personal things that she had to sort through and decide what to keep and what to give away. She'd shed a few tears as she'd started to go through them. Jason had dropped by on Wednesday night to check she was okay and taken Bailey's cage away for her. 'It will only upset you seeing it empty,' he'd said. He'd given her a big hug and promised that they would still see her regularly. And today Cathy was coming over to help Mary pack boxes. She really was blessed, Mary reminded herself. She had three wonderful children and had had a loving marriage. It was more than a lot of people had. Now she was ready to move on to the next stage of her life.

# 36

## *Cathy*

The smell of baking wafted out as Mary let Cathy in on Friday. 'I've made a walnut cake. I know you enjoy them,' Mary told her, kissing her on the cheek. 'And I've got a lovely bottle of red, we can enjoy a glass while we watch the film.'

'And I have these.' Cathy gave her a box of chocolates. 'But they are just for you. Eat them one of the evenings when you're on your own.'

'I most certainly will not! Nice things are much better shared,' Mary said, taking the box from her. 'Now do come in and make yourself comfy. Dinner won't be long.'

Cathy took off her coat and headed for the kitchen to help. She took out the plates, and two glasses for the wine and two trays. She and Mary always ate their meals on a tray in front of the TV.

An hour later, they'd finished their meal and were on their second glass of wine when they heard the key turn in the front door. 'Only me, Mum!'

'It's Joanne! That's a surprise for a Friday evening,' Mary said. She called out, 'We're in the living room, love.'

The door opened and Joanne appeared in the doorway. She looked flushed. And angry.

'Goodness, what on earth has happened?' Alarmed, Mary got to her feet. 'Have you and Damien had a row?'

'No we're fine. I wanted to make sure that you were okay,' Joanne said. She looked at Cathy. 'I might have guessed you'd be here.'

'Do sit down, Joanne, you're not making sense. Why wouldn't I be okay?' Mary looked really concerned. 'Cathy has come to have dinner and watch a film with me.'

Joanne was glaring at Cathy as if she hated her. Cathy felt uncomfortable. What had she done? Was it because she was spending time with Mary?

'Proper little dutiful daughter, aren't you?' Joanne's eyes were cold and accusing. 'Shame that you're not a truthful one.'

Cathy's heart missed a beat. What had she found out?

Mary's gaze swept from Joanne to Cathy. 'What on earth do you mean? What are you insinuating?'

'I'm not insinuating anything. I'm telling the truth. Cathy here hasn't told you the truth about herself, have you, Cathy?'

Cathy swallowed. 'I don't know what you mean...' What did she know? Had Jason been talking?

'Don't you? Well, I was in FashionMart yesterday with Kelly, late-night shopping, and I saw Cathy with a young girl. She was about Kelly's age. They both had loads of shopping. They were spending money like it was out of fashion.'

'Really, Joanne, it's none of our business if Cathy wants to buy presents for a friend's daughter...' Mary reprimanded her.

'Only it wasn't a friend's daughter, was it, Cathy?' Joanne retorted. 'It was your daughter. Don't bother to deny it. I heard her call you Mum.'

# 37

## *Mary*

Cathy had a daughter? 'Is this right, Cathy?' Mary asked, puzzled.

Cathy met Joanne's gaze coolly. 'Yes, you're right, Hannah is my daughter. She's fifteen. In fact, I was going to tell you about her tonight, Mum.' She turned to Mary. 'I thought it was time you both met.'

'Liar! You're just saying that because your lies have been found out,' Joanne retorted.

'You did say that you didn't have children, Cathy.' Mary looked disappointed. 'Why did you do that?'

'I know.' Cathy admitted. 'I'm sorry, I felt awful hiding the fact that you have a granddaughter from you but Hannah has been through such a lot.' She took a tissue out of her pocket, wiped her nose and squeezed it into a ball in her hand. 'Her father and me, we're divorced and Hannah took it badly. We're on good terms,' she said hastily. 'Hannah is with him now. He's a lovely man but I'm not good at relationships. I have trust issues...' She hesitated.

*Is that because of me? Because I abandoned her, she can't trust anyone*, Mary thought sadly. She was pleased that Cathy had a daughter, though, that she'd had a husband and family even if they were now divorced. She hated to think of her being all alone.

'What's that got to do with telling bare-faced lies? Denying your own daughter exists?' Joanne snapped.

Cathy jerked her head up, her eyes blazing. 'I told you, I did it to protect Hannah. I don't want her to get hurt, to get to know a grandmother, a new family, then to lose them. Don't tell me that you wouldn't do the same?'

'I wouldn't lie. I would say I had a child but I wasn't ready for them to meet you yet. I wouldn't deny the existence of my own daughter!'

Cathy swallowed. 'So what if I'd told you all about Hannah? Are you telling me you wouldn't have wanted to meet her? Mum certainly would. I had to make sure that we all got on first before I let you into her life.' She levelled her gaze at Joanne. 'When I went to meet Mum, I had no idea if she was married, if we would hit it off, if she had children and they or her husband would resent me. This had the potential to go drastically wrong. If it did, I could handle walking away, but Hannah, she would be devastated. All she has is me and her dad.'

Mary nodded. 'I can understand that, and in the circumstances I think that it was very wise. But you say you were going to tell me about her tonight?'

'Yes, I've brought some photos of Hannah to show you.' Cathy opened her handbag and took out some photos. 'I printed them out in case you wanted to keep them.' She held them out so Joanne could see them. But she didn't seem convinced.

'This is just an excuse. I bet you always carry them around with you,' she said.

'Let me see.' Mary ignored Joanne's outburst and held her

hand out for the photos. 'She's beautiful,' she said as she looked at them. 'I would very much like to keep them and to meet Hannah. Will you tell her that I'm her grandma or do you want me to pretend to just be a friend?'

'I want her to know who you are. I'm sorry that I didn't feel ready to at first. I didn't mean to deceive you. Hannah has always known about my... beginnings... and how desperate I was to find my birth mother. She would have been so excited for me. I was just scared that she would be disappointed if things didn't work out. I didn't want that for her.' Cathy brushed a lock of hair out of her eyes. 'But now... Now I want her to meet her family.'

'That's wonderful. Perhaps I should meet her first, before introducing her to everyone else,' Mary suggested. 'So that she's not overwhelmed.'

Cathy blinked back the tears. 'That sounds good to me.'

'That's settled then,' Mary said. 'Now will you join us for a drink, Joanne, or do you need to get off?'

Joanne could barely conceal her anger. 'I have to go, Mum. I'll see you on Sunday,' she said.

# 38

*Alison*

'She can think on her feet, I'll tell you that,' Joanne said. 'She had her excuse off pat.'

Joanne had come straight around after visiting Mary and had been ranting for almost half an hour now and Alison had a headache. She could understand Joanne being angry at finding out Cathy had lied about not having children, but her excuse for doing so seemed credible to Alison.

'I think I'd be a bit wary about introducing my kid to a new family. I'd want to check them out first and make sure everything was okay,' she ventured.

Joanne snorted. 'You should have seen her. She's such an actress! She's got Mum twisted around her little finger!'

'Maybe I should go over and have a word with Mum,' Jason said.

'Good luck with that. Cathy is always there, she's helping Mum to clear the house. Seeing what she can take, more like!' Joanne was furious. 'Damien thinks she's up to no good too. She's out for what she can get.'

'I don't trust her either but I do feel sorry for her. She didn't have the best start in life. How do you think she feels seeing how you and Jason were brought up? Private schools, wanting for nothing. Then along she comes, the cuckoo in the nest,' Alison said. She knew what it was like to be an outsider in this family, although she adored Mary.

'She's a cuckoo all right. She's nothing like Jason and me, it's hard to believe that we're related. She must take after her father.'

'Oh come on, Jo, give her a break...'

'It's all right for you to be so complacent about it, it's not your mother. Maybe you don't mind that this stranger has come along and wormed her way into the family, is Mum's confidante and has even persuaded her to put the house up for sale and a deposit down on a new bungalow.'

'That's great. That's a good thing, isn't it? You and Jason have been trying to get her to do that,' Alison pointed out.

'Yes and she's promised to share the profit with us! And we could do with the money, Jo,' Jason pointed out.

'Well, we won't be getting as much as you think. Mum told me the other day that she has decided she is going to split the money left over from the house sale and bungalow purchase three ways – between me, you and dear Cathy.'

'What?' Jason stammered, his face darkening.

Alison knew that would get him. Money was the only thing Jason cared about.

# 39

*Mary*

'Oh, Paul, it's so wonderful. I have another granddaughter.' Mary sat in bed later that night, talking to her beloved husband's photo, as she often did. 'It's a bit of a mess, though, as Cathy didn't tell me. It sounds as though she was really wary about meeting me, thinking I might reject her again. And now Joanne has accused her of lying like that.' She sighed as she recalled the scene earlier that evening. Cathy had been so apologetic and upset, while Joanne, tight-lipped and scornful, obviously hadn't believed a word she said.

Paul's blue eyes stared lovingly back at her from the photo and she could almost hear his reply in her head. *That's our Jo, jump straight in. But you know she was only looking out for you, don't you? It comes from a place of love.*

And it did, she knew that. Joanne drove her mad sometimes, but Mary knew that she cared for her, and was trying to look out for her now that her father wasn't here. She could see that it had looked suspicious when she'd seen Cathy with Hannah, but Cathy's explanation had been completely credible; in her shoes,

Mary would have done exactly the same. After all, she had abandoned her daughter once, how could Cathy know that she wouldn't again? And she had to face it, Joanne and Jason hadn't exactly made Cathy welcome. It was obvious that they resented her.

'I don't know what to do, Paul. Joanne and Jason seem to resent Cathy.' She gazed at his face. 'Oh, I wish I hadn't kept it from you. You were so kind and loving. I'm sure you would have understood. And would have known how to deal with all this. You always did.'

She kissed her two fingers and placed them on his lips in the photo before putting it back on the bedside cabinet. Then she reached for her phone and played his answerphone message as she did every night, feeling comforted by his voice saying, 'Love you.' If only he was here now, if she could cuddle up to him and talk about the situation, get his advice. Joanne had been so angry when she left. She'd clearly expected Cathy to feel embarrassed, to make excuses, not to stick up for herself like that. Mary sighed. All she wanted was for her children to get on. Was that too much to ask?

Then, as she was about to drop off to sleep she had an idea. It was her sixtieth birthday in October and Joanne and Jason were anxious for her to mark it in some way but she was reluctant, not wanting to celebrate her first birthday without Paul – well they could go away together, have a family holiday. She could rent a cottage for the half-term weekend for the whole family, Cathy and her daughter too. It would give them all a chance to relax and bond together. She'd take a look online first thing in the morning.

---

As soon as she'd had breakfast, Mary switched on her iPad and researched holiday cottages, finally deciding on a large stone farm cottage in Dartmoor. There were enough rooms for everyone and the surroundings were beautiful. She secured it with a deposit and then messaged both Joanne and Jason to let them know, saying that it would mean a lot to her if they could join her. She was going to tell Cathy about it personally when she came by later today. She had promised to bring Hannah to see Mary this afternoon. She was really looking forward to meeting her granddaughter.

The morning passed quickly. Mary tidied around and did a bit of weeding, then baked a chocolate sponge, so that she could offer Cathy and Hannah a slice when they arrived. She'd just taken it out of the oven when the bell rang. They were here. She felt ridiculously nervous, what if Hannah hated her for abandoning her mother as a baby?

She took a deep breath and went to the front door. Cathy was there, smiling, her arm around the shoulder of a beautiful teenage girl with long jet-black hair, dressed in jeans and a black T-shirt. She looked so much like Robbie it took Mary's breath away.

'Mum, this is Hannah,' Cathy said proudly.

Hannah gave Mary a lazy grin – Robbie's grin – and said, 'Hello, Nan. I'm so pleased to meet you.' Then she was hugging her and they were both crying. When they finally parted and Mary took out a tissue to wipe her eyes she saw that Cathy had tears in her eyes too.

'Come in. Come in, both of you,' Mary said, stepping aside.

Hannah was a bundle of delight. Her eyes darted everywhere, admiring the furniture, the patio windows leading to the lawn, the family photos – 'your husband looks such a lovely man' – and squealing in delight when she saw the chocolate cake – 'my favourite'. She was so outgoing, so different to Cathy that she took Mary by surprise. Perhaps her outgoing character was her father's influence, although the love between mother and daughter shone through.

They ate cake, drank coffee – juice for Hannah – and chatted for hours, swapping memories, giggling over stories of Hannah as a child. How Mary wished she had stories to tell about Cathy as a child – although Hannah coerced a few stories of Joanne and Jason's mischievous deeds out of her. Then Mary gave Hannah a tour of the house.

'It's adorable!' she declared.

Finally, when they sat down for another drink, Mary told them both about the holiday cottage she'd booked. 'I was hoping you would both come,' she said.

'Of course we will. That will be amazing.' Hannah's eyes were shining. 'Please say yes, Mum.'

'I know you sometimes work weekends but as it's not until the half-term holiday in October I was hoping you could arrange that weekend off,' Mary told Cathy. 'I really would love you both to join us. I want all my family to be together.'

Hannah shot Cathy a questioning look and Cathy shook her head slightly. Was she saying she couldn't come?

'There's plenty of room for everyone. I realise that things have been a little awkward with Joanne and Jason but it's only because it was such a shock to find out about you. Once you all get to know each other better you will get on well, I know you will. You're all wonderful people. Please say you will come.' Mary waited anxiously for Cathy's reply.

'Can we go? Please, Mum!' Hannah said eagerly.

Cathy seemed a bit hesitant but Hannah's enthusiasm must have won her over because she eventually nodded. 'We'd love to. Thank you, Mum.'

Hannah squealed and clapped her hands in delight. 'Now let's have a selfie of us all before we go.'

She took a selfie stick out of her backpack, similar to the one Kelly used, Mary noticed, and placed her phone in it. 'Last chance to check you look okay,' she said, fishing out a mirror and checking her own appearance. Cathy exchanged an amused look with Mary. 'Right, here we go.' Hannah pressed a couple of buttons on her phone then held out the selfie stick. 'We've got ten seconds, huddle up!'

They all placed their arms around each other and smiled as the camera flashed. 'We'll do a couple, just in case,' Hannah said.

They all checked out the photos. They were lovely, the three of them were smiling so happily. Her daughter and granddaughter.

'Could you send one of those photos to me please?' Mary asked, wanting a copy of this precious moment for herself.

'Of course,' Hannah told her.

'Send them to me and I'll pass them on to your nan,' Cathy said.

A few minutes later the photos pinged onto Mary's phone. Then they all hugged goodbye and Cathy and Hannah left with a chorus of 'See you tomorrow'.

# 40

## *Cathy*

'Nan is lovely and I get why you didn't tell her about me at first,' Hannah said when they were back home. 'But...' Little lines formed between her thick black eyebrows as she frowned. 'But why did you tell her you have a job?'

She didn't add, 'That's another lie,' but Cathy guessed that's what she was thinking. She sighed and sat down on the sofa next to her daughter. 'It's complicated, Hannah.'

'Why is it? Nan abandoned you because she was young and scared and couldn't look after you. I get that, she was only a bit older than me. I'd be terrified if I got pregnant... not that there's any chance of that,' she added hastily as Cathy shot her a look of panic. 'But she's desperate to make it up to you. And I'm sure she won't care that you haven't been able to work because you've been ill. It doesn't seem right to lie to her. What will she think when she finds out?'

Cathy was trying not to think of that. Mary had been really understanding about Cathy's lie that she didn't have children, but would she be if the whole truth came out? If all the lies

Cathy had told unravelled? Hannah knew that Cathy hadn't been able to work for a couple of years because she'd had a breakdown, but she didn't know why, or why they had suddenly moved from the area she had grown up in to a different part of the country. She didn't know how close Cathy had come to being imprisoned. Jason knew, though. And if they spent this weekend in the cottage with Mary and the rest of the family, Cathy was worried that her secret might come out.

Jason had something to hide too, she reminded herself.

'I don't want your nan to feel sorry for me, and think that she has to give me money, that's why I pretended I was still working,' she told Hannah. 'And I will be working soon. I'm going to get myself another job. I feel much better now. Strong enough to work.'

'You do look better, you seem so much happier since you found your mum. And she is lovely, isn't she?'

'Yes she is.'

'What are your brother and sister like?' Hannah asked. 'I can't believe that I have an aunt and uncle and loads of cousins I've never met.' Her eyes were sparkling now. 'You've got a family now, Mum.'

'They're... nice. We're all still trying to get used to each other, though. Joanne's daughter Kelly is fifteen, like you. She goes to a private school, though, and is a bit...'

'Snobby?' Hannah wrinkled her nose and laughed. 'Don't worry, that won't bother me, we've got some snobby girls at school too.'

It probably wouldn't bother Hannah, she had so much confidence and always had a comeback.

'Besides I'm going to meet them tomorrow, aren't I? So it's not like they'll be strangers when we go away,' Hannah pointed out. 'Oh Mum, please! We must. It's Nan's birthday and this is your family. You've always wanted a family.'

If only she hadn't been forced to tell Mary about Hannah,

Cathy could have gone alone. She could have handled that. She didn't want Hannah caught up in any unpleasantness. She loved Hannah more than she had ever loved anything or anyone and hated her to be upset. She nodded. 'Okay, we'll go. But if there's any drama, we leave right away. Agreed?'

'Sure.' Hannah planted a kiss on Cathy's forehead. 'I'm off to meet Sammie now. She's dying to hear all about my nan. She thinks it's really cool that I've got this long-lost family.'

Hannah was a glass half-full person. She had always seen the sunny side of everything – as a child a rainy day was an excuse to splash into puddles and look for rainbows. Cathy wondered what she would be like if she hadn't got Terry for a father. Would she have become introverted, isolated, awkward around people like Cathy had been until she decided that the best way to deal with bullies was to front it out, act confident, bully them first?

She wished that she hadn't had to ask Hannah to lie about her having a job. It wouldn't be for much longer. She would start looking for work next week.

# 41

*Mary*

Sunday lunch had gone well yesterday, thank goodness. Kelly and Hannah had hit it off right away, which made things a lot easier. Both girls had been happy to keep an eye on Oliver and Nicholas in the garden while they chatted, Connor had been glued to his tablet as usual, and the adults had really made an effort to get on. Both Joanne and Jason had been to check out the development where Mary was buying the bungalow and had approved. 'At least you'll have neighbours, Mum,' Joanne said.

Jason seemed a bit worried about it not being available until just before Christmas. 'That's a long time, Mum. Can't you sell your house sooner and move in with us? I don't like you being here on your own.' Mary had pointed out that she needed that long to sort out this house, and Cathy had said that she and Hannah were happy to stay over a couple of times a week to help her and keep her company. All in all it had gone very well, and Mary was looking forward to the holiday now.

Mary had agreed to meet Stella, Daphne and Penelope for lunch today and was going to tell them about her forthcoming move too. She dressed in mauve linen slacks and a white top, knowing that Daphne and Penelope would be dressed to the nines, and decided to wear her Pandora bracelet. It comforted her to finger the assorted charms – Paul had bought her a new one every birthday – and remember his love for her. There was no sign of it in her jewellery box, though, or in any of her dressing table drawers. She tried to think of the last time she had worn it. When she was presented with the Villager of the Year award, that was it, and she thought she'd put it straight back into the jewellery box, but she must have absent-mindedly put it away somewhere else. Well, she didn't have time to look for it now, she would be late, so she slipped on her gold bracelet instead and set off.

'Well hello, stranger.' Stella kissed her on the cheek and sat down next to her. 'I'm the first one here then,' she remarked, glancing at the empty seats on the other side of the table.

'Penelope and Daphne are trying to find a parking space,' Mary told her. Daphne had messaged to let her know they were on their way a couple of minutes ago.

'Good, it gives us time to have a quick chat before they arrive. How are you, darling? How are things going with your new daughter?'

'It's going really well, and I've got some good news.' She had been planning on telling them all together but Stella was her oldest friend. 'I've put an offer in for a new bungalow on the Meadow Farm development. My house will be up for sale soon, and my bungalow will be ready to move into before Christmas.'

'That's brilliant, darling. That house is too big for you and holds too many memories. It's best for you to have a new start, and so good that you're remaining in the area.' Stella patted Mary's hand. 'I hope that means we'll be seeing a bit more of you now that things are starting to settle down.'

'You will,' Mary promised. 'We're all going away for a weekend in October for my birthday, and I'll be moving soon after that, but once I'm settled you and Ralph must come round. I'll have a housewarming evening for a few friends.'

'That would be delightful,' Stella said, smiling. Then she glanced over Mary's shoulder. 'Ah, here are Penelope and Daphne.'

As soon as the other two joined them, Mary repeated her news and it was congratulations all around. She felt a flood of happiness as she sat talking to her friends. Paul had gone, and the hole he had left in her heart would never fill, but she had her family and friends. She was so lucky.

They chatted over lunch, filling each other in on their news, and the other women seemed genuinely interested in how things were going with Cathy and thrilled to hear about Hannah. 'You must be chuffed to have found them both,' Stella said. 'I do love a happy ending.'

None of Mary's friends had passed judgement on her past, not to her face anyway, and they seemed really pleased for her. She wished for the umpteenth time that she hadn't kept it a secret for so long, that she had looked for Cathy before. She would have loved for Paul to have met her and Hannah. But what was done was done, as Mary's mother used to say.

The lunch hour extended into two as they chatted, finally saying their goodbyes and promising to do it all again before too long.

The waiter brought their bill, and Mary reached for her bag to pay her share. She took out her purse and opened it.

'No, no, this is our treat,' Stella said. 'We're all covering your share.'

'That's very kind of you. Are you sure?' Mary asked.

'Absolutely,' Daphne agreed.

Mary didn't argue. She was relieved because looking in her

purse she saw that the notes she'd withdrawn from the cash-point yesterday had disappeared.

This was the second time this had happened. She always seemed to be misplacing things just lately. Was the thing she had always dreaded happening? Did she have early-onset dementia like her mother?

# 42

## ONE MONTH AGO – SEPTEMBER

The next few weeks flew by in a flurry of sorting out the house, packing, taking things to the charity shop and all the other things involved in moving from a large house to a two-bedroomed bungalow. Everyone mucked in – Jason, Joanne and Cathy. Mary gave the three of them first choice of whatever furniture they wanted, and, of course, allowed Jason and Joanne to choose anything of their father's that she wasn't taking with her. She tried not to notice that Jason and Joanne rarely came to the house at the same time as Cathy. They would all gel a bit better during the weekend away next month, she told herself. At least they were all polite to each other, although it was clear from the odd remark that both Jason and Joanne made that they still didn't trust Cathy.

She'd had a few viewers but so far no one had made an offer yet.

'Perhaps you should drop the price of the house, Mum,' Jason suggested when he and Joanne came over to help Mary sort out Paul's study and see if there was anything they wanted to have for themselves.

'It sounds a good idea to me; you want to be in your

bungalow before Christmas, don't you Mum? That's only three months away,' Joanne agreed.

'But it's only been on the market a few weeks. Surely I'd be more sensible to wait a little longer,' Mary pointed out. 'The estate agent said that now everyone has finished going on their holidays things should pick up, as buyers will want to be in for Christmas too.' There had been no more incidents and she was feeling quite safe here again now. It seemed like the police were right, and the culprits had been kids, bored in the summer holidays. Cathy stayed over a couple of nights a week when Hannah was at her father's and they had also both stayed over last weekend. She always enjoyed their company. Mary was looking forward to moving, but no longer felt desperate. She was enjoying this time sorting things out and choosing new furniture and furnishings for her new bungalow.

By the end of September, the bungalow was coming on well and the developers thought it should be ready for early December, a little sooner than originally expected. Mary took Stella with her when she went to choose the kitchen fittings and her friend was full of admiration. 'It's really lovely,' she said, gazing around. 'And a perfect location.'

Mary was pleased that she'd made the decision to move. She was sure that she would be happy in the new property, with neighbours and shops nearby. And she had decided to get a little dog when she moved in, as Cathy had suggested, it would keep her company and taking it for walks would keep her fit.

After choosing the kitchen fittings, Mary waved goodbye to Stella and set off home. As she pulled up into the drive, she was suddenly aware of smoke coming from the side of the house. Stopping the car, she jumped out and hurried over to investigate. To her horror, flames were leaping out of the wheelie bin, which was resting against the side wall of the house. How on earth had that happened? She had to put it out quickly before the whole house went up in flames. Hurrying over to the hose pipe that she kept fixed on the tap at the back of the garden, to make it easier to water the garden, she turned the tap on and hauled the thick pipe over to the burning dustbin, alarmed to see that thick black smoke was billowing out of it and a couple of flames were now licking up the wall of the house. Standing as far away as she could so that she didn't inhale the smoke, she turned the spray on full and doused the flames. When they were finally extinguished, she leaned against the wall, all her strength draining out of her. There was no way this was accidental, she never put anything flammable in the dustbin. Someone had deliberately set it alight and if she hadn't come back when she did, the flames would have spread and her home would have caught fire. Was that what the culprit had intended?

Then another thought hit her. What if this had happened when she was in bed? She could have been burnt alive.

Was someone out to kill her?

*Don't be silly, who would want to kill you? You've been watching too many detective films on the TV,* she told herself. Shaken and wanting reassurance, she called Joanne, who immediately said, 'Oh Mum, have you been putting candle stubs in the bin again? I've told you that you need to wet the wick to make sure it's completely out.'

'I haven't,' Mary protested, but even as she said the words she tried to remember the last time she'd put a candle stub in the bin. It had been a few days ago, she was sure of it, and she had doused it in water first, she always did. 'I think someone set my bin alight, Jo,' she said, her voice quivering. 'Should I call the police?'

'Oh Mum, surely not!' Joanne sounded really worried. 'Have you checked the CCTV, that'll show you if anyone came up the drive and put something in the bin. If they did, then yes, call the police right away. Otherwise, I don't see what they can do.'

Why hadn't she thought of that? Mary logged onto her laptop and checked out the CCTV. The screen was blank.

Jason dropped by after work, as Joanne had told him about the dustbin fire. He studied the blackened, melted bin thoughtfully. 'These plastic bins go up in no time, ' he said. 'It must have only just set fire. It's a good job you came home when you did, Mum.'

'Do you think someone set it alight on purpose?' Mary asked him worriedly. 'The CCTV isn't working again, the screen was blank.' Jason had never found the time to replace the CCTV system.

'I don't know. It is a bit strange that your dustbin should suddenly go up in flames, but why would someone do that? Unless it's kids again.' He thrust his hands in his pockets and surveyed the drive. 'The trouble is, you are bit exposed here, Mum. The drive is open and you're secluded at the end of the lane. I do worry about you. I'll be glad when you sell the house and move.'

'Me too,' Mary agreed. 'I think it's time I dropped the price. My bungalow will be available a bit earlier than originally planned so I need to get things moving. I'll phone the estate agent tomorrow and tell her.'

Jason checked out the garden and the house to reassure Mary that it was all safe, and stayed for a while to keep her company. 'Give me a call if you feel nervous, Mum. I'll come over any time,' he told her as he kissed her on the cheek goodbye, after trying – unsuccessfully – to persuade her to stay with him and Alison for a few days. 'You're not a nuisance, I promise.'

'Thank you, dear, but I'm sure I'll be fine,' Mary said. When Jason had gone, though, she sat in the lounge, feeling anxious and vulnerable. The only feasible explanation for that dustbin catching fire was that someone had deliberately set fire to it. She thought back to the other incidents, the punctured car tyre, the trampled plants, the brick through the window. Someone had it in for her, she was sure of it. She no longer felt safe living here. The sooner she moved out the better and if she had to drop the price of her house to do that then so be it. Better to lose a few thousand pounds than her life. She shuddered. She could hardly believe it but she actually felt that her life was in danger.

# 43

## *Cathy*

Cathy had resigned herself to not finding Robbie. It had been weeks since she had replied to the message from the person who knew him, asking if she wanted Robbie to contact her. Robbie obviously didn't want to know. He was probably married now, and didn't want an illegitimate baby popping up from his distant past. That was okay, she had Mary. Cathy spent every spare minute she could at Mary's, helping her clear out the big house and pack the boxes. Hannah sometimes came over too. They got on so well, the three of them. And surprisingly, Hannah and Kelly got on too. Hannah had been delighted to learn that she had a cousin the same age, and Kelly had been very welcoming. The two girls were now firm friends and often messaged each other.

They had a family now, she and Hannah. What did it matter if Robbie didn't want to know?

And then, just as she'd forgotten all about it, a message popped into her inbox. It was from Robbie and he wanted to meet her. She smiled to herself as she read the message. He was surprised but delighted to know that he had a daughter and couldn't wait to meet her.

Perfect. He was the missing piece of the puzzle. Now she would be secure at last, with both parents. The perfect family.

# 44

## THREE WEEKS AGO

### *Mary*

Mary was surprised to see Joanne's car parked in her drive when she returned home.

Joanne opened the front door as Mary pulled up. 'I dropped in on the off chance that you'd be in,' she said, stepping out to meet her. 'I was just about to drive off again.'

'Hello, darling, what a lovely surprise,' Mary said. 'Have you come to congratulate me on selling the house?'

'Yes, it's marvellous news. Well done, Mum.' Joanne gave her a hug. 'I've got the kettle boiling,' she said.

Mary could sense that there was something her daughter wanted to talk to her about. 'Oh good, I'm dying for a cuppa,' she said as they walked over to the house. Mary sat down at the table and waited as Joanne reboiled the kettle and made a cup of tea for Mary and coffee for herself. What could it be? Had Damien been gambling again and Joanne needed some money? Had they decided not to come to the cottage for her birthday? She hoped not, she was looking forward to spending some quality time with all her family.

Joanne put the two cups on the table and sat down. 'Mum, I have to tell you something more about Cathy,' she said.

Mary suppressed a sigh. What now?

'She's been feeding you a pack of lies. She's doesn't work in a supermarket at all.'

'How do you know this?' Mary asked, puzzled. Why would Cathy make it up?

'One of Kelly's friends has a sister who lives in the same area. She said that Cathy doesn't work. She had a mental breakdown a few years ago and hasn't worked since,' Joanne said. She looked earnestly at Mary. 'I've been talking to Damien and we think she's after your money, Mum. That's why she is always here. And why she's persuaded you to sell the house and buy something smaller.'

Mary had to admit that she'd wondered about Cathy's job. She did seem to have a lot of time off, and whenever Mary enquired about her work, Cathy evaded the subject. Hannah had given her mother a strange look the other day when Mary had asked Cathy what shifts she was doing this week. She guessed Cathy was embarrassed to say that she was too unwell to work, but there was nothing to be ashamed of. Mary had seen the effect of these breakdowns a lot in her nursing career. She'd seen parents who kept strong while helping their children fight their disease, collapse mentally if the child died, or sometimes even when they recovered. It was as if they had used all their strength trying to hold it together and then couldn't do it any longer. Perhaps that was what had happened to Mary's dad when her mother had died – he simply couldn't cope any longer, maybe that was why he had been so withdrawn from Mary. The mind was a strange and powerful thing. She was concerned to hear that Cathy had suffered a breakdown and hoped that her daughter had recovered now. She seemed fine but Mary knew from her years as a nurse that people often put on a front.

'So Cathy didn't want to tell us that she's out of work because she had a breakdown. That's perfectly understandable and not something that I'm going to judge her for,' she said gently. 'And being out of work doesn't mean that she's after my money, Jo. Cathy's never asked me for anything, what I've given her I've given freely. Like I do to you and Jason.'

Joanne let out an exasperated sigh. 'You're so full of guilt for abandoning Cathy that you're blinkered about her, Mum. Can't you see how much she's wheedled her way into your life? And how little she's told you about her own?'

'She's entitled to her privacy, she's an adult. I don't want to know anything that she isn't ready to tell me,' Mary replied firmly. 'And yes, I do feel guilty for abandoning her. She is my child, just as much as you two are. And I do wish that you'd accept her instead of always trying to look for faults.' She swallowed. 'Don't you realise how much it means to me to have Cathy and Hannah in my life? It doesn't mean that I love you less, for goodness' sake.'

'We're not kids, Mum. We're not fighting over your attention. We're just saying that Cathy isn't all she seems,' Joanne said curtly. 'I wouldn't leave your purse lying around when she's here.'

'That's enough,' Mary said sharply. 'Just because Cathy is unemployed it doesn't mean that she's a thief.'

'Oh, Mum, I'm only trying to look out for you,' Joanne said with a sigh. She gave Mary a hug. 'Of course I'm glad you've found Cathy, so is Jason. It's just it's all happened so quickly and we don't know much about her, but I did also come to say congratulations for selling the house. It just shows that it was the right decision to drop the price. Will you come back with me for something to eat and a celebratory drink? Jason and Alison are coming over too. Why not stop the night and you can have a couple of glasses of wine? I'll bring you back in the morning.'

Mary's outrage faded away. It was only natural that Joanne would be concerned and be looking out for her. This was all strange for her and Jason too, their father dying, an older sister appearing who they had known nothing about, and now their mother was moving out of the family home. And it was so thoughtful that they wanted to celebrate with her.

'I would love that, thank you. Let me grab an overnight bag and I'll be with you,' Mary said.

Joanne's face broke into a wide grin.

---

They had a lovely evening, chatting about past family times and reminiscing about Paul. It was bittersweet and Mary was pleased that she'd accepted Joanne's offer to stay overnight. Perhaps she had neglected her and Jason a little while she was trying to bond with Cathy, she thought, as she climbed into bed in the spare bedroom, contented but weary. She'd left the others downstairs chatting. Joanne had opened another bottle of wine, the boys had fallen asleep on the sofa and it looked like it was going to be a late night, but Mary was too tired to stay up any longer.

She had almost fallen asleep when something flashed into her mind. There were a couple of times just lately when she'd misplaced money and had worried that she was getting dementia. The uncomfortable thought that maybe Cathy had taken the money wormed its way into her mind. She recalled Joanne saying she'd seen Cathy and Hannah with a load of shopping bags, two days after Mary had had lunch with Cathy and misplaced the money she'd taken from the cashpoint. And now some money had disappeared from her purse again, when Cathy had been at her house most days this week.

'Don't leave your purse around,' Joanne had warned.

Surely Cathy wouldn't steal from her?

She had to face it, though, money had been going missing. And there was her Pandora bracelet too, she'd searched high and low but there was no sign of it. And everything had only started happening since Cathy had come into her life.

# 45

*Alison*

Alison read the text from Joanne again.

> *Will you and Jason come around on Friday for a drink and something to eat? We need to discuss plans for Mum's birthday in the holiday cottage.*

She groaned. She didn't really fancy going and was sure that Jason wouldn't either, but this was a big birthday for Mary, and her first one without Paul, so she guessed they did need to talk about it and make sure it all went to plan.

Jason agreed too, so Friday evening they went over to see Joanne and Damien for pizza and wine. As soon as they walked in, they could see that there was an atmosphere and Joanne had obviously already started on the wine.

'Anyone want topping up?' Joanne asked when the pizza had been eaten and one bottle of wine emptied.

'Don't you think you've had enough?' Damien snapped.

'I need something to wind down after the day I've had. You've no idea what it's like, you're never here,' Joanne retorted.

Before Damien could reply, Kelly came in. Her friend's father had dropped her off. Damien's eyes widened as he looked at her. 'What's that stuff plastered all over your face?' he growled. 'And your skirt is no wider than a belt.'

'Chill out, Dad, everyone wears makeup and short skirts,' Kelly told him. She looked around at the open bottle of wine and empty glasses. 'I can see you're having a boozy night so I'm off to bed.' She gave a little finger wave and went straight upstairs.

Damien turned to Joanne. 'I can't believe you let her go out like that. And Connor is stuck up in his room all night. You've got no control over these kids!'

'I don't want to "control" them. I'm their mother, not their gaoler,' Joanne snapped.

Alison and Jason exchanged awkward looks. Joanne and Damien were always arguing over Kelly and Connor. Joanne was fairly relaxed with them, claiming if you were too strict teenagers would rebel so you needed to choose your battles, whereas Damien always went head to head with them, insisting they do as he said. Joanne often told Alison that life was like a battlefield when Damien was around. Alison didn't like him, although she tried hard not to show it.

'You think these days are hard, at least you know where your kids are every night, and they do as you tell them,' Damien said, glancing over at the boys fast asleep on the sofa. 'Kelly and Connor shut themselves in their room every evening, apart from weekends when Connor turns the kitchen into a disaster zone while he practises another recipe. Mind you, I prefer Kelly to stay in her room. When she does go out she dresses like a tart and disappears for hours saying that she's "with friends".' He knocked back a swig of wine. 'And muggins here stands for it.'

Joanne scowled at him. 'They only stay in their rooms to get away from you!'

'Now, now, play nicely,' Jason teased although Alison thought he was secretly enjoying seeing them at loggerheads. 'I hope you two aren't going to be arguing all weekend when we're away.'

Damien grimaced. 'I'm dreading that, aren't you? Three whole days stuck in a cottage with Cathy Cuckoo.'

Damien had christened Cathy 'Cathy Cuckoo' as soon as he had met her though he just about managed to hide his dislike of her when Mary was around. Alison guessed that was because he needed to be in Mary's good books in case he had to tap her for another handout. Joanne had confessed to her a couple of weeks ago that she thought he was gambling again. She'd had letters from the schools saying that fees hadn't been paid that month, but apparently when she'd confronted Damien, he'd said it was a bank mix-up, and the fees had been paid a couple of days later. Alison didn't trust him. She didn't trust Jason either.

'I can't say I fancy it either,' Jason said, 'But it's what Mum wants and I'm sure we can all rub along for a couple of days.' He put down his glass. 'Anyway, we came to discuss Mum's birthday plans, not listen to you two having a domestic.'

Joanne threw him a frosty look. 'We are not having a domestic.'

Alison wished Jason wouldn't wind Joanne up like that, he always had to stir things. She didn't fancy being cooped up with everyone in a cottage in the middle of nowhere either, but the boys would enjoy it. She needed an afternoon with Hugh before she went, though, to give her the strength to get through. He was the only thing that kept her sane. Joanne's next words jolted her out of her thoughts.

'Actually, I asked you over because Mum told me yesterday that she's changing her will to include Cathy. And that she wants to give a bigger share of her money to Cathy to make up for abandoning her. She said that we've had a better start in life than Cathy so she thinks that she deserves more.'

There was a dead silence then Jason slammed his glass down so hard that Alison thought he'd break it. 'Bloody Cathy!' He scowled.

'For once I agree with you,' Joanne said.

# 46

## TWO WEEKS AGO

### *Cathy*

She'd just settled down to watch the TV with Hannah for the evening when the phone rang. Cathy glanced at the screen, surprised to see that it was an unknown caller, then hesitated for a moment before answering.

'Cathy, it's me. Jason,' a male voice boomed.

Jason? Mary must have given him her number. What did he want? 'Cathy? Are you there?'

She glanced anxiously at Hannah, who was still engrossed in the film. 'I'll just take this,' she whispered, getting up to go out of the room.

'Are you there, Cathy?'

'Yes. What do you want? I'm sure you haven't called for a chat.'

'That's exactly what I do want. A chat. I think we need to clear the air. But not now.' She could hear Nicholas and Oliver shouting in the background. He was at home then. 'Let's meet tomorrow. Twelve o'clock. I'll WhatsApp you the location.'

'And if I don't want to meet you?'

'Oh I think you know that it's in your best interests if you do. We've got things to sort out. Don't be late. I've got a busy day.' He ended the call before she even had time to reply. Cathy went back to join Hannah, her mind still going over the conversation. She'd been expecting Jason to say something ever since the first time when it was evident he'd recognised her, but it still shook her that he wanted to meet her. She guessed that it was because Mary's birthday weekend was fast approaching and Jason was getting nervous about them spending so much time together so wanted to make sure that Cathy didn't let the cat out of the bag about the first time they had met each other. She'd better go, she decided. Later that evening Jason WhatsApped the location over, telling her it was a hotel where he was attending a business conference.

She'd been half-expecting him to threaten or blackmail her but he was actually very pleasant.

'Let's not beat about the bush,' he said as she sat down to join him for a coffee. 'I know you recognised me that first time, just as I recognised you. I think it's in both of our interests not to mention where we met, don't you?' He smiled before continuing. 'There's no need for Alison, or anyone else to find out about it.'

So he was playing the friendly approach. 'I had no intention of mentioning it. The past is the past as far as I'm concerned,' she assured him.

'I'm glad that's settled. I didn't want any awkwardness when we all go away for Mum' s birthday and are thrust into each other's company for a long weekend.' He took a sip of his drink. 'How are things going? Are you starting to get used to us all yet?'

She was surprised at his question, not expecting him to be interested in her feelings. 'Yes, but I have to admit it's strange to have a mum – and siblings – after all these years.' She ran her finger around the edge of the cup before adding, 'It must be strange for you and Joanne too.'

He shrugged. 'A bit. Well, to be honest it was a total shock.' He gave her a rueful smile. 'But, well, we get why Mum didn't say anything, and how hard it must have been for her – and you. It's good that there's been a happy ending to it all.' He raised his cup. 'Good to have you in the family. And Hannah too, of course.'

For a moment she was taken aback. Then she smiled. 'Thank you.'

He looked, and sounded, like he meant it. She had been nervous about meeting him today, prepared herself for him to threaten her to keep quiet but he was being pleasant, friendly even. So why drag her all the way over here to talk? He could have said this over the phone.

Almost as if he had read her mind, he said, 'I thought it would be pleasanter to have a drink together and discuss things, face to face is always better than on the phone.' He smiled a wide smile. 'Glad we're on the same wavelength.' He supped the last of his drink and put the cup down. 'See you then.'

She nodded. 'Bye.'

It was in the past. Over with, although it had almost destroyed her at the time. She pushed the thought away. It was over, all of it. She'd been acquitted.

# 47

## ONE WEEK AGO

### *Alison*

Alison groaned when she saw the message from Hugh that had come in just as she pulled into the hotel car park.

*Sorry I've been delayed, there's been a break-in at the office.*

Not that Hugh could help that but she wished she'd received his message before she left home, now she'd have to sit here like a dummy waiting for him.

*I'm already at the hotel, I've just parked up. Will you be able to join me or shall I go home?*

She'd be gutted if he couldn't come. She'd been so looking forward to spending an afternoon with Hugh, the last time she would meet him before the birthday weekend. She didn't want to waste all the time she'd spent getting ready, and the expensive lingerie she'd bought. She wanted to be making hot, sensuous love in the hotel room with Hugh. She'd been looking forward to it all week.

*I'll be there. The room is booked, number 204, in the name of Simon Turner. I'll message you details of the booking and have let the hotel know you're on the way. Get the key and go and make yourself comfortable.*

Alison smiled. Thank goodness for that. The receptionist handed her the key and she went up in the lift. She opened the door and caught her breath when she saw the luxurious room with its soft cream carpet, stunning four-poster bed, the jacuzzi in the corner... Hugh really had pulled out all the stops.

She poured herself an orange juice, it was tempting to raid the mini bar and add vodka to it but she had to drive back home later, so she switched on the TV to find a film to watch.

Hugh arrived an hour later, looking a bit flustered, which was very unlike him. One of the things she liked about Hugh was that he was always calm and composed, not like Jason, who often veered from being on a high to being moody and snappy.

'Is everything all right? Was much taken?' she asked.

'Nothing was taken, that was the strange thing. The burglar was obviously looking for something, all the cupboards and drawers were ransacked. You should have seen the place. But as far as we can tell nothing is missing. Jason seems to think it's a rival firm. We're working on a bid for a lucrative new project, the program we're doing is highly innovative and he thinks the burglar might have been after that. Luckily we're both working on it on our home computers.' Hugh took off his jacket and tie, putting them on the back of the chair.

She stood up and walked over to him. 'Need help?' she asked, undoing the top button of his shirt.

He groaned and pulled her into him so close she could smell

his expensive aftershave, feel his toned body beneath the suit. Hugh was ten years older than Jason, handsome, suave, dynamic, experienced. Jason seemed so immature beside him. And Hugh certainly knew how to pleasure a woman whereas she and Jason only had functional sex now and again. Two young children and busy working lives did that to you. Most nights Nicholas would have a bad dream and come into their bed, so Jason would immediately get out and go into Nicholas's bed, grumbling that he needed to sleep. As if she didn't. She didn't care, though, she'd rather cuddle up to Nicholas than listen to Jason snoring, and now she had Hugh to put the sparkle in her life. She loved Hugh but she didn't want to split up her family, especially while the boys were so young, even though Jason was cold, calculating and selfish.

'Sorry I'm late,' he said softly.

'Not your fault.' She slowly unbuttoned the next button of his shirt.

'That's what I like about you, you're so calm and undemanding,' Hugh said.

'Well, I don't know about undemanding,' she replied, her lips curving into a smile.

His eyes met hers and she saw the desire she felt mirrored in them. 'Shame we're both driving and can only have a soft drink,' he said. 'We really must arrange a night away soon. Then we could have some champagne delivered to our room and enjoy ourselves.'

Her body tingled in anticipation. Hugh always did this to her. He was like a drug. They had both agreed that they would end it if Jason got suspicious but she wondered if she could. Without Hugh, her life would be so dull, meaningless.

*You've got the boys*, she reminded herself. She adored her boys. But she also needed something else, something for her, and Hugh provided that.

'But for now, let's enjoy the afternoon. We've wasted enough time.' Hugh pushed her up against the wall, his body pressed against hers, his mouth claiming her. 'I love you,' he murmured huskily. 'I want to be with you every minute of every day.'

For a moment Alison froze. Was he asking her to leave Jason for him? He knew she couldn't do that much as she longed to. Hugh pulled his head back and looked into her eyes, waiting for her response.

'I love you too,' she said and wound her arms around his neck.

# 48

## TWO DAYS AGO

### *Mary*

'It's so pretty, like a Hansel and Gretel cottage in the wood,' Hannah said in delight.

Kelly shuddered. 'Well, I think it's a bit spooky. We're really isolated.'

The cottage was very picturesque, nestled in a section of the moor, surrounded by trees. But Mary could see why Kelly thought it was spooky too. They'd all travelled down that evening, after work, and it was already dark so the cottage, standing on its own with the full moon shining down on it, did look a little eerie. There was a large drive at the front of the cottage, big enough for the three cars they'd come down in – Mary had travelled with Cathy and Hannah – and a large garden at the back which backed onto the wood – according to the details anyway. They had only just arrived so hadn't checked out the back yet.

'There are other cottages a few minutes away,' Joanne told her. 'And it will all look a lot different in the daylight. 'Come on, let's go inside and get ourselves settled.'

She was being overly bright and cheerful but Mary was pleased that she was making the effort. This birthday weekend spent with her family meant a lot to Mary, she was so delighted to have all her children around her and hoped that the closeness would encourage them to stop arguing and get on for once.

It was half-term so everyone had booked the Monday off work – although Mary was sure that both Damien and Jason would be glued to their mobiles as they were both workaholics. The lady who Mary had rented the cottage from lived nearby so had been in and lit a fire for them and the cottage was really warm and cosy when they stepped inside. They all wandered about, checking out the downstairs rooms – a large living room with a fire burning in the grate, and two huge comfy sofas, plus a few other armchairs scattered about, a dining room with a large wooden table big enough for twelve people to eat around, a fully fitted cottage kitchen with a rustic wooden table and chairs – ideal for the children to eat their breakfast – and an AGA, plus a conservatory (or sun room, as the brochure called it) and a utility room.

'This is great, at least we won't be tripping over each other,' Alison remarked. She glanced at Nicholas, who was almost asleep on her shoulder. 'How about we sort out the bedrooms now? This little one could do with going to bed.'

'Good idea, you all carry on and I'll put the kettle on,' Mary said. 'I don't mind which room I'm in. They've all got an ensuite.' She wanted everyone to be happy and have a good time together as a family.

'Neither do I,' Cathy said.

'Can me and Hannah choose our room?' Kelly asked as they all headed in the direction of the stairs. The girls had already decided that they wanted to share. Mary was surprised and pleased at how well they got on. They seemed such different personalities, but they had gelled instantly and kept in regular touch with each other since that first meeting. When they were together they spent their time huddled together in a corner, giggling and chatting, or pouting and taking selfies for Instagram. Connor ignored Hannah – he was that age – but Nicholas and Oliver adored her as much as they adored Cathy.

'Oh good, an electric kettle,' Cathy said, filling it up and switching it on. Mary went over to the fridge to put away the food and drinks they'd brought with them and was delighted to see that the landlady had left milk, bread, eggs, tea and coffee. She'd also pinned a note to the fridge door saying she was away for the weekend, leaving a number to contact her in emergencies, and directions to the nearest shop and informing them that there were leaflets on the table in the hall detailing the local attractions, and a map. It was too late to do much apart from settle in and maybe have a drink now but at least they had two full days to explore.

Damien and Jason went straight outside to check out the garden and surroundings, coming back in a few minutes later to inform everyone that it was a huge garden but completely fenced in so the boys would be safe to play out there.

'Thank goodness, I don't want them under my feet all weekend,' Alison said. She had just come back down to get some hot milk for Oliver and Nicholas.

Mary put the beef casserole she'd made earlier into the oven and Joanne opened one of the bottle of wines she'd brought, poured everyone a glass then set about laying the table. Cathy had brought a homemade fruit cake with her, so that was the meal sorted.

They all sat around the dining table and tucked in heartily. It was a happy, fun atmosphere.

'I think the men should do the washing up as we've prepared the meal,' Joanne said. She reached over for the opened bottle of wine in the ice bucket and poured herself another glass of wine. 'Anyone else want one?'

'Me,' said Kelly, holding out her glass. She, Hannah and

Connor had been allowed a small glass of wine diluted with lemonade.

Damien glared at her. 'You're not old enough to drink at all. Your mother shouldn't have allowed it. Alcohol rots your insides.'

'No chance, we said one glass only,' Joanne told her, then turned to glare at Damien. 'Since when were you Mr Teetotal?' she demanded.

'I drink, yes, but in moderation.' He stood up and started collecting the plates. 'Seeing as I've spotted the dishwasher in the kitchen, I'm quite happy to load it,' he said. 'Come and give me a hand, Jason. We'll show these women how to stack a dishwasher correctly.'

Joanne raised a glass. 'Go for it.'

Alison and Cathy laughed and held out their glasses for Joanne to refill as Damien and Jason took the dirty plates into the kitchen.

Mary went in to check on the men and found them talking football as they expertly loaded the dishwasher. Joanne and Alison often complained that they did the majority of the household chores because of the long hours the men worked, but at least they were willing to help when they were at home. She loved how couples both mucked in nowadays, not like back in her day when the children were little. Although Paul was a kind man, he left the chores and childrearing to her – most men did back then. She was lucky to be able to afford help and to not need to work full-time until the children were older.

Table cleared away and dishwasher loaded, they all drifted into the living room and sat chatting for a while, then Kelly and Hannah went up to bed and Jason and Damien opened a bottle of whisky. Mary could see that it was going to be a long night. 'I'm going to bed, I'll leave you younger ones to it,' she said, with a yawn.

'Night, Mum, and thanks for this. It was a lovely idea.'

Joanne was a little red-faced now, the wine no doubt, but at least she was happy. It was good to see her relax. Mary looked around for Alison then remembered that she had gone up to check on the lads. She'd pop her head in and whisper goodnight.

As Mary walked up the stairs, she could hear the giggles from the girls' room and a murmur from Alison's room. She walked along the corridor, stopping outside the slightly open door to say goodnight – then halted as Alison's whispered words floated out to her.

'I miss you too, Hugh. I'll make it up to you on Wednesday. Usual place. I can't wait to spend a whole afternoon with you.'

Mary froze as the meaning of the conversation registered with her. She recognised the name Hugh. That was Jason's business partner. And by the sound of it, Alison was having an affair with him. She was stunned. She was very fond of Alison and had thought that she and Jason were happy together, she was the last person Mary would have expected to cheat. The enormity of the situation hit Mary like a brick. If Jason found out what was going on, the marriage would be over. Those two little boys would no longer live with their father, their lives would be changed forever.

# 49

For a moment Mary stood there, dazed, wondering what to do, then the door swung open and Alison came out. She smiled at Mary. 'Are you off to bed now? The boys are fast asleep already so I think I'll go back down and join the others.'

Mary hesitated, tempted to pretend that she hadn't heard anything but then she thought of her precious grandsons and knew that she had to try and stop this before Jason found out. 'I was just about to go to bed – but I heard your conversation,' she said firmly.

She saw the panic in Alison's eyes. 'I don't know what you mean.'

' How long has this affair with Hugh been going on?' Mary demanded.

Alison's face flushed and she jutted out her chin in defiance, obviously determined to continue denying it. 'I don't know what you think you overheard...'

'Please don't take me for a fool, Alison. I know exactly what I overheard.' Mary looked around, it was too public out here to talk. 'Look, we can't discuss it here – let's go into my room.'

Alison folded her arms. 'I don't think—'

'Do you really want Jason – or anyone else – to overhear this conversation?' Mary asked, aware that Cathy had already gone up to bed and, although she was at the other end of the corridor, could come out of her room any minute. She walked along the hall to her room, opening the door and turning to Alison. 'Are you coming in?'

As she'd guessed she would, Alison followed her, closing the door behind her. 'I think you misunderstood, Mary—' she started to say but Mary raised her hand.

'I wish I had never heard your conversation but I did and I can't unhear it.' She sat down wearily on the chair in her bedroom. 'You said you missed Hugh and couldn't wait to spend an afternoon with him. There is only one conclusion I can draw from that remark.'

Alison went pale and sank down on the edge of the bed. 'Are you going to tell Jason?'

Mary hoped she wouldn't have to. The last thing she wanted was for her son's marriage to end so she kept her voice stern. 'I should but I don't want you both to split up. You're good for Jason, at least I thought you were. And I would hate for Oliver and Nicholas to grow up in a broken home.'

'So would I,' Alison said quickly, leaning forward and clasping her hands together anxiously. 'I didn't mean this to happen but Jason...' She turned her head to the side. 'Well, he and I, we don't...'

Mary had an idea what she was going to say. She knew how easy it was for couples to grow apart with the demands of a young family. 'It's no excuse, Alison. How would you feel if Jason was cheating on you?'

Her eyes met Mary's, the resentment clearly visible in them. 'I wouldn't be surprised,' she said sadly.

This was worse that she had realised, Mary thought. 'Look, I know that it can be difficult when your children are little but do you really want to end your marriage?'

Alison shook her head. 'Of course not. I just felt lonely and unloved and Hugh...'

Mary bit back the angry retort that sprang to her lips. She was prepared to overlook this for the sake of saving Jason's marriage but she didn't want to hear her son criticised. It was bad enough Alison cheating on him, but to do it with his business partner...

*We all make mistakes. We all deserve a second chance*, she told herself. She'd had one, hadn't she?

'I won't breathe a word of this to Jason or anyone. I will never mention it to you again.' She saw the relief flare in Alison's eyes. 'Providing you promise to end it with Hugh right now. Message him immediately and tell him it's over.'

Alison stared at her, aghast. 'You can't order me about like that.'

'I'm not standing by and watching you cheat on my son and ruin my grandsons' lives. Either message Hugh now and tell him it's over, and promise not to see him again, or I'll go downstairs and tell Jason what's going on,' Mary said firmly. 'I adore you, Alison, you are like a daughter to me, but if push comes to shove, my loyalty is with Jason.'

Alison's lips tightened and Mary could see that her daughter-in-law was assessing whether she would do as she had threatened. Finally, Alison nodded slowly. 'Fine. I was going to end it anyway. It's only happened a couple of times, and only because Jason doesn't give a damn about me. He's always out and I get lonely being alone with the boys.' She raised her eyes defiantly to meet Mary's. 'He's not the perfect husband you think he is.'

'I'm sure he isn't. None of us are perfect. But he is my son and you are cheating on him. And with his business partner of all people. Now send the message then show it to me so that I know you've done it.'

Alison looked as if she was about to break down, Mary

thought worriedly. Surely she didn't actually have feelings for Hugh? It was just a meaningless affair, wasn't it? Well, whatever it was, she had to make Alison end it. 'I'm not going until I see that message, Alison,' she said firmly.

Alison pulled her phone back out of her pocket and thumbed a message. Mary heard the ping as she sent it then Alison showed her the screen.

> *I can't do this to Jason anymore, Hugh. Sorry but I'm ending it. Don't contact me again.*

'Satisfied?' she asked, her voice wobbling a little.

Mary nodded. 'I'll keep your secret but only because I know it will break my son's heart and I don't want my grandchildren to grow up in a broken home. But if you ever cheat on Jason again I will tell him. You get one chance only. Don't make a fool of my son, or take me for one. Understand?'

Alison nodded. 'I'm sorry. I promise it won't happen again. And thank you for not telling Jason.' She got up and walked out of Mary's room, closing the door quietly behind her.

'Oh Paul.' Mary picked up his photo from the bedside table. 'I hope I'm doing the right thing.' She knew that Jason would be furious if he ever found out about Alison's affair, and even worse if he discovered that his own mother had known too and not told him. She had to do what she felt was right, though.

In the distance an owl hooted and Mary shivered. She'd been so looking forward to this weekend away but already things were going wrong. She pulled herself together. *Stop looking on the negative side*, she told herself. It was a good thing that she had overheard Alison and could put a stop to this. At least now it would be over, and Alison did love Jason, Mary was sure she did. Her daughter-in-law was lonely and bored and Hugh had come along and given her the attention she longed for.

Mary was angry at Hugh too. He was Jason's business partner and Jason trusted him. How could he betray him like that? She felt like telling Hugh that she knew what was going on and warning him to back off, but she didn't want to make the situation worse now that Alison had done the right thing and ended it. Tomorrow she'd suggest to Jason that he should try and spend more time with his wife and family. She remembered how lonely she had felt sometimes when Joanne and Jason were little and Paul worked away. She had never been unfaithful, though. She was so grateful to have Paul in her life, for how he had given her the chance to turn her life around after what had happened, that she would never have risked doing anything to spoil things between them. She wondered briefly if Paul had ever strayed while he was away, lonely in his hotel bedroom. She looked down at the photo. She was sure he hadn't. He wouldn't have done that to her.

If he had, though, she would have forgiven him. She would have forgiven Paul anything. If only she had been so sure of his unconditional love for her, she would have told him about Cathy earlier. Then maybe things would have been different and the children would have all accepted each other.

Or Paul would have left her and then the children would have hated her.

# 50

## ONE DAY AGO

Mary had a restless night, worrying about Jason and Alison, finally getting out of bed at six-thirty, showering and heading downstairs. She was surprised to see Oliver and Nicholas sitting watching the TV. There was no sign of anyone else up and about.

'Morning, boys, you're both up early. Are your mum and dad still asleep?' she asked.

'They're tired and said we could come down and watch the TV,' Oliver replied without glancing away from the cartoon on the screen.

Mary wondered if Alison was too embarrassed to come down and face her, but thought it was far more likely that she was sleeping off the wine. The four of them had looked like they were in for a heavy session. Well, they were on holiday, it was only natural that they would want to let their hair down and relax a little. Cathy hadn't joined them, though, she had gone up early just before Mary. She guessed that she still felt a little like an outsider, but hopefully this holiday would bring them all closer together. At least Kelly and Hannah got on well. 'Have you had breakfast yet?' she asked the boys.

They both shook their heads. 'Turn that off and come into the kitchen – I'll do you some,' she told them. She didn't want them to spend the entire weekend stuck in front of the TV.

'Oh Nan, it finishes soon, can't we see the end?' Oliver pleaded.

It was a reasonable request. 'You can if you promise to turn it off as soon as this cartoon finishes and come straight into the kitchen,' she agreed.

'We will,' they chorused.

The boys kept their word and came into the kitchen five minutes later. They were both sitting at the table eating a bowl of cereal each when Cathy came in, showered and dressed in jeans and a jumper.

'Morning, Mum. Childminding already?' she said, giving Mary a kiss on the cheek. She had made a couple of comments recently about how much Alison expected Mary to look after the boys. Mary had insisted that she didn't mind, but after what she'd overheard last night, she wondered if Alison had used her to look after the boys while she dallied with Hugh – the affair could have been going on for ages. *It's over now,* she reminded herself. As soon as she got the opportunity she would talk to Jason and suggest that he give Alison a bit more support, and maybe take her out for a meal every now and then. While she didn't intend to babysit so Alison could meet Hugh, she was more than happy to look after the children for her and Jason to go out for the evening. She would suggest that he bought Hugh out of the business too, or set up on his own. It would be better if they no longer worked together. Thank goodness her house sale was almost through, maybe Jason could use that money to buy Hugh out.

'I don't mind giving them breakfast while Jason and Alison have a bit of a lie-in,' she told Cathy. She went to stand up. 'Would you like a cup of tea or coffee?'

'You stay there, let me do it,' she said. 'Tea, I take it?'

'Please,' Mary said, sitting back down.

Cathy squatted down by the boys. 'Hello, you two, do either of you want a drink?' she asked.

'Yes please,' they both said. One thing Mary had to say about Alison was that she instilled manners in the boys.

'Two apple juices coming up,' Cathy said, going over to the fridge and taking out the carton of the boys' favourite drink, then flicking on the kettle before taking two beakers and two mugs out of the cupboard. She was very efficient and always did tasks smoothly, as if she was used to looking after people, Mary noticed.

'You look troubled. Is everything all right?' Cathy asked as she put the kettle on then poured juice into both beakers and handed them to the boys.

'I'm a bit tired. I didn't sleep well.' Mary mustered up a smile. 'You know what it's like sleeping in a strange bed.' She wished she could confide in Cathy about Alison's affair but it would be disloyal, and the fewer people who knew about it the better.

'Why don't you go and sit yourself down in the living room and rest? I'll bring your cup of tea in. I can supervise these two until one of their parents comes down.'

'Thank you.' Mary went into the lounge and sank down in the armchair. She really did feel weary.

She must have dozed off because when she opened her eyes again it sounded like the whole family was in the kitchen. She got up and went in to find them all sitting down at the table, chatting away. Alison studiously avoided Mary's gaze as she concentrated on talking to the boys.

'Right, who wants to come for a walk over the moors?' Damien asked enthusiastically when breakfast was finished and everything cleared away.

Oliver and Nicholas were eager but the older children were more reluctant. 'How long a walk?' Connor asked dubiously.

'A couple of hours there and back. Dartmoor is a really interesting place you know. There's lots of wild animals. You might see the Dartmoor ponies. There's sheep, goats, Highland cows...'

In the end they all decided to go except for Jason, who said he had some business phone calls to make. Mary couldn't help but notice the look of fury Alison gave him. 'It's a weekend, Jason, and we're meant to be on holiday,' she told him. 'Surely work can wait?'

'Sorry, but if I want to keep my business afloat I need to get more customers, and these calls are to potential customers that can bring a lot of business our way. I'll come for a walk later, I promise.'

'Don't worry about it. I'll handle the boys by myself, as usual,' Alison said, storming out.

Kelly and Hannah exchanged looks, and followed her, no doubt to help with the boys.

'Are you coming, Mary?' Damien asked.

She shook her head. 'I'm rather tired. I'll have a rest and leave you young ones to wander the moors.' She was looking forward to a bit of peace and quiet for an hour, and hopefully the chance to talk to Jason alone.

She guessed they would be out for an hour or so, so she gave Jason half an hour then made them both a cup of coffee. She peered through the door of the conservatory where he was holed up making his phone calls and noticed that he looked really agitated as he spoke into his mobile. Oh dear, it looked like things weren't going well. Jason glanced over at her and held his hand up for a moment, indicating that she shouldn't come in. She waited until he'd finished the call then opened the conservatory door. 'I've brought you a coffee,' she said, handing him the mug. 'I can go back out if you have other calls to make. It looked like that one was a bit tricky.'

'Another sale lost and things are a bit tight at the moment.' He looked fraught she thought anxiously. 'Thanks for this.' He took the mug and sank back into his chair. 'We desperately need to drum up more business.'

She sat down opposite him. 'Are things really that bad?'

'We took a battering in the pandemic, Mum, and it's been a hard haul ever since.' He grimaced. 'You know, to listen to Alison you'd think I was out enjoying myself all the time instead of working to look after my family. And yes, I know that Alison works too but that's only a few hours here and there. It's my money that pays the mortgage.'

'She has the boys to look after too, Jason,' Mary reminded him. 'What about Hugh? Is he pulling his weight? Does he work as many hours as you do?'

'It's a bit of a bone of contention between us at the moment. I don't think Hugh is putting in enough hours and the business is suffering through it.' He looked down into his coffee for a moment, as if deep in thought. 'It's not really working out between us, to be honest.'

This was going to be easier than she'd expected. 'Then why don't you buy him out?' she suggested. 'I'll have the house money through in a few weeks; there should be seventy thousand coming your way. That will help, won't it?'

He shook his head. 'I'm grateful, Mum, I really am. But, well, we've got a few debts to pay as well and I desperately need a new car so while your money will help, it won't give me enough to buy Hugh out. It's just a shame...' He paused.

'What?'

'Well, originally the money was going to be between me and Joanne, which would have meant another thirty-five thousand for me. That would have been enough. Still, Cathy is here now...'

Mary frowned as she tried to assess whether this was a ploy to get her to not give any money to Cathy. Both Jason and Joanne had made it clear that they weren't happy about that decision.

'I'm sorry if me sharing the money with Cathy means you're going to get less than you expected, Jason, but she is my daughter too. It's the least I can do after not being in her life all these years.'

'Of course, I understand that, Mum. And it's your money, your decision,' Jason said. He put the mug down and got to his feet, looking defeated. 'Well, maybe I'll just have to sell the business and try to get a regular nine-to-five job where I can go in late enough to take the boys to school every morning and put them to bed at night. At least then I might be able to save my marriage. Alison has already told me she might as well be a single mother for the amount of time I'm at home.'

'Don't say that...'

He shook his head. 'It's the truth, Mum. I have to face it. My marriage is on the brink and so is my business.'

Mary watched worriedly as he walked away, shoulders slumped, head down. He looked depressed. Why hadn't she noticed it before?

She sat deep in thought, wondering what to do. She'd promised Cathy a third of the money now, and she didn't intend to go back on that promise. Cathy deserved it. She'd shown Mary nothing but forgiveness, love and kindness since they'd met. But she was worried about Jason's financial situation and wracked her brains trying to think of a way she could help. Paul had bought her some nice pieces of jewellery throughout their marriage; she could sell some of them – they might raise the cash that Jason needed. It would be a shame for him to lose his business after all the years of hard work. And that could be the final straw for Alison.

# 51

Mary was sitting out in the garden, enjoying the solitude, when she became aware of something jumping onto the chair beside her. Surprised, she glanced down and saw a black cat. It was curled up on the seat, looking very comfortable and at ease. She gathered it must belong to the owner of the cottage. It fixed its green eyes on her face and miaowed. 'Hello there, you look friendly. Have you come to keep me company?' she asked, reaching over to stroke its head and it purred happily. After a few more strokes the cat climbed onto her lap and went to sleep. *Well, I wonder what your name is*, she thought as she caressed the silky black fur, feeling the tension melt out of her. Maybe she'd get a cat when she moved as well as a dog, she thought. She could imagine sitting in front of the TV in the evenings, a dog lying at her feet and a cat curled up on her lap. Pets made a place feel more like home.

She was still sitting there, fussing the cat, when they all returned from their walk. The boys were muddy but red-cheeked and cheerful. Kelly and Hannah were chatting away happily. They looked like they'd all had a good time.

'Pussy cat!' Nicholas shouted and ran over to stroke the cat but before he reached it the cat jumped off Mary's lap and disappeared into the bushes. Nicholas looked really disappointed and Mary felt sorry for him.

'I'm sure the cat will be back. I think it lives here,' she told him.

'I hope not!' Joanne exclaimed. 'It's probably covered in fleas and might scratch or bite. You shouldn't have encouraged it, Mum. A girl at my school was blinded in the eye by a cat scratching her.'

Nicholas looked worried. 'I won't touch it, Auntie Jo,' he promised.

'I'm sure it won't hurt anyone. It's been lying on my lap all afternoon,' Mary told Joanne, annoyed. Her daughter really did overreact sometimes.

Joanne gave Mary an exasperated look then rubbed her hands together. 'It's chilly, isn't it? How about a mulled wine to warm us up?'

'Not for me thanks, it's a bit early for wine,' Alison said, shaking her head. 'I need to get these two cleaned up, they're filthy.'

'It's never too early for Jo to drink wine,' Damien remarked, catching Alison's comment as he and Connor walked into the garden.

'Sod you, we're on holiday,' Joanne said, heading for the back door. 'I'll be in the conservatory if anyone wants to join me.' They all piled into the house, apart from Damien, who thrust his hand through his hair and looked at Mary ruefully. 'Sorry, Mary. I just wish Joanne wouldn't drink so much.'

*And I wish you wouldn't be so critical all the time*, Mary thought, but she didn't want to make waves, especially when they were all cooped up together for the next couple of days. 'I guess she's just trying to unwind. We are on holiday and it's only one glass,' she replied.

He sighed wearily. 'It won't stop at one glass. That's the

problem.' He wiped a hand across his brow. 'Jo's an alcoholic, Mary.'

'Joanne?' Mary stared at him as her mind tried to process this information. How could cool, calm, collected Joanne, who kept the house spotlessly clean, as well as working and looking after the children, be an alcoholic? It was ridiculous! 'Goodness, Damien. What are you saying? I know Joanne enjoys the occasional glass of wine – who doesn't – and maybe it is a bit early in the day, but we've all come here to relax and she's just making the most of the weekend away.'

'Occasional?' He raised an eyebrow and Mary noticed for the first time how pale and strained he looked. 'She can't go a day without a drink. Okay, yes, she's a functioning alcoholic but she's an alcoholic nonetheless. I know she's got her hands full with working and running the home. I help out as much as I can but my job is very demanding. I work long hours. I can't babysit my wife and earn money.'

Was he serious?

Damien sank down into the chair next to Mary. 'I'm sorry, I shouldn't be burdening you with this but I really don't know what to do.' He rested his elbows on the black-and-white mosaic table and sank his head into his hands.

Mary struggled with her emotions. She didn't want to be disloyal to Joanne, remembering how she had stuck by Damien when he had gambled so much they had almost lost the house. Paul had always felt that Damien wasn't good enough for his precious daughter, and Mary had to admit that she didn't particularly like him either. He was pompous and condescending, but he did really look distraught. She bit back the retort that if Joanne was drinking too much he had probably driven her to it and instead said softly, 'If you want to talk about it, I'm willing to listen and promise that it won't go any further.'

She listened silently as Damien poured it all out. How Joanne opened a couple of bottles of wine as soon as she got home from work and didn't go to bed until she'd finished it. 'It started with a glass with every evening meal, she said she needed to relax...'

'It is difficult working and bringing up children,' Mary said gently. 'And, as you said yourself, you work such long hours. I expect she just wants to wind down in the evenings.'

'If I want to get a promotion I have to put in the hours, Mary. I'm sorry, I know that Joanne's your daughter but she's an adult, she should be able to cope with a few evenings alone. And we have a cleaner to help her with the housework. It's not too much to expect her to remain sober while she's looking after our children, is it?'

'Surely she doesn't actually get drunk, Damien?' Joanne was always the picture of poise and sophistication. Mary couldn't imagine her teetering about, slurring her words. She couldn't be an alcoholic, it was absurd. Damien must mean that Joanne had a drink too many now and again.

'Mary, I've come home twice in the last fortnight to find Joanne sprawled out on the sofa, an empty bottle of wine on the table, too drunk to wake up and go up to bed. I've had to leave her there all night. Then I've got up the next morning to find her showered and dressed and about to drive to work, even though I was sure she was still over the limit. Thank goodness the kids go on the school bus. I've begged her not to drive but she always insists that she's only had a couple and I'm exaggerating.'

Mary's blood ran cold at this, at the danger her precious daughter was putting herself in. And what if something came up and she had to take Kelly or Connor to school? She could crash and kill them all. She closed her eyes tight, blocking out the terrible image. Joanne adored the children. Surely she wouldn't risk anything happening to them. She opened her eyes again and focused on Damien, whose face was etched with despair. He was either a very good actor or he was genuine.

'I'm sorry, Mary. I didn't want to tell you this, especially on your birthday weekend but I really am at my wits' end. I don't know what to do.'

'Can't you persuade Joanne to get help? There are people she can talk to, who will give her support.'

'She won't admit that she has a problem. She says she has a drink or two to unwind and that I'm exaggerating things.' He rubbed his eyes with the back of his hand, like Paul used to do when he was stressed. 'I'm getting scared to go to work and leave her, Mary.'

Was it really that bad? Mary's mind whirred, seeking a solution. 'Perhaps if you could cut down your work in the evenings? Then Joanne wouldn't be so lonely and wouldn't reach for the wine.'

'How can I do that? Our outgoings exceed our incomings at the moment. Jo always lives above our means. Why do you think I started gambling all those years ago? And why do you think she stayed with me? She knew that she drove me to it.'

Mary was stunned. She knew that money was a bit tight, it always was when you had a family to look after, but she hadn't realised their situation was that bad.

'Don't forget neither of us were on full wage in the pandemic, we were both lucky to keep our jobs. We've been trying to make up the shortfall ever since,' Damien pointed out. 'We've got debts, Mary. Joanne will be mad that I've told you but I need you to understand why I have to put in so many hours.' He looked beseechingly at her. 'Please don't let Joanne know that I've told you. She's very proud.'

'Of course I won't. Look, my house sale will be through soon and I'm sharing the surplus money between you all. Won't that pay off your debts?' she asked. 'Then you can cut down the hours you work. It will be through in a month or so.'

Damien shook his head. 'It's really kind of you, Mary, and it will help, but it won't be enough.' He paused. 'Especially now it's being split three ways.'

So Damien and Joanne resented her sharing the money with Cathy too. 'I'm sorry but I have to do this, Damien. Cathy is also my daughter and I feel so guilty about giving her away and not trying to find her earlier. I want to make it up to her for not being part of her life.'

'That's perfectly understandable.' He sighed and gave her a rueful smile. 'Look, this isn't your problem and I shouldn't have said anything to you. I'm sorry. I don't want to ruin your birthday weekend. I'm sure this is a phase Joanne's going through and we'll both sort it. Don't worry.' He patted her arm. 'I'll grab Jason and we'll both rustle up some lunch, you women have a break.'

Mary's mind was a whirl as she watched him head over to the back door. She didn't want to believe that Joanne was an alcoholic but Damien sounded so convincing. He would never make up something like that, surely. She could see that he felt bad confiding in her.

This weekend wasn't working out as she'd thought. However, now they were all together under the same roof, perhaps she could talk to Joanne and Jason – separately of course – and prevent things getting worse. The last thing she wanted was for either of them to divorce.

# 52

Mary made herself a cup of coffee and took it back out into the garden, pondering it all over. She had been really looking forward to everyone being together to celebrate her sixtieth birthday but now she was wishing she hadn't suggested it. There was so much tension in the air, although fortunately the grandchildren seemed unaware of it. It was clear both Jason and Joanne's partners were unhappy. As she sipped her drink, she thought of how different this birthday would have been if Paul was alive. Maybe he would have booked a cruise for them both, he would certainly have spoilt her. She missed him terribly. She was lucky, though, she reminded herself, for the first time ever she got to celebrate a birthday with her firstborn, the child she had given away and never thought she would see again. And she had a new granddaughter too. Thank goodness the grandchildren were getting on, even if the adults weren't.

'I hope I'm not interrupting.' Cathy pulled out one of the chairs and sat down. 'Have you come out here to escape? It's like a battlefield in there, isn't it?'

'So you noticed it too?' Mary replied wearily.

'It would be hard to miss it. Damien and Joanne are having

a bit of a ding-dong now. He doesn't like her drinking. Seems to think that she's an alcoholic.'

'I know, he's been talking about it to me. I thought that Joanne was just relaxing because she's on holiday but Damien reckons she's always drinking.' Mary rubbed her temple, where she could feel a headache building. 'It seems that both my children have problems.' She paused as she saw the look on Cathy's face and realised that she had said 'both my children' instead of 'two of my children' and wished she could take the words back. Cathy was now looking concerned, though.

'I'm sorry to hear that,' she said sympathetically. 'But try not to worry, they both will sort it out.'

Mary shook her head. 'I'm not so sure. Jason desperately needs a cash injection into his business. I'm glad I made the decision to sell my house and scale down, although his share of the money isn't enough to completely solve his financial problems.'

Cathy narrowed her eyes. 'Did Jason tell you that? Is he trying to get you to give him more money?'

'No, of course not. It's just that a financial injection would mean he could buy out his business partner. They aren't getting on.'

'Won't that mean he has to work even more hours, though?' Cathy asked.

Mary hadn't thought of that. 'He could always get a new business partner, or hire a manager,' she replied.

Cathy leaned across the table. 'It's very kind of you to help Jason and Joanne, but they aren't your responsibility now, they're adults. I hope that isn't why you've downsized.' She sat back suddenly, a look of dismay on her face. 'Oh goodness, I hope you don't think I encouraged you to sell because I wanted a share of your money.' Her hand flew to her mouth. 'You said the house was too big for you so I wanted to help you find something smaller and I did think it might be better for you to move after... everything that had happened but maybe I shouldn't have done that. Maybe it's not what you want. I'm so sorry.' She looked horrified.

'There is nothing to apologise for, I did want to move.' The incidents Cathy had alluded to – Mary's car tyre being punctured, the plants trampled on, the broken window, the fire in the dustbin – had all made Mary feel unsafe in her own home. 'I'm very grateful for your help. It's a bonus that moving means I can help my children too, all three of them.' She emphasised the word 'three' and squeezed Cathy's hand. 'Take no notice of my fretting.'

'If you're sure?'

Mary nodded. 'I'm positive.'

Cathy looked relieved. 'Well, please don't think that you have to give me any of the money. Me and Hannah are fine. Share it between Joanne and Jason just like you were going to do before I came along.' She twisted her hands together. 'No wonder they resent me. They think I've stolen part of their inheritance.'

' I'm sure they don't think anything of the sort.' Mary replied, even though she knew that was exactly how they did feel. She was ashamed to admit that they were so selfish, and didn't want Cathy to feel bad. She patted Cathy's hand. 'You're my daughter, part of the family, and you'll all be treated equally. Now let's go and see what everyone wants for lunch.'

Cathy slipped her arm through Mary's as they walked in together. It was a comforting gesture and Mary couldn't help thinking how Cathy was being more supportive of her than Joanne and Jason. They were both so wrapped up in their own problems that neither of them had stopped to consider how it affected Mary, how much finding Cathy had meant to her, how scared she had been and what a big upheaval it was for her to move house after all these years. Cathy and Hannah had become such a comfort to her. She wondered if that was part of the reason Jason and Joanne resented Cathy, because they could see how close she and Mary had become, but surely they should be pleased that she had someone else to turn to for support as they were both so busy? She and Paul had spoilt their children, she acknowledged. They had given them everything they could, a lovely home, a good education, the deposit for their first homes, whereas Cathy hadn't even had her mother's presence. Someone else had nursed her, comforted her, fed and clothed her. How could anyone begrudge her this time with her mother now?

'I've got a nice recipe for cheese tortellini and sausage bake on my phone that I was going to make for lunch,' Mary said as they walked into the kitchen. She went over to the shelf where she had put her phone. It wasn't there.

'I could have sworn I put it here,' she said. 'I must have left it in the living room. I'll go and get it.'

'I'll get the pasta out ready,' Cathy told her. 'We can make it together.'

Cathy was always so helpful, Mary thought as she went to find her phone. She was going to get a share of her money whether the others liked it or not.

# 53

## *Alison*

'Have you lost something, Mary?' Alison asked as Mary went over to the sofa and lifted up one of the cushions to look underneath it.

'Yes, my phone – I want to check a recipe on it. Has anyone seen it?' she asked. 'I put it on the shelf in the kitchen this morning but it's not there now.'

'I'll phone you,' Alison offered. She dialled the number. 'It's going straight to answerphone,' she said. 'Either you've got it switched off or your battery is dead.'

'I've got it charged up, I know I have.' Mary looked puzzled. 'I'll go and check the kitchen again.'

'I'll search the rooms down here, you check your bedroom. Maybe you've left it there,' Alison told her.

'Perhaps. I'm sure I brought it down with me, though,' Mary said, heading upstairs.

'Anyone seen Mary's phone?' Alison asked, going into the kitchen.

'She's not lost it again!' Jason sighed. 'She had us turning the living room upside down for it last week and she'd left it in the car.'

'Mary does seem to be getting more and more forgetful,' Damien said with a concerned frown. 'It's rather worrying.'

'Lots of people lose their phone. Not everyone keeps theirs glued to them like you do,' Joanne retorted. Jason was the same, Alison thought, he never let his phone out of his sight.

'It's not just her phone, is it, though?' Damien pointed out. 'Mary's always misplacing things. She couldn't find her house keys the other week. They turned up in the fridge.'

They were right, Mary really was getting forgetful, Alison thought. 'It was probably Mary who forgot to close Bailey's cage, you know. It was too high up for the boys to open but she insisted it was them,' she said.

Joanne frowned. 'You could be right, I thought that was strange. I hope she isn't getting dementia.'

'Surely she's a bit young for that,' Alison said. 'I'll go and see if she's found her phone yet.'

Mary's bedroom door was open. Alison peered around it to see Mary on her knees looking under the bed. 'It's not here. I know I had it this morning. I can't understand where it's gone.'

'Don't stress yourself, Mary. It's not good for you. The phone will turn up. You can use mine to check the recipe, if you want to,' Alison told her.

Mary's bottom lip wobbled. 'It's not just that, Paul left me a voicemail and I listen to it every morning and night, have done every day since he died.'

'Oh Mary!' Alison gave her a hug. 'We'll find it, I promise. It has to be here somewhere.'

'I hope so. It's so comforting to hear his voice. I won't be able to sleep tonight if I can't find my phone.' Tears sprang to Mary's eyes. 'I'm sure I took it downstairs with me this morning and left it on the shelf in the kitchen.'

'Let's retrace all your steps,' Alison told her. 'We've checked upstairs and downstairs and it's not there. Maybe we should take a look in the garden.'

'I didn't take it out in the garden,' Mary protested.

'Are you sure? Wouldn't you have taken it outside with you when we all went for a walk, in case we called?'

Mary looked a little confused. 'Why would I? Jason was here too so you could have contacted him.'

'Panic over!' Cathy shouted. She came into the bedroom, holding up Mary's phone. 'It was outside under the table. It must have fallen off. You're lucky that it didn't rain and get wet.'

Mary's face lit up as Cathy handed her the phone. 'I must have taken it outside after all.' She shook her head. 'I could have sworn I left it in the kitchen.'

'Well, we've found it now, so no worries,' Alison said. 'I'll go and let the others know.'

'Trust miss goody-two-shoes to find Mum's phone,' Joanne muttered when Alison gave them the news. 'She's all over Mum like a rash and Mum is besotted with her.'

'Cathy's okay. I guess it's only natural that your mum wants to make it up to her,' Alison said.

'Make it up to her? She's pulling out all the stops,' Damien retorted. 'I wouldn't be surprised if she didn't change her will to make Cathy the main beneficiary.'

'What made you say that? Has she said something to you about it?' Joanne asked him.

'Not in as many words, but she's told me she feels guilty about giving Cathy away and not trying to find her earlier, and wants to make it up to her. She said we're all comfortably off with good jobs, while Cathy rents and isn't financially secure. She blames herself for that.'

Joanne scowled. 'That would be so unfair. I bet Cathy put that idea in her head, hinting about how much she's struggled, how hard it was to grow up not knowing her real parents. She lied about not having any children, lied about having a job. It was obvious that she would say anything to get Mum's sympathy – and money.'

'Strange that she was the one to find the phone too,' Damien said.

'You know, the problems with Mum's memory have got worse since Cathy came along,' Jason said thoughtfully. 'You don't think she's behind some of the stuff, do you? That she's trying to confuse Mum so that she would rely on her, and she could manipulate her?'

Alison considered this. Joanne had suggested that Cathy might be responsible for some of the things happening at the house, and now Jason thought she was trying to make Mary look like she was losing her mind. Could they be right?

# 54

## *Mary*

After lunch Mary suggested that they all go for a drive to a local village to have a look around. She could see that the children were already bored, and wanted to keep the adults busy too so that no one had a chance to bicker. Kelly and Hannah wanted to travel in the same car so went with Cathy, and Joanne insisted Mary went with them. 'You don't want to listen to the girls chatter all the way, Mum. You can sit back and relax,' she said.

'I need a wee,' Nicholas suddenly announced as they were all about to get in the cars.

'Oh Nicholas, you could have told us before!' Alison groaned in exasperation.

'It's okay, I'll take him. I could do with going myself,' Mary offered. 'We'll be quick, we'll use the downstairs toilet.'

Mary opened the front door and Nicholas ran to the toilet. 'Can I go back out to the car, Nanny?' he asked when he'd finished.

'Okay,' Mary agreed. Quickly using the toilet herself, she

washed her hands and dashed out of the front door, firmly pulling it shut behind her, listening for the click as it tended to stick, then hurried over to the car. Nicholas was already strapped in his seat and Jason was about to drive off. She could imagine Damien drumming his fingers on the steering wheel as he waited for her.

'Sorry. Ready now,' she said as she got into the back of the car.

'Great. Let's get going before anyone else needs the loo.' Joanne sounded curt but she glanced over her shoulder and smiled at Mary. *Relax, it's going to be a pleasant afternoon,* Mary told herself.

---

The village was gorgeous, really quaint like a picture postcard. They took lots of photos, selfies for Kelly and Hannah so they could put them on Instagram. Then Alison spotted a play-ground. 'I'm going to stop here so the boys can let off steam, for a few minutes,' she said. 'If you want to carry on looking around we can meet you in the tea room later.'

'I quite fancy looking at the Doll Museum,' Cathy said. 'Anyone else?'

'Not for me but I'm going to check out the pottery,' Joanne said. 'What about you, Mum?'

Mary opted to stay with Alison and Jason. 'I can have a rest on the bench while the boys play,' she said. Kelly and Hannah went off together, with strict instructions to be at the tea room for four.

They boys played happily for half an hour or so. Jason was checking his phone non-stop, Mary noticed, and Alison was clearly irritated with him but said nothing, concentrating on playing with the boys. Mary guessed that she felt awkward now that Mary knew about her affair. She hoped it didn't strain her and Alison's relationship, she was fond of her daughter-in-law but she couldn't turn a blind eye to her actions. She had to be firm and insist that Alison stopped seeing Hugh for everyone's sake. She caught Alison glancing at her and she gave her a smile, which was hesitantly reciprocated. Hopefully they would be able to put this behind them.

Joanne and Damien were already in the tea room when they arrived, having secured a large table by the window. Joanne waved to them as they walked in. 'Kelly and Hannah are on the way; they've been buying souvenirs, apparently.'

Damien rolled his eyes. 'More clutter!'

'Don't be such a grump,' Joanne snapped.

Mary pulled out a chair before Damien could retaliate. 'Have you ordered yet?'

'No, we've only just arrived and thought we'd wait for you all,' Joanne said. 'We're going for tea and scones.'

'That sounds good,' Mary said.

Alison and Jason agreed, as did Cathy and the girls when they all arrived a few minutes later. Everyone seemed in good spirits and they all sat chatting together amicably, to Mary's delight. She loved it when her family got on. Kelly and Hannah proudly showed the souvenirs they had bought, and the photos they'd put on Instagram. They were a bit of a rowdy bunch, though, and Mary saw a couple of people glance their way, thankfully with a smile on their lips.

Scones and drinks finished, and a quick trip to the loo, then they all piled back in the cars. 'Want to jump in with us this time, Mum?' Cathy asked. 'The girls can show you the pictures they've taken.'

Mary gratefully accepted. There seemed to be even more underlying tension between Damien and Joanne and she didn't want to be caught up in the middle of it. Cathy turned on the radio and they all sang along to the songs. It was a pleasant journey.

Damien reached the cottage first and strolled over to the front door, keys out ready to open it. Jason and Cathy both pulled up alongside each other and everyone piled out of the two cars and headed for the house.

'What's the matter with Damien?' Jason asked.

Mary looked over and saw that the front door was open and Damien had stopped dead and was staring at something on the ground.

'What's up?' Jason called, striding over.

Damien turned around. 'Mary mustn't have closed the door properly and that perishing cat she was fussing has left us a present,' he said. 'Don't let the kids in yet. I'll go and get a shovel to clear it up.'

'I did close it,' Mary protested. She distinctly remembered hearing the door click.

Alison told the boys to wait by her but everyone else went over to see what was going on. Kelly and Hannah screamed as they reached the half open door, their hands flying to their mouths as they backed away.

'What is it?' Joanne asked, hurrying over. 'Oh, gross!' she exclaimed with a shudder.

Mary was right behind her. She recoiled in horror when she saw the huge dead black rat lying motionless on the mat. It was massive but thankfully wasn't half-eaten as cats tended to do. She guessed they should be grateful that the cat had left it here where they could find it easily rather than somewhere in the house.

'Oh Mum, you should have checked that you closed the door!' Joanne scolded her.

'I did!' Mary protested. She turned to Jason. 'I heard it click shut...' Then she stopped as she saw that he was staring at the rat in sheer horror. She hadn't realised that he was still terrified of rats. He had hated them as a child but she thought he might have outgrown his fear by now.

'Then how come it's open?' Damien demanded. 'Unless someone's broken in!' A worried look crossed his face. 'I'd better go and check. You all wait here!'

'I'll come with you,' Jason said. He still looked pale but had managed to pull himself together now.

Everyone else stepped back as the two men went inside to search the house.

# 55

They returned a few minutes later. 'No sign that anyone's been inside,' Damien said. 'You must have left the door open, Mary.'

Mary wanted to deny it again but she saw the look Damien and Joanne exchanged and wondered if she had. Was she getting confused?

'Right, let me get rid of this creature and then we can all go in.' Damien headed over to his car.

'That's so gross! Why has the cat left it there?' Hannah wrinkled her nose. She and Kelly were keeping a safe distance. Alison and the boys were standing by the car.

'Cats kill rats and other creatures and often bring them to their owners as a present. I guess this must be for you, Mum, as you were stroking the cat earlier,' Joanne said.

Mary felt guilty for making a fuss of the cat now. Who would have thought it would have latched onto her that quickly? Or maybe it brought presents for all the holidaymakers who came to the cottage whether they fussed it or not.

'Stand back, everyone.' Damien had returned with the spade he always kept in the back of his car and an empty box. He scooped the rat up into the box and went off to dispose of it.

They all breathed collective sighs of relief and went into the cottage.

Thankfully the rat was soon forgotten, although Mary vowed not to make so much fuss of the cat if they saw it again. The children disappeared upstairs, then Mary put the kettle on and Joanne opened a bottle of wine and they all retreated into the living room to relax. After an hour or so Joanne went into the kitchen to warm up the curry she'd brought with her yesterday and when they'd eaten Alison suggested a game of charades. Nicholas and Oliver went to bed, tired out from the excitement of the day, but Kelly, Hannah and Connor all joined in enthusiastically.

'It's so lovely to have a family,' Hannah said. 'I'm really pleased that Mum and Nanny found each other.'

'Me too.' Kelly smiled at her. 'I bet it's strange to be part of a big, noisy family when you've been an only child all your life, though.'

'It is a bit, but I like it,' Hannah said with a grin.

'What a shame that Nan couldn't keep your mum; it must have been so lonely growing up in care,' Kelly said. 'I'd hate that.'

Mary paused at this remark and turned to look at the girls. They were huddled together talking and hadn't noticed her and she couldn't make out Hannah's mumbled reply. What made Kelly said that about Cathy growing up in care? She had been adopted. Maybe Kelly had just assumed then Hannah had put her right. She shrugged and carried on up to bed.

All in all it had been a good day, Mary thought as she let herself into her room. It had been a good idea to bring everyone to the cottage after all. Yes, they'd got off to a wobbly start but now everyone was relaxing and getting on. Even Damien and Joanne seemed more friendly with each other this evening. She was looking forward to her birthday tomorrow. They had booked Sunday lunch at a pub not too far so that no one had to cook. They could all enjoy a leisurely meal then they could sit and relax and enjoy their final evening together.

Mary sat down on her bed and picked up Paul's photo. 'I think the family are coming together, Paul. There's been a lot of laughter this evening.' She ran her finger over his lips. How she wished she could feel them on hers just one more time. 'I'm worried, though. I seem to be getting really forgetful. I lost my phone this afternoon. And then I was sure I closed the front door when we went out but we came back to find it open and a dead rat on the mat.' Paul's eyes stared warmly back at her as if he was telling her to stop fretting, everything would be okay.

*I've just been stressed, what with Paul dying, and finding Cathy, and now moving house. I've a lot on my mind. No wonder I'm forgetting things*, she told herself. She went into the ensuite to freshen up and brush her teeth, then changed into her pyjamas and pulled back the duvet. She was so tired she was sure her eyes would close as soon as her head touched the pillow.

She reached for her phone, anxious to hear Paul's comforting voice telling her that he loved her. She laid her head down on the pillow and selected the answerphone.

*'You have no answerphone messages.'*

*What?* She sat up and stared at the phone. There must be some mistake. She'd listened to the message this morning. It was there. It must be a blip. She tried again. Same message.

How had this happened? Had she accidentally deleted it?

Tears filled her eyes. How could she have been so stupid as to accidentally delete Paul's precious last message to her? Now she would never be able to hear his voice again. She really was losing her mind. She was going to end up like her poor mother. Tears sprang to her eyes as she thought of what lay ahead, getting more and more confused, losing precious memories, becoming a shell of herself. She couldn't bear it. She would prefer to die than suffer that.

That's what her mother had thought, she realised. That was why she had killed herself. She had always wondered what had driven her to it.

# 56

*Alison*

'I'm really worried about Mary,' Damien said later to Joanne, Alison and Jason. Alison suspected that the others had been waiting for Mary, Cathy and the children to go to bed because they wanted to discuss Mary. Jason had already mentioned his worries to her earlier. 'She seems to be getting very forgetful. It's just one thing after another.' Damien counted out on his fingers, 'First, it's money going missing, then the bird cage being left open, then her phone. And today she didn't close the door properly and we ended up with a disgusting dead rat on the mat. Thank goodness it wasn't anything worse. We could have been burgled. I know that Mary's been through a lot but she seems to be getting really confused and forgetful. I'm not sure it's safe for her to continue living on her own.'

Alison considered this. If everyone thought that Mary was getting confused and forgetful, she could use that to her advantage if Mary ever spilled the beans about her and Hugh's affair. Mary had no proof and both Alison and Hugh would deny it.

She'd say her mother-in-law was imagining the conversation. Alison felt a weight lift from her. She had been dreading not seeing Hugh again, she loved him so much and he loved her. He was the only good thing in her life right now. Apart from the boys, of course, who she adored but were such hard work. She couldn't bear to think of life without Hugh.

'She has been behaving a little strangely. And she's always losing things,' she added.

'I think...' Damien paused, a pained expression on his face as if he was about to say something he really didn't want to. 'Well, I think we need to keep an eye on Mary. She could be a danger to herself. I'm not even sure if she should drive. What if she loses concentration and crashes?'

'I agree. Mum's really vulnerable at the moment and someone could take advantage of her,' Jason said. 'Don't you all think that it's strange how Mum has been worse since Cathy arrived on the scene? I don't trust her. She's got far too much influence on Mum. We've been talking to Mum for ages about downsizing but she wouldn't even think of it, then Cathy comes along and suddenly all sorts of things are happening at the house that make her too scared to live there so she agrees to sell up and is about to change her will.'

'You mean you think that Cathy is behind that stuff? The car tyre punctured, plants trampled on, the brick through the window?' Joanne asked. 'And the fire? Mum could have been killed in that if she'd been at home.'

'Surely not?' Alison asked, horrified at the thought.

Jason shrugged. 'I don't know. But Cathy definitely has too much influence on Mum, and if she's got wind that Mum is getting dementia, she could be exploiting that.'

'You're right.' Damien stood up. 'I hate to say this but as a family I think we need to persuade Mary to see a doctor. And one of us should go with her to make sure she tells them everything. Also, we need to take control of your mother's finances before she gives all her money away.' He looked around at them all. 'I know it isn't something that we want to do but she needs our protection.'

The others all nodded their agreement.

# 57

## EARLIER TODAY

### *Mary*

Mary awoke with a start, her sleepy eyes trying to focus in the dark room. She glanced at the digital display on the clock: three o'clock. It sounded as if a storm was brewing outside. The window panes rattled as the rain hammered against them, the wind battered through the branches of the trees, whistling down the chimney, shaking the old cottage to its foundations. She reached out to switch on the bedside lamp and a comforting glow lit up the room. She got out of bed and went over to the window, peering outside at the bleak moor that had now descended into darkness. Suddenly a sense of foreboding shuddered through her, and she quickly pulled the thick velvet drapes shut then padded across the room to the ensuite, the sound of the rain making her want to go to the loo.

As she reached the bathroom door, a foul smell filled her nostrils and her bare foot touched something cold and furry. She stepped back in horror and glanced down, screaming in terror as her eyes rested on a huge dead black rat lying on the floor by her bed. It was almost identical to the black rat that they'd found in the hallway when they had returned home yesterday and smelt so bad she was sure it had been dead for some time. Even so, her whole body was shaking and in flight mode, worried that the creature was still alive and would suddenly lunge for her. She could almost feel its claws in her, its teeth biting into her neck. *It's dead. Dead*, she repeated in her mind, her petrified eyes fixed on the hideous creature, her hand over her mouth to stifle another scream as she backed away from it. How had it got here? Had the cat left it for her? Had it been here ever since they returned from their walk?

It couldn't have been here last night, she'd used the bathroom when she came to bed, she remembered. Could she have forgotten to close her bedroom door and the cat had somehow got into her room in the night and left it there? Another present for her?

She looked over at the bedroom door. It was closed.

Her heart raced as she realised what that meant. Someone had sneaked into her room in the middle of the night and put the dead rat there for her to find. Who would do such a terrible thing? And why?

She felt a sudden sharp pain in her chest, as if an invisible band was tightening across it.

*Oh God, I'm having an angina attack.*

She had to get her GTN spray. She walked slowly backwards to the chair where she had left her handbag the previous night, scared to take her eyes off the creature in case it somehow leapt back to life. She reached out and grabbed the straps, pulling the handbag to her and frantically opening it then shaking out the contents onto the bed behind her. Her purse, comb, lipstick, tissues, notebook all poured out. There was no GTN spray.

It had to be there. She always kept it there. Panic-stricken, she double checked the contents and shook her empty bag again. The spray had gone.

The pain was intensifying. She clutched her chest and took deep, steadying breaths.

*Calm down. Think!*

The spare spray! She always carried two with her and had put the other one in the drawer by the bedside cabinet when she arrived on Friday evening. Slowly, almost bent double with pain, her breath coming out in painful gasps, she inched over to the cabinet and pulled out the drawer, desperately feeling inside with her right hand for the small spray which she had put within easy reach right at the front. It had gone too.

Her chest was so tight it was like a clamp was closing in around it. She could hardly breathe. Her legs buckled underneath her and she collapsed onto the bed, gasping as she realised that someone had taken her sprays. Someone had sneaked into her room in the night and put the rat there for her to find, hoping it would give her a heart attack, then they had taken her GTN sprays to make sure that the heart attack killed her.

Someone wanted her dead.

# 58

'Nan! Nan! Wake up!'

The sound of Kelly's voice gave Mary the strength to flicker her eyes open. Kelly and Hannah were both kneeling down beside her, their faces white with fear.

'Nan! What's happened?' Kelly asked anxiously.

'My heart,' Mary managed to croak, her hand still clutching her chest; the pain was agony. 'Get help. Please.'

'Quick! Go and fetch someone. I'll look for Nan's spray,' Kelly shouted to Hannah. Hannah jumped to her feet and dashed out of the room.

'It's gone,' Mary gasped as Kelly looked wildly at contents of the handbag scattered all over the bed, then at the open drawer. She closed her eyes as another pain squeezed her chest. she heard Kelly's voice as if it was in the distance. 'Nan. I've found it. Here it is.'

She wanted to take it from her but she hadn't got the strength. It was too late. She was going to die. *To join Paul*, she thought fleetingly as her eyes closed.

'Open your mouth,' Kelly urged. 'I'll do it for you.'

*Not yet. Not like this.* Paul's voice came into her head.

She wasn't going to die. Someone had tried to kill her but she wasn't going to let them win. Dragging up every ounce of strength her weak body possessed, Mary opened her mouth and lifted her tongue. She heard the hiss of the spray and felt the cold liquid shoot under her tongue. *Thank you, Kelly.* She closed her mouth, concentrating on breathing through her nose instead as the spray started to take effect.

'Mum! Oh God, Mum!' She could hear Joanne's voice but was too weak to open her eyes. 'Take it easy. Keep breathing through your nose,' she urged. Then she heard Joanne's scream. 'Oh My God! There's another rat! Go and get your dad, Kelly.'

Mary took a few more breaths through her nose. The pain was easing so she slowly opened her eyes. Her whole family were now in her bedroom, crowded around her. 'The rat?' she croaked.

'Don't worry, it was dead. Damien's got rid of it,' Joanne told her. 'Just lie there for a while and rest, Mum. You've had a bad angina attack. Thank goodness Kelly and Hannah heard you scream.'

Thank goodness indeed, and that Kelly had found the GTN spray. She could have died. Mary could feel the familiar headache already forming and knew that soon she would be feeling nauseous too. But at least she was still alive.

'What's going on in here? It looks like you've been burgled,' Alison asked.

'Nan was looking for her spray. I found it under her bed, it must have rolled there when she emptied out her handbag,' Kelly explained.

'Oh Mum, you must be more careful. I thought you kept a spare one too?' Jason looked really worried.

'Couldn't find it,' Mary explained weakly. She just wanted to lie down and rest in peace until this headache had gone.

'Shouldn't we call an ambulance?' Hannah asked.

'No, she'll be fine now she's had the spray. She just needs to rest but I don't think she should be left on her own. I'll stay with her,' Cathy offered.

Mary was grateful for that. She didn't want to stay in the room by herself. She didn't feel safe. Someone wanted her dead, and they might come back.

Cathy got into the spare bed and, exhausted, Mary closed her eyes and drifted off to sleep.

Mary woke a few hours later to see Cathy still asleep in the other bed. She lay there for a moment, her mind going back over all the things that had happened since Paul had died and how she had got more and more forgetful. Perhaps it was the grief and the stress but she had to face it, her mind clearly wasn't what it was. She didn't even know how much money she had lost – hundreds. And her precious Pandora bracelet. It was probably her fault her beloved Bailey had gone too. She mustn't have closed the cage properly after she'd fed him that morning, but she'd blamed her grandsons. And things had got worse since they'd been at the holiday cottage. Losing her phone, deleting Paul's message, leaving the front door open – although she could swear she'd heard it click shut. She shuddered as she thought of the two dead rats. The cat might have dumped the one on the doorstep but it couldn't have got in her room when the door was closed. Damien had said the cat must have left the rat earlier and she hadn't noticed it, but how could she miss it right by the ensuite door like that?

And now, losing her GTN spray. She could have died. Was it all really an accident? It had to be. That alternative was that someone had brought the dead rat into her room and taken her sprays, hoping she would have a heart attack and die, like she'd thought last night when she was almost out of her mind with fear. If that was true it could only be one of her family, and none of them would do that. Yes, they argued, families did, and

Jason and Joanne weren't happy that she was sharing the money with Cathy but neither of them would harm her. They loved her and had always been supportive of her.

Cathy murmured and as Mary looked over at her, it suddenly struck her that everything had got worse since Cathy had come into her life. Cathy had lied to her from the beginning, about her job, and Hannah. She hadn't trusted Mary with the truth and had plenty of reason to resent her – after all Mary had abandoned her right after her birth when she was so fragile and defenceless. But Cathy had always been kind and helpful, and she wouldn't gain from her death, would she? Mary hadn't changed her will yet so Cathy wouldn't get a penny if she died.

Unless it wasn't the money she was after, but revenge. Mary recalled their first meeting, how hostile and bitter Cathy had been. How she had said that she was Mary's 'dark and dirty secret'. Had she been playing her all this time? Pretending she had forgiven her when she really resented her for abandoning her but keeping Joanne and Jason? For giving them two such a good life and not going back for her firstborn when her life was more settled and she could have cared for her. Resented her so much that she was determined to make her pay?

So much had happened since Cathy came into her life. Was she behind it all?

# 59

Cathy must have sensed Mary staring at her because she opened her eyes and smiled sleepily. 'Happy birthday, Mum,' she said softly. Then she added, 'That's the first time I've ever been able to say that to you.'

Her birthday! Goodness, with everything that had happened she'd forgotten. A lump formed in Mary's throat at the knowledge that Cathy had remembered. Cathy seemed to genuinely love her. Was she wrong about her?

'Our first birthday together,' Cathy continued. 'I'm so pleased we found each other again, finally.'

Mary sat up and rubbed her eyes. 'So am I,' she said.

'I've got you a present. I hope you like it. I didn't know what to get you, and well, it was Hannah's idea. We did it together.' Cathy reached down by the side of her bed – she must have brought the present in with her last night, Mary realised, as Cathy pulled a wrapped parcel onto the bed then leaned over and handed it to Mary. 'Happy birthday, Mum,' she said again.

'Thank you, darling.' Mary kissed her on the cheek then took the present. As she looked down at the carefully wrapped parcel with the envelope saying 'Mum' stuck on the top she felt very emotional, recalling all the birthdays they had both missed. Then she reminded herself of everything that had happened since Cathy came into her life, the things she feared Cathy was responsible for. *I can't let her know I suspect her*, she thought, *but somehow I've got to think of a way to set her up so that I know for certain if it's her.*

Mary carefully pulled the sticky tape off the envelope and opened it up. She swallowed the lump in her throat as she read the loving verse and message. Was it all an act or did Cathy mean those moving words?

'It's lovely. Thank you.' She gave Cathy a wobbly smile and then opened the parcel. It was a pretty white photo album with a rainbow on the front. She must have looked puzzled because Cathy quickly said, 'We chose a rainbow because it comes after the rain, like us all. We've all had the rain and now we have our rainbow – each other.'

Mary flipped open the first page, her eyes resting on the top photo – the one of Cathy as a newborn baby that she'd shared with her, followed by a photo of her as a toddler, then her first day at school. Then there were photos of Hannah as a baby, Hannah and Cathy together. Mary's eyes were swimming with tears by the time she got to the final one of the three of them together, taken that day she'd first met Hannah. She felt so mixed up; Cathy seemed so genuine.

*Look how she's lied to you. Remember the things that have happened.*

'I hope you like it. Me and Hannah have the same album. We thought you might like the memories...' Cathy's voice was halting, unsure.

'I love it,' Mary told her. 'It's a wonderful present. Thank you so much.'

They hugged tightly and Cathy whispered, 'I love you, Mum.'

'I love you too,' Mary said. She did too, so very much. It broke her heart to think that Cathy could be using her, had tried to kill her. Was she like her father? Robbie had said he loved her too. And look what he had done.

Cathy gently pulled away and looked at her, her brown eyes full of concern. 'How are you feeling now, Mum? You gave us all such a scare last night. Thank goodness Kelly found your GTN spray. Do make sure you keep it with you all the time, won't you? You never know when you might need it.'

'I will, don't worry. I certainly won't risk that happening again.' Mary got out of bed. 'Thank you again for your lovely present. I think we should get ready to go down and join the others now. They'll be waiting to give me presents too.'

'Of course.' A flicker of something crossed Cathy's face but it was gone before Mary could assess it. 'Are you okay in here by yourself while I go to my room to shower and get dressed?'

'I'll be fine,' Mary assured her. She wasn't going to be intimidated, she was stronger than that. She was going to find out if Cathy was causing trouble and if she was, she would send her packing.

'Happy birthday, Mum.' Joanne greeted Mary as she walked into the kitchen a little later. 'How are you feeling today?'

'I'm okay darling, I've just got a bit of a headache. Nothing to worry about,' Mary told her.

'I'm not surprised. Sit down and take it easy. We're all going to spoil you today.' Joanne took a card and present off the table. 'Here you are. It looks like I'm the first one to give you a present,' she said with a big smile.

'Actually I've already given Mum mine,' Cathy said, coming into the room, now showered and dressed.

Mary saw the flash of annoyance on Joanne's face which she

quickly replaced with a smile. 'That's nice. Well, I'm second then.' She nodded at Mary. 'Go on, open it.'

Mary opened the exquisitely wrapped present, feeling Joanne's eyes on her as she unwrapped each layer. *She really wants me to like this*, Mary realised. *She must have taken a lot of time considering what to buy*. She removed the last layer and picked up the little gold box, decorated with a white satin bow. *It must be jewellery*, she thought, opening it up. A beautiful gold locket lay on a white satin cushion.

'Open up the locket,' Joanne urged.

Mary carefully removed the pin securing the pendant and opened it up to reveal a photo of Paul and herself, it had been taken on their last anniversary. She gulped back a sob and a mist formed over her eyes as she remembered that precious evening.

'I thought you might like it. You do, don't you?' There was a worried edge to Joanne's voice.

Mary wiped away the tears with the back of her hand. 'I love it. Thank you for such a thoughtful present.'

Joanne smiled in relief and hugged her. 'I know how much you miss Dad. I miss him too. And we could have lost you as well last night. I couldn't bear that.'

'Neither could I. I've only just found my mum,' Cathy said.

She sounded so genuine, Mary thought. But then Robbie had too, hadn't he?

The rest of the family came down then, all bearing presents for Mary, a Pandora charm for her bracelet – she hadn't told them that she'd lost it yet – chocolates from the boys, a fluffy white dressing gown from Kelly and a gorgeous crystal vase from Hannah with a note promising to always keep it filled with fresh flowers. She thanked and hugged them all. Then they sang 'Happy Birthday' to her at the top of their voices – Nicholas and Oliver with much gusto – and finally, after more hugs, they sat down for breakfast. Mary was overwhelmed, she felt so loved her heart was fit to burst. She should be so happy, all her family together, celebrating with her on this special day. But as she smiled and chatted away her heart was breaking. She had been so desperate to find Cathy but now she had she was terrified that her long-lost daughter was a danger to her, just as her father had been.

# 60

## ONE HOUR AGO

### *Alison*

'Can't you turn that thing off? It hasn't stopped since we got here,' Alison said irritably as another message pinged into Jason's phone.

'I do have a business to run, you know. When you're self-employed, every day is a working day,' Jason snapped as he turned away to read the message, which was a sure sign it was bad news.

'Don't tell me, another deal lost,' she snapped. When they got back home she had to have a serious talk to Jason about the company and find out exactly how they stood financially, she thought as she watched the boys racing their cars on the carpet.

'Hey, take a look at this.' Joanne came into the living room carrying her iPad.

Jason looked irritated as she sat down on the sofa next to them. 'It seems that our darling half-sister has been keeping even more secrets.' She handed the iPad to Jason.

He frowned as he started reading it. 'How did you find this?'

Joanne tapped her nose. 'Let's say I was suspicious about her so thought I'd do some research. Cathy's never mentioned being a carer, has she? She's always said she worked in a supermarket. Now we can see why.'

Alison peered over Jason's shoulder. 'Bloody hell!' she exclaimed as she read the newspaper article on the screen. 'We have to tell Mary about this.'

'That's what Damien said. Proper little dark horse, isn't she?'

Jason frowned. 'It says she was acquitted,' he pointed out.

Joanne's eyes narrowed. 'No smoke without fire, I reckon. And how come you're team Cathy all of a sudden? Damien agrees that Mum needs to know about this. Cathy could be a danger to her. Mum could have died last night when her GTN spray went missing.'

'I agree. But not today, it will ruin her birthday,' Jason said. 'Let's all get together in the week and tell her then.'

Alison nodded. 'Jason's right, Jo. This will be a shock for Mary. We can't tell her today.'

'Okay.' Joanne nodded. 'We'll wait until we return home and all go around on Tuesday evening to break the news then. Agreed?'

'Agreed.' Jason stood up and thrust his hands in his pockets, gazing up out of the window at the rain. 'Actually, I think it might be best if we go home today. It seems like this rain is here to stay and the sky looks really dark. We're isolated here. If there's a storm it could take the electrics out and the kids will be scared in the dark.'

Joanne nodded. 'To be honest, we've all had enough. Let's ask Mum if she minds us going back a day early.' She put the iPad down on the coffee table. 'Anyone want a cuppa?'

'Let me give you a hand, the boys could do with a snack, it's a couple of hours until lunch,' Alison said. 'Come on you two,' she called to the boys and they followed Joanne into the kitchen.

When Mary and Cathy came down a little later, they agreed it was a good idea to leave early. 'It's been lovely but I think we're all ready to go,' Mary said. 'We can go after my birthday lunch.'

'Then let's all pack now, save us coming back to the cottage. We can leave the cases in the car while we have lunch.' Alison and Joanne both got up to leave the kitchen then froze at the doorway when they heard Hannah shout.

'I hate you! I wish my mum had never found your nan. You're all horrible!'

'And your Mum is a liar. It says here that she's been on trial for murder!' Kelly retorted.

'They must have found my iPad! I left it on the coffee table.' She turned to Alison, her eyes wide. 'I forgot to close the page down.'

She spun around as she heard Cathy gasp behind her, then saw the colour drain from her face.

Now it was all going to kick off, Alison thought. 'Come on boys, let's watch the TV for a bit,' she said, not wanting them to hear the inevitable argument.

# 61

*Cathy*

Cathy bolted out of the room and up the stairs where Hannah and Kelly were both glaring at each other. Hannah's eyes were flashing with anger, Kelly was holding Joanne's iPad.

'You take that back!' Hannah ordered, seething.

'Why should I?' Kelly demanded. 'It's the truth.'

'Because I was found not guilty, Kelly,' Cathy said sternly. 'The old lady died of natural causes. So it's not very kind of you to spread nasty rumours.'

'I wasn't spreading rumours. I told the truth. You were charged with murder.' Kelly tossed her long hair back. 'You can't stop people from telling the truth.'

'I was *falsely* accused and acquitted,' Cathy repeated firmly. 'So, if you must gossip about it, please state all the facts.'

Hannah looked like she was struggling to hold back her tears. 'I want to go home. I hate it here. They're all so horrible.'

'Then we will leave right now,' Cathy told her, reaching out and enveloping Hannah in an embrace.

'Can someone please explain to me what's going on?' Cathy turned to see Mary standing behind them. 'It's my birthday and I really want my family to celebrate my birthday lunch together. I'm sure that Kelly is sorry for any hurt she's caused, aren't you, Kelly?'

'No I'm not. Her mum has been lying to you, Nan, to all of us.' Kelly shot Cathy a look of pure venom. 'She's not the manager of a supermarket off ill with stress. She is – was – a carer and lost her job because she was accused of murdering an old lady in her care. That's why she's not working. No one will employ her.'

Mary looked as if she'd been smacked across the face. 'Is this true?' she demanded, her gaze fixed on Cathy.

'It was a few years ago and I was acquitted. If Kelly had read all about the case instead of the headlines she would have seen that the old lady died of heart failure. It was nothing to do with me,' Cathy said defiantly. 'And I did work in a supermarket for a while after that, until I got bad depression and had a breakdown.'

'You withheld her medicine. That's what it said,' Kelly retorted.

'I was accused of withholding her medicine,' Cathy corrected her. 'And I was acquitted.'

'It was all lies. My mum would never hurt anyone!' Hannah said, her voice breaking as she hugged her mum.

'Strange how Mum couldn't find her GTN spray yesterday, and how she has been getting confused. Just like the old lady you were accused of murdering,' Joanne said, her arm now around her daughter's shoulders.

Cathy turned to Jason as he joined them. 'Is this your doing? Did you tell everyone?'

'What do you mean?' Joanne's eyes narrowed. 'You knew about this, Jason? And didn't tell any of us. Why the hell not?' she demanded.

'Because...'

Jason was floundering so Cathy finished the sentence for him. 'Because he was in court the same day, weren't you, Jason? And while I was found innocent, he was found guilty.'

There was a stunned silence.

# 62

## *Mary*

Jason in court? Mary stared disbelievingly at her son but she could tell by the expression on his face that Cathy was telling the truth. What on earth had he done?

'For what? Speeding? A driving offence?' Joanne demanded.

'Possessing drugs,' Cathy retorted. She glanced at Jason. Blame your sister and niece for your secret being exposed, not me.' Her arm still around Hannah's shoulder, she turned to Mary. 'I'm sorry, Mum, but I think it's best if me and Hannah go. We're obviously not wanted here and I don't want to spoil your birthday.'

She always seemed so genuine, even now, Mary thought. And she had to admit that it wasn't Cathy who had caused this upset, and that she wasn't the only one who had a secret. Jason had too. 'I don't think there's any need for you to go,' she said quietly. 'You've explained why you went to court and that you were acquitted. I understand why you didn't tell any of us. I, above anyone, can understand why people keep secrets.'

'Thank you,' Cathy said quietly.

Mary turned to Jason, her mind was still reeling about his conviction for drugs. 'You, however, were found guilty.' She shook her head. 'I can't believe this, Jason. Does Alison know about it?' Alison was still downstairs with the boys so hadn't heard the conversation.

He ran his hands through his hair, looking defeated. 'No.'

'Then you had better tell her,' Mary said. 'I don't think you owe an explanation to the rest of us, it's none of our business. It obviously wasn't a heinous crime as you are free and still in charge of your business.'

'So you're just taking Cathy's word that she wasn't guilty?' Joanne demanded.

'She was acquitted, Joanne. Which means she was found by a court of law to be innocent. I don't think we need any more proof, do we?' Mary asked.

'She's lied to us from the beginning,' Joanne said.

'I know but she has explained why and it has no bearing on this.' Mary sighed. Honestly, their arguments were wearing her down. 'Now can we please let this go. We are all family and should be supporting each other.'

She was exhausted with them all. It was one thing after another. And now this. Her son convicted of possessing drugs. It was too much. All she'd wanted was to celebrate her birthday with all her family around her. Her first birthday with Cathy. And now it was all going dreadfully wrong. She was relieved that they'd decided to go home after lunch. She couldn't bear all the stress and tension any longer.

'So Cathy was acquitted but you have to admit that it looks suspicious. And she's told one lie after another.' Joanne pointed accusingly at Cathy. 'She even lied about her upbringing. She told you that she was adopted by a loving family.'

'I was!' Cathy protested.

'Yes but they died when you were seven, didn't they? And

don't bother to deny it, it's all in this article. It says that you spent your childhood in a succession of children's homes. No wonder you resent us all.'

Mary was dumbfounded at this new piece of information. 'Is this true, Cathy? Did you really end up living in various children's homes?'

Cathy nodded. 'My adoptive parents died in a car crash when I was seven. I then spent most of my childhood in a home,' she admitted. 'I didn't tell you because I didn't want you to feel bad about it.'

'More like you didn't want her to know that you had a big chip on your shoulder about your childhood compared to ours. Then she would realise how much you were manipulating her,' Joanne retorted.

Joanne was right, it was one lie after another, Mary thought. Was Cathy manipulating her? Was she responsible for all the things that had happened? 'Oh, Cathy, I don't feel like I can believe anything you say!' she said sadly. 'I can't trust you anymore.'

'Really? And yet you trust your precious son who was found guilty of possessing drugs and given a suspended sentence?' Cathy retorted.

Mary's eyes misted over. 'I can't take any more of this,' she said.

Leaving them all still arguing on the landing, she went back downstairs, then grabbed her waterproof coat, pulling it on and going out into the back garden, wanting to get away from them all. She could feel her heart galloping and was glad that her GTN spray was in her trouser pocket. She wasn't taking any chances after last night.

She wiped the seat with the sleeve of her coat and sat down, deep in thought. What a weekend this had turned out to be. Joanne was an alcoholic, Jason had a drug conviction and now she'd discovered that Cathy had been feeding her one lie after another. She couldn't trust any of her children.

A sudden gust of wind blew through the bushes and she shivered and looked around. An eerie air had descended on the garden and she couldn't shake off the feeling that someone was watching her.

# 63

*Alison*

Alison listened to Jason in horror. When Kelly had come down to look after the boys so that Jason could talk to her alone, she had thought he was going to fill her in about all that performance with Cathy. She hadn't expected his confession that he had been to court and found guilty of an offence himself.

'It was a one-off.' He chewed his bottom lip. 'I needed to make some money fast and someone asked me to get some drugs for them. It was quick money. I kept them in the office. Only the police were tipped off and the office was raided.'

'Drugs? You take drugs?'

He shook his head vehemently. 'No. Well. I have taken the odd line of coke,' he admitted. 'But not for ages now.'

'So you mostly just deal them? You're a drug dealer?'

'No! I told you it was a one-off! I needed the cash. I didn't think there was any risk.' He looked defiant. 'If you weren't going on about wanting this and wanting that all the time, we wouldn't be in so much debt.'

'That's right, blame it on me. If you weren't so hopeless at running your business you wouldn't have lost the Rowington deal and we'd be okay for money,' she retaliated, stung. Then she saw Jason's eyes narrow and realised the big mistake she'd made.

'And how do you know about that?' he demanded.

Damn. Hugh had told her.

'You mentioned it to me,' she said, thinking on her feet. 'Don't say you're losing your mind as well as your business acumen.'

'I didn't tell you,' he said firmly.

The only thing she could do was bluff it out. 'Really? Then how do I know about it?' she asked, lacing her voice with heavy sarcasm. Then she added for extra effect, 'Does Hugh know about your drug conviction?'

Jason still looked puzzled but he nodded. 'Yes, he got me a good lawyer, that's how I got off with a suspended sentence. I thought I was facing prison, Ali.'

'And you were too ashamed to tell me? What if you had got sent down? You'd prefer me to face the shock of a policeman knocking on my door to tell me that my husband had been sent to prison for a crime I didn't even know he'd committed than tell me yourself?'

'I tried to. I did. But I couldn't find the words.'

'Couldn't face me knowing the truth, more like.' Alison was so furious, she shoved him in the chest. 'You make me sick.'

'I was scared that you would leave me. I couldn't bear to lose you and the boys.'

'Shame you didn't think of that when you were taking and dealing drugs!' she shot at him.

She spun around and stormed upstairs, consumed with fury, not just at Jason but at Hugh too. He had known about this and hadn't told her. She had sent him a message straight after the one Mary had made her send the other night, telling him what had happened and saying that although she loved him and wanted to keep seeing him they would have to lie low for a while. He'd replied saying that he'd go along with however she wanted to play it, he didn't want to lose her.

And it was all down to Cathy. Nothing had been the same since she came along. Mary wouldn't have it, though; she was still sticking up for her. Her guilt at abandoning Cathy was blinding her to what she was like. Well, Cathy didn't fool her. She was up to something, and Alison was going to find out what it was and expose her. Then Mary would have to open her eyes to what her precious eldest child was like.

# 64

## NOW

### *Mary*

'Get off me!'

Terror gave Mary strength and she kicked the man in the shins, wrenching out of his grasp, her hand reaching for the door handle and thrusting it open. She hurtled herself in, then slammed it shut behind her, pulling the bolt across.

'Mary?'

She turned around, leaning her back against the door, her hand defensively across her chest as her racing heart threatened to explode. Joanne, Cathy, Jason and Damien gaped at her as if she was mad.

'Mum, what were you doing out there in the rain?' Joanne demanded, her face creased in concern. 'You're soaking wet and you look as if you've seen a ghost.'

'Come and sit down, Mary, before you have another angina attack,' Damien said, taking her arm and leading her over to the table

Mary's heart was thudding so much, her breath gasping out,

that she feared she would have an angina attack too. She slipped her hand in her trouser pocket and took out her GTN spray then sprayed it under her tongue, closing her eyes as she waited for it to take effect.

'What happened? Who's out there, Mum?' Jason asked urgently. She opened her eyes and saw that he was hunched down in front of her, his eyes wide, the whites clearly visible, as he looked into hers. 'Who's scared you?'

Mary gasped, still trying to catch her breath. 'It's Robbie.'

'My father? He's come here?' Cathy asked.

Mary swirled around and gaped at her, astonished that she knew her father was alive.

'Have you been in contact with him?' she asked, stunned. Had Cathy brought him here? Why? And how had she found him?

'Yes I've met him, but I didn't tell him we were here...'

'Hang on, I thought you said Cathy's father was dead...' Jason got to his feet and looked from Mary to Cathy in bewilderment. 'What's going on?'

'I was hoping he was...' Mary felt the room sway. She was going to faint.

'Drink this, Mum. I've put you extra sugar in it.' Joanne placed a mug of tea on the table in front of her. Mary stared into the light brown liquid, trying to calm herself down. Joanne squeezed her shoulder comfortingly. 'I can understand why you don't want to see this man again as he left you in the lurch and you had to deal with the pregnancy alone but why are you so terrified of him? You're shaking.'

She was terrified. There was only one reason Robbie was here. She dragged her eyes from the cup to Cathy, who was looking really angry. 'How could you bring that man back into my life?' she demanded.

'How could you pretend that he was dead? That's a terrible lie to tell me!' Cathy countered.

'For good reason! You have no idea what kind of man he is.' Her throat was so dry it was a struggle to speak. She swallowed. 'I never wanted to see him again. Not after...' She closed her eyes again, her last image of Robbie flashing across her mind. The raw anger on his face, his heavy black leather motorbike boot raised as he landed another kick. She shook at the memory.

'Mum, take it easy. You're safe. You'll have another heart attack.'

Mary swallowed. Joanne was right, she was trembling all over.

She took a deep breath. She was inside the house, the door was locked and her family were all here. She was safe now. Robbie had hopefully gone. And they were all going home soon, miles away, where he would never find her. Unless Cathy had told him where she lived.

'Mum, are you okay? I promise you that I didn't bring Robbie here. I just wanted to meet him, see what he was like.' There was a tremor in Cathy's voice and when Mary opened her eyes she saw that her daughter looked worried.

'How did you find him? You haven't told him where I live, have you?'

Cathy shook her head. 'I found a photo of you both in your tin,' she confessed. 'So I took a picture of it with my camera, cropped you out, and put it up on my Facebook account asking if anyone knew anything about Robbie. Someone replied and said they knew him. Later he contacted me and said he wanted to meet me. So we met up. He seems really nice. He asked about you.'

Oh dear God, she'd gone to meet him. Then she realised Cathy had said she found the photo in the tin; she'd been snooping in her wardrobe. Was that when Nicholas said that he'd caught Cathy playing hide and seek in her bedroom? If she was in the wardrobe, that's what he'd have thought she was doing, wasn't it? And had Cathy caused the bruise on his arm by pushing him away? Then she recalled how she'd tripped up on the handbag the same night, Cathy must have knocked it out of the wardrobe when she was looking for the tin.

'Why has he come here?' Joanne asked. 'You must have told him Mum was here. Look at the state of her! How could you do this?' She glared at Cathy.

'It wasn't my mum, it was me.' Hannah's voice came from the open doorway. 'I wanted it to be a surprise for your birthday, Nan. Grandad said he wanted to meet you, that you had both been planning on running away to Gretna Green and getting married but he lost touch with you, and then you moved away. He said he had no idea you were pregnant and wanted to see you again to apologise.'

Fear flooded through Mary. Robbie had got to them, worked on them, fed them a sob story to get to her.

'You have no idea what you've done, Hannah,' she told her. 'Or you, Cathy. Or the terrible danger you've put me – all of us – in.'

'What do you mean?' Hannah asked. 'Why are you so terrified of him?'

Mary stared at her, her breathing ragged, unable to voice the words.

'I guess it's because he's a criminal,' Cathy said quietly. 'I found the newspaper article too, about his arrest. And he said that he was sent to prison; that's why he lost touch with you. That's why you pretended he was dead, isn't it?'

'What? Is this true?' Hannah asked, her eyes wide as saucers. 'My grandad's a criminal!'

Joanne looked aghast. 'This is getting worse and worse.'

Cathy nodded. 'He confessed to it. He said that it was for stealing cars and that he was little more than a kid. It was wrong what he did, I'm not excusing it, but he regrets it. And he regrets what happened to Mum. He told me so. He wants to make it up to you, Mum.'

'Stealing cars?' Mary croaked. 'It was more than that. It was murder!'

# 65

*Cathy*

Her father, a murderer? Cathy stared incredulously at Mary, who was literally trembling with fear. It was obvious that she was terrified of Robbie.

There were gasps of horror from the others and Joanne bent down and put her arm around Mary's shoulders. 'Don't upset yourself, Mum,' she said softly, but Mary had now closed her eyes as if she couldn't bear to remember the terrible thing she had witnessed.

'You really think that he wants to kill you?' Jason asked.

Mary slowly opened her eyes. She looked exhausted. 'I'm certain of it.' Her voice was weak as if she was forcing the words out.

Joanne sat down by her and handed her the still undrunk cup of tea. 'Drink this, Mum. 'You've had a dreadful shock,' she said gently.

Mary took a long sip of the now-cool liquid.

'I don't know what you were both thinking of, Hannah, bringing that man here without checking that your nan actually wanted to see him first,' Joanne scolded Hannah. 'Look at the state of her.'

'I thought it was romantic,' Hannah whispered. 'Grandad is so desperate to see Nan.'

'Well, Mum isn't desperate to see him,' Jason retorted. 'Can't you see that she's terrified of him!'

'I'm sorry! I didn't know!' Hannah's hand flew to her mouth. 'We didn't mean to upset you. Mum just wanted to find her dad. He seems nice.'

Cathy went over to her daughter and hugged her. 'It's okay, darling.' She glared at Mary. 'You should have told us! You've had a go at me for lying but you've told the biggest lie of all.'

'I was protecting you. You shouldn't have looked for him behind my back. You shouldn't have told him where I was.' Mary's voice was little more than a whisper.

Alison glared at Jason as another text pinged into his phone. Jason scanned it, shot Alison an apologetic look and slipped the phone into his pocket.

'Look, this has all been a lot for Mum. I think we should forget lunch and go home now,' he said. 'You can come and stay with us tonight, Mum. You probably won't feel safe on your own.'

'Does Robbie know where I live, Hannah? Have you and your mum told him my address?' Mary asked, looking a bit stronger now she'd drunk some of her tea and calmed herself down.

'No, Nan, honestly we haven't. He knew it was your birthday today and wanted to come and surprise you. He came around the back way because I was going to let him in when you blew out the candles on your cake. I thought you'd be pleased. Now I've ruined everything.' Hannah turned on her heel and ran out of the room.

'Hannah didn't mean any harm,' Cathy said. 'Neither of us did. We didn't know. If Mum had told us the truth...'

'I had convinced myself that he was dead. So why tell you the horrible thing he'd done?' Mary whispered. 'I didn't know you'd go snooping in my bedroom, and find the newspaper clipping, and the photo of us and put it on Facebook.'

Alison pounced on this. 'So Nicholas was telling the truth – you were in Mum's bedroom. Did you bruise his arm to frighten him so he wouldn't tell?'

Cathy looked shocked. 'Of course I wouldn't. I would never hurt a child.'

'Really?' Joanne rounded on her. 'I bet all the other things were you too. I bet you let Bailey out, you wanted to make sure Mum stopped looking after the boys so that you could have her all to yourself. You've done nothing but monopolise Mum and try to drive a wedge between us all since you arrived!'

Jason joined in. 'Jo's right. You've been trying to freeze the rest of us out ever since you arrived. I reckon you tried to phone your dad hoping to get him and Mum back together, so you could all play happy families.'

Tears sprang to Cathy's eyes. 'I did not! It's okay for you two with your perfect lives. I never had a mum or dad, my adoptive parents died when I was seven. I was pushed from pillar to post then.'

'You lied about that too!' Alison pointed out. 'You've done nothing but lie. Mary had a reason for not telling the truth; she is obviously petrified of your dad. But you, you've lied for the sake of it. You obviously can't be trusted. You've used us all.' Then she heard another message ping into Jason's phone. 'For God's sake, can't you turn off that phone for a while? It's done nothing but ping all weekend!' she shouted.

Jason opened the message; his eyes widened and the colour drained from his face.

'What's the matter?' Alison reached for the phone and took it out of his shaking hands. She gasped as she stared at the screen, then her eyes darted over to Cathy. 'Has Hannah gone outside?'

Cathy looked around. 'She must have done. Why, what's the matter?'

Alison and Jason both exchanged horrified looks but neither of them answered.

'Tell me!' Cathy stepped forward and grabbed the phone from Alison's hand. She swiped the screen then screamed as she saw the photo of Hannah sprawled out in the garden, her eyes closed as if she was dead. While they'd been arguing her precious Hannah had slipped outside unnoticed, probably to talk to Robbie and now she was lying on the floor, maybe dead. Hannah, the only person who had ever loved her unconditionally.

'Oh my God. I've got to find her!' Cathy raced to the back door and slid open the bolt.

'Cathy! Come back!' Mary called but Cathy ignored her. She had to help Hannah. She grabbed the handle of the door and flung it open, stumbling back as a burly man, his face covered by a balaclava dashed in, pushed Cathy back against the wall and kicked the door shut behind him.

'Where is he?' the man yelled, pointing a gun at her. 'Where's that two-faced snake?'

Cathy shook with fear as she stared into the barrel of the gun. Who was he? Had he hurt Hannah? She had to go to her daughter.

'What's going on...' Damien stepped forward and the man swung the gun around at him.

'Get back!' the gunman ordered.

'Hey.' Damien backed away, his hands in the air. 'I don't know who you're looking for, mate, but I think you've got the wrong house.'

'I've got the right house. I've been tracking him.' The man brandished the gun. 'Everyone move away from the back door, put your hands on your head and get back against that wall. Now!' he shouted.

Sweat pouring down her forehead, Cathy backed against the wall, her eyes darting towards the now closed back door. Her daughter was lying out there injured. She had to help her. Hannah was her life, her reason for living. *Please God, let her be alive.*

# 66

## *Mary*

Mary could hardly believe that this was happening; it was like something in the films on TV. They were all being held at gunpoint in a remote cottage in Dartmoor and someone had taken Hannah. The man had come for her, she was sure of it. Robbie had sent him. He was going to make sure that she didn't live to tell the tale of what he did. Well, she had lived a good life, she would prefer that he killed her than all her family.

'Is it me you're looking for?' she asked, her voice trembling a little. 'There's no need for this. I won't say anything. I haven't said anything all these years.'

The man laughed. 'You? Why would I want an old lady? It's Jason Hudson I want.'

He pointed his gun menacingly at them all. 'I won't tell you again. Stand against the wall.'

They all obeyed instantly. 'What do you want with my son?' Mary asked, trying to keep calm.

'He owes me big time. I told him if he didn't pay up by

Friday morning I'd come for him. Now where is the two-timing rat?'

'What does he owe you?' Alison's voice was trembling.

'Fifty thousand pounds,' the man snarled. 'So I've come to collect it.' He turned to Damien. 'Where is the two-faced rat?'

Damien looked petrified. He glanced around the kitchen. 'I don't know. He was here a minute ago.'

Mary guessed that Jason had sneaked out and gone straight upstairs to look after the children. She hoped that he'd managed to get them out of the house and call the police. The best thing to do was to keep this man talking until the police arrived. 'If you give us a little time we could get the money together,' she said.

'I want the money now or Hudson pays.' The man uttered a twisted evil laugh. 'Oh don't worry, I won't kill him. He'll be alive. Just.'

Mary shuddered. The dreadful man sounded like he meant it. What was Jason thinking of borrowing money from a man like this? He'd said his business was in trouble but this! Was Hugh involved too?

'Don't worry. I'll find him but first I need to deal with you lot,' the man said menacingly.

Suddenly the back door was thrust open and Robbie stepped in, a spade in his hand. The man spun around but Robbie was quicker than him. He lifted his arms high in the air and brought them quickly down, whacking the man on the head. The man groaned and sank to the floor.

# 67

Mary screamed and Joanne rushed to put her arms around her. 'It's okay, Mum. We're safe now.'

'He's going to kill us. He's going to kill us all.' Mary pointed at Robbie.

Robbie stared at her incredulously. 'Christ, Mary. I would never hurt you. It's this monster I'm after.' Robbie turned to Cathy. 'Hannah's safe. I saw that creep knock her out and lock her in the shed but I unlocked it and checked on her as soon as he'd gone. She's okay, just a couple of bruises. I've told her to stay in the shed until I come back for her.'

'Oh thank goodness!' Cathy threw her arms around Robbie's neck.

'Let just get this animal tied up first. I've already called the police,' Robbie said, patting her back.

Damien crouched down by the unconscious man and checked his pulse. 'He's alive,' he said. 'I noticed some rope under the sink earlier, we can use that to tie him up.'

'I'll get it.' Joanne dashed to the sink, returning a couple of minutes later with the rope. Robbie had now picked up the gun and put it on top of the cooker hood. Then he and Damien tied the unconscious man's hands and feet together.

'We'd better go and check on the kids upstairs. Thank goodness they didn't come down while this was going on,' Alison said.

'The police are coming?' Mary asked weakly as Joanne and Alison went upstairs to check on the children. She could hardly believe this was happening. And still didn't trust Robbie, even if it did seem that he had rescued them all.

'They're on their way,' Robbie said. He stood up and nodded to Cathy. 'Let's go and get Hannah.'

'Where's Jason?' Damien asked, looking around.

'I'm here.' Jason pushed open the broom cupboard door and stepped out, looking a bit shame-faced.

'You hid in there while that man threatened us?' Damien retorted. 'What a cowardly thing to do!'

'I thought it would be safer for everyone if he didn't find me,' Jason said, his face was deathly white. 'He might have killed us all.'

When Cathy came back in with Hannah, who had a bruise on her forehead and was pretty shaken up but thankfully uninjured, Kelly threw her arms around her and told her how sorry she was for falling out with her. 'You could have died!' she said, her voice trembling.

'I'm okay, Grandad saved me,' Hannah said weakly. The two girls huddled up together, sobbing quietly.

Alison and Joanne took the children into the living room and put a film on the TV, some snacks and drinks on the table and left the boys with Connor to watch the film, with strict instructions not to tell them anything that had gone on.

The police arrived shortly afterwards and took the injured man – and the gun – away. A couple of officers remained to take statements from everyone, finally leaving to say they would be in touch. Robbie left too, saying they needed time as a family to discuss everything. 'You know where I am if you want to get in touch,' he told Cathy.

Cathy stormed over to Jason, her arms crossed, voice icy cold. 'Now I want to know exactly what has been going on. And you'd better tell the truth. Thanks to you my daughter was attacked and could have died.'

'We all want to know, your actions put us all in danger,' Damien agreed. 'So spill, Jason. Why did you owe that man so much money?'

Jason sat down at the kitchen table and sank his head into his hands. 'He's part of a drug gang that have been blackmailing me for months,' he confessed. 'I owed them a few grand and I didn't have the money so they blackmailed me into keeping a stash of coke for them at work.' His voice broke. 'I desperately needed money for the business so I pretended that someone broke into the office and stole the drugs, so I could sell them myself. The gang somehow found out that I was lying and said I needed to pay it all back or they'd kill us all.'

Alison glared at him. 'You're still involved with drugs?' she demanded. 'How could you, Jason? First I find out you've been convicted of possessing drugs and given a suspended sentence but instead of learning your lesson, you decide to become a drug dealer!' She paused. 'So that's why your offices were broken into and it seemed like nothing was taken.'

'I wouldn't have done it if it wasn't for you,' Jason retorted. 'You and the kids are always wanting something. I can't earn enough money to satisfy you. Then you moan that I'm working too much.'

'Don't you dare blame this on me! I work too,' Alison told him.

'When you're not sleeping with my business partner!' Jason shot back at her.

Alison looked shocked. 'You knew?'

'I didn't, until I borrowed your phone this morning and found a message to him!' Jason looked at her coldly. 'How long has it been going on?'

'You promised me you'd finished with him,' Mary scolded Alison.

Jason swung around incredulously. 'You knew too! How could you keep this from me, Mum?'

'Christ, Jason. Adultery is the least of your worries! You could have got us all killed!' Damien said. 'What the hell are you playing at?'

'I didn't know they'd put a tracker on my phone.'

'So that's why you kept getting all those texts. It was from this man wanting his money,' Alison said accusingly.

Jason nodded. 'He kept sending me messages threatening me with what he would do if I didn't get it. I kept begging him to give me more time. He wouldn't, though. He said I had to have it this weekend.' He looked desperate. 'I think it was him who left the dead rat on the doorstep. It was a warning to me.'

'So you decided to hide the rat, then sneak into Mary's room later and take away her GTN spray, hoping to give her a heart attack. Then you could pay your debt with the money she left you in the will,' Cathy said.

Mary could see by the guilty look on Jason's face that Cathy had guessed right. 'It was you. All the time.' Her head was swimming; she couldn't take it all in. Feeling as if she was about to faint, she sank down into the chair. Jason was the one responsible for her almost fatal angina attack. 'And you tried to blame Cathy for it.' The thought that her son had tried to kill her made her feel physically sick. 'Were you responsible for all the other things too?' she asked quietly. 'Did you steal money from my purse? Have you been playing with my mind, trying to make me think I was losing my faculties?' She couldn't believe that Jason, her beloved son, had done these awful things.

'Not the money... but the other stuff,' Jason sank his head in his hands. 'I'm sorry. I didn't want to do any of it. I was desperate. You've seen what this guy is capable of. And he doesn't work alone. He threatened to kill all my family if I didn't pay up. He took Hannah, I guess thinking she was my daughter, to make me pay up. I thought...'

'That I'd had my life? Better an old lady die than yourself,' Mary cut in.

Jason's hands were wet with tears. 'I was in over my head, Mum. I didn't know what to do. I'd never hurt you. I was just desperate.'

'You could have tried telling us the truth,' Joanne retorted. 'It would have been better than trying to kill our mother.'

'I didn't.'

'Did you hide Mary's GTN spray?' Alison demanded.

'I didn't mean anything to happen to her. I just thought that if she went to hospital I could go with her, get away from the drug gang. They've been threatening me all weekend.'

'You wanted her to die so you could have your share of the money, more like, before Mum changed her will to include Cathy!' Joanne said. 'How could you do such a terrible thing, Jason?'

'Not only did you try and kill our mother, you put us all in danger. That man had a gun. If it wasn't for my dad – the one you all think is a criminal – we would have all been dead,' Cathy told him. 'You should go to prison for what you did. If it was left to me, I'd report you.' She stood up. 'You all decide what you're going to do. I don't want any part of it. Now I'm going to see my dad and thank him for saving Hannah's, and all of our lives.' She looked at Mary. 'I don't know why you think he's a murderer, but if you could ever find the strength and compassion to hear him out, I think he would love to talk to you.' She kissed Mary on the cheek and walked out.

# 68

## TWO WEEKS LATER

### *Mary*

The drug dealer had told the police of Jason's involvement and the police came back to take Jason in for questioning. He had confessed everything and due to his suspended sentence was refused bail. His solicitor was hopeful that he would escape a custodial sentence as he was blackmailed into keeping the drugs and was willing to give evidence against the drug gang. Apparently the police had been after them for ages. Alison wouldn't forgive him for putting them all in so much danger, though, and was filing for divorce.

Before the police had arrived to arrest him, Jason had confessed everything, how he had had turned off the router so the CCTV wouldn't work, then punctured the car tyre, killed the plants, put the brick through the window all to try and make Mary feel unsafe in the house so she would sell it. It was Jason who had started the fire in the dustbin, insisting that he had known Mary was out so wouldn't be harmed but wanted her to be able to claim the insurance money so she could give him enough to clear his drug debt. The others had wanted to turn him in so he could be charged for this too, as well as the drugs offence, but Mary refused. She couldn't, wouldn't give evidence against her own son. But she was finished with him.

She'd spoilt him, Mary realised. He'd always been her blue-eyed boy, always been able to wrap her around his little finger. He'd fooled her. Paul had told her a few times that she was too soft with Jason and she knew that Joanne had felt edged out since he was born, but he'd always been such a good little lad, eager to please, always so attentive whereas Joanne was headstrong and confrontational. Jason insisted that he hadn't stolen her jewellery, and taken money out of her purse, so she guessed that she had lost them herself. Just like she'd erased Paul's last telephone message. She hoped that it was stress that was making her forgetful. She'd confided her fears to Joanne, who told her she could have some tests to see if she did have dementia, and reassured her that if she had there were steps she could take to slow down the progress.

Joanne had become closer to Cathy over the last couple of weeks, probably because of her guilt at blaming her for all the things Jason had done. She had stopped drinking too, and she and Damien seemed to be making more of an effort to get on, which Mary was pleased about. The terrifying incident at the cottage had changed them all.

Cathy and Hannah had both sat down and told her how they had met Robbie and really liked him. 'He spoke so well of you, Mum. As if he really cared about you. And he's upset that you're scared of him. He swears that he never killed anyone,' Cathy said.

'Please meet him and talk to him, Nan. We'll come with you if that makes you feel safer,' Hannah added.

Mary thought about it a lot and finally agreed to meet Robbie and hear him out. She guessed that she owed him that much after saving their lives. The awful thing he had done was a long time ago, she reminded herself. Perhaps he deeply regretted it. So she agreed to meet him in a local café.

'You can drop me off, and pick me up,' she told Cathy. 'But I want to speak to your father alone.'

Cathy agreed.

When Mary walked into the café, Robbie was already there, sitting at a table in the corner. He stood up when he saw her, his gaze fixed on her as she walked towards him. 'Thank you for coming,' he said, pulling out a chair for her.

'I did it for Cathy and Hannah,' she said bluntly. She sat down, feeling awkward. It had been forty-five years since she had last spoken to Robbie but looking into those deep brown eyes that had always mesmerised her, it seemed like yesterday.

'Thank you for giving me a chance to explain,' he said. His eyes held hers. 'I had no idea you were pregnant, Mary. I was shocked when Cathy found me and told me that she was my daughter, and how you had given birth alone and abandoned her. You must have been so scared and desperate.' His eyes were full of compassion. Had he changed, or was he fooling her, as he'd done before? As Jason had done.

They both paused as the waitress came over to take their orders, both requesting white coffee with sugar. Then Robbie continued. 'I'm sorry that you had to go through that. If I'd known I would have stood by you but I guess I wouldn't have been any help to you in prison.'

The waitress brought the coffees over and left to serve someone else. Robbie stirred two sugars into his coffee before gazing earnestly at her. 'I really loved you, Mary. I promise I did. I had no idea you were pregnant. Why didn't you tell me?'

'I didn't know myself for ages. I refused to accept it, I guess. I kept telling myself that I was late because I was stressed. But then I had to face it. I came to tell you...' She stopped as the memory of that awful night flooded back.

'But what? What is it? Why are you so convinced that I murdered someone? I went to prison for car theft, nothing else.'

Mary ran her finger around the rim of her cup, trying to form the words she wanted to say.

'You said you came to tell me you were pregnant. What stopped you? Couldn't you find me?'

'Yes, I found you.' Mary forced herself to meet his gaze, wanting to see his reaction. 'I thought you'd seen me too. I guess you were too busy kicking someone to death to notice me.'

# 69

The colour drained from Robbie's face. 'So that's it. You saw that? I am so sorry. But it wasn't what it seemed.'

The image of his leather boot taking a swing at the lad on the floor shot across Mary's mind. 'I know what I saw so if you're going to lie I'll leave right now.'

'I'm not denying it, Mary. I'm just saying that I didn't attack that lad, he attacked me. He and his gang jumped us.' Robbie pulled up the sleeve of his jumper and showed her a long scar running down his arm. 'He stabbed Jordy in the leg and knifed my arm.' He sat back, his face clouding over. 'So what you saw was me defending myself. And yes, I can understand that it looked bad but if you had stopped a little longer you would have seen that someone pulled me off him. And the lad got up, bruised but not badly injured.'

'But in the paper the next day it said someone had been killed in a rival gang attack.'

'That was Jordy. The knife cut through a major artery. I was so mad when I saw the lad knife him, that's why I kicked him. He was bruised but not badly hurt but Jordy died.' Robbie's face darkened at the memory. 'I was grief-stricken and angry, I could see he was bady hurt. I called the ambulance, stayed with Jordy until they came then took off, hot-wired the first car I came across and sped off. Of course the police followed and cornered me. I was up in court the next day. And as it wasn't the first time I'd been charged with car theft I got a custodial.'

Mary gazed at his scar and thought back to the scene. She'd turned and run as soon as she'd seen the fury on Robbie's face as he kicked the lad lying on the floor. She'd been petrified that he was like her dad. Violent. She was convinced he had killed the lad. Had she got it badly wrong?

'There's no excuse. I was pretty wild back then. I know I was. But Jordy's death – and my stint in prison – taught me that I needed to change.' He laid his elbows on the table and leaned forward, his expression earnest. 'I never forgot you, Mary. I told my mates that if they saw you, they had to tell you where I was and that I loved you. I had no idea you were pregnant.'

'No one did. I hid it. Then gave birth alone.' She swallowed the lump in her throat. 'Have you any idea what that was like? How absolutely terrified I was?'

'I can imagine.' His voice was soft, tender. 'I did look for you when I came out of prison but you'd moved away and no one knew where. I thought you didn't want to know me, seeing as I was a criminal.' His eyes clouded over. 'I realise now that you ran for your life because you believed that I was a murderer and would come after you because you thought I knew you'd witnessed me kill someone. Well, I didn't see you, I was too busy and angry to focus on anything other than the guy who killed Jordy. And I would never harm you. Never.'

They both drank their coffees in silence for a while, then something occurred to Mary. 'If you didn't know I was pregnant, why did you reply to Cathy?' she asked.

Robbie winced. 'I was curious. I was a bit of a lad back then, a player. I guessed it was possible that I could have fathered another child.'

'Another?' Of course, he was probably married with a family. Like she was.

'Yes, I've got two sons. We split up years ago. My wife found someone else, moved miles away taking my sons with her.' He looked a little ashamed. 'I miss them, but I got on with my life. We meet up now and again but we're not close. When Cathy put a message up saying she was looking for me, one of my mates saw it, contacted her and she said she thought I was her father. I did my sums and wondered if she could be yours. If that's why you went away. We met up and clicked right away. She's lovely and so is Hannah.'

'She is,' Mary agreed.

'I told her that I would like to meet you and could she arrange it but she was worried. She said that you were reluctant to talk about me and had said I was dead. She said you were going away for the weekend and she'd talk to you about it when you came back.' He took another sip of his coffee. 'Then Hannah contacted me and said that you were all going to spend your birthday weekend at a cottage in Dartmoor; it was only an hour's drive from where I live, so she invited me over. We wanted to give you a birthday surprise.'

'You did that all right,' Mary told him.

He reached out and put his hand on hers. It felt so comforting that she didn't pull it away. 'I really am very sorry for everything you went through,' he said softly. 'And I want you to know that my feelings for you were genuine. I really loved you and wanted to marry you. I was devastated when I heard you'd moved away. I hope you can find it in your heart to forgive me.'

He was telling the truth, Mary could see it in his eyes. She was so relieved that he wasn't the violent murderer she'd feared for years. And he *had* loved her too, he hadn't just been using her. She had meant something to him. If only he hadn't gone to prison, maybe she would have found out the truth about that night and they would have run away together, brought Cathy up instead of giving her away. But then she wouldn't have met Paul, and they had been so happy together. She wouldn't have had Joanne and Jason either, and devastated and angry as she was with Jason, he was her son and she still loved him. 'It doesn't matter now. It was all such a long time ago, we were so young,' she replied. 'Of course I forgive you.'

Robbie looked relieved. 'Cathy said that you got married, that you had a good life.'

'I did. Paul was a wonderful man. I never told him about Cathy, though. Did you know I named her Hope when she was born? I guess I was scared his love for me wasn't strong enough to cope.'

They sat talking, exchanging news, and it felt so good to catch up.

'Can we keep in touch, just as friends?' he asked. 'We've got a daughter and granddaughter together now, after all. It would be great to share special occasions sometimes. Meet up and swap news?'

She looked at this man who she had once loved and saw the kindness in his eyes. He'd made mistakes, hadn't they all? But he had paid for those, and had fought for them when they had needed him. The love she'd had for him had long gone, as she was sure had his for her, but yes, they were family now. They had Cathy and Hannah. She didn't think that Joanne and Alison would mind her including Robbie, they were all so grateful for his intervention when their lives were at risk. She had been terrified of him for so long, it was time to put the past to bed.

'We're having a family party for Cathy's birthday in a couple of weeks,' she told him. 'Why don't you join us?'

He smiled and nodded. 'I'd be delighted to.'

# EPILOGUE

## 21ST NOVEMBER

### *Cathy*

'I'm so glad that we found Nan. And Grandad. Wouldn't my auntie Sarah have been happy? I wish I'd known her too,' Hannah said on Saturday afternoon as they set off for the birthday party Mary was having for Cathy. Mary had even invited her friends and neighbours. And Robbie. She said it was a 'goodbye house' party too as she was moving into her new bungalow on Tuesday.

'I do too.' Cathy nodded.

Cathy and Sarah had been inseparable in the children's home, they had clicked straight away when they first met at seven years old and went everywhere together. Everyone said they looked like sisters with their dark hair and brown eyes, although Cathy was a little smaller. They began to call each other sisters and asked to be given a home together.

No one wanted to take on the two of them, though, and when one of them got a foster family, she missed the other so much she was eventually sent back and was delighted to be reunited. They got a flat together when they were both old enough to leave the foster home, and Sarah got a job in the local care home while Cathy got a job in a sales office. They'd both said they wanted to find their birth mothers and both had registered with an agency and started looking on the boards. Then Cathy had come down with leukaemia when Hannah was a few months old. 'Look after Hannah for me, please,' she'd begged her best friend. 'And try to find my mother so she has family.' So she had agreed.

The years had ticked by, with occasionally someone replying to the messages but it never turned out to be anything. Until Mary.

No one knew that the woman who now called herself Cathy was really Sarah. That Cathy herself was the one who had died. She had begged Sarah to become her, to use her birth certificate. They were born only two days apart anyway. That way she could pass herself off as baby Hannah's mother. The real Cathy had been terrified that otherwise Hannah would be taken into care and she didn't want that for her daughter. They always looked similar and neither of them had any family so no one would know, and Sarah adored Hannah so had agreed. So, as far as everyone was concerned, Sarah was now Cathy Stokes, Hannah's real mother. The real Cathy had written down all the facts she knew, given Sarah the mementos her birth mother had left and put some strands of her hair in an envelope for a DNA test, begging Sarah to keep trying to find her birth mother so Hannah could have a family.

Mary's message on the boards had come out of the blue. Sarah hadn't known what to do. Should she go along and meet her, and explain about the real Cathy's death? But that would mean she'd have to tell Hannah she'd lied to her for her whole life, though. Maybe she'd let her friend's birth mother know what she thought of her abandoning her new baby in a telephone box? But then the idea wormed into her head. Maybe she ought to get revenge on this affluent middle-aged woman who had abandoned her friend, leaving her fate in the hands of strangers?

Even now she had the shivers when she recalled the evil men in the care homes who had tried to force their attentions on her and the real Cathy when they were in their teens. She decided that she would pretend to be Mary's long-lost daughter, get close to her, then abandon her, walk away and never see her again. See how she liked it! She'd started to take her revenge too, stealing the odd bit of money from Mary's purse, thinking that the woman was so rich she would never miss it.

She hadn't expected to grow fond of Mary, and to feel sorry for her when she heard her story and saw how selfish her grown-up children were. As the weeks went by, Sarah had started to realise how much Mary had longed to find the daughter she had abandoned, how sorry she was, and it had been more difficult for her to walk away. Then Mary had found out about Hannah and wanted to meet her, and Hannah had loved her grandmother straight away, so Sarah felt that she had to go along with the story.

And what harm was Sarah doing anyway? She'd gone by the name Cathy for Hannah's whole life now. The real Cathy was dead and Hannah was her child so technically Mary was Hannah's blood family. No one knew that she, the woman calling herself Cathy, wasn't who she said she was. No one would ever find out. Besides, Cathy would have been pleased for her, Sarah knew that. All she had wanted was for Hannah was to be safe and financially looked-after, and to have her blood family. And, with the money coming into her bank account from Mary in less than a week, Sarah had found that for her.

She had kept the promise she'd made on her best friend's deathbed. No one would ever know the truth.

# A LETTER FROM KAREN

I want to say a huge thank you for choosing to read *The Family Reunion.* If you enjoyed it, and want to keep up to date with all my latest releases, just sign up at the following link. Your email address will never be shared and you can unsubscribe at any time.

*www.bookouture.com/karen-king*

I always find family dynamics interesting to explore and for this story I chose to explore the dynamics between a young mother who abandoned her baby at birth and the child she abandoned. There are many reasons why babies are abandoned and my heart goes out to both the mother and child involved. As a mother myself I know that this isn't an easy decision and must be an act of hopelessness and desperation, a mother wanting the best for the child she isn't able to look after herself. I love watching programmes such as *Long Lost Family* on TV, and always have tears in my eyes when the families are reunited and there is a happy ending. But, as a psychological thriller writer, I can't help looking at the other angle, and asking myself what would happen if things didn't quite turn out as everyone wanted. What if the birth mother's existing family resent the long-lost sibling? Or if the long-lost sibling has struggled in life and resents the way their birth mother abandoned them but went on to marry and look after other children? Then, of course, I have to take this a little bit further; what if the jealously between the other siblings simmers and explodes, resulting in someone getting hurt? What if the long-lost child returns to get revenge on the mother who abandoned her? What if instead of a 'happy ever after' there was a terrible tragedy? This was the springboard for the plot of this book.

I hope you loved *The Family Reunion*, and if you did, I would be very grateful if you could write a review. I'd love to hear what you think, and it makes such a difference helping new readers to discover one of my books for the first time.

I love hearing from my readers – you can get in touch on my Facebook page, through Twitter, Goodreads or my website.

Thanks,

Karen

karenkingauthor.com

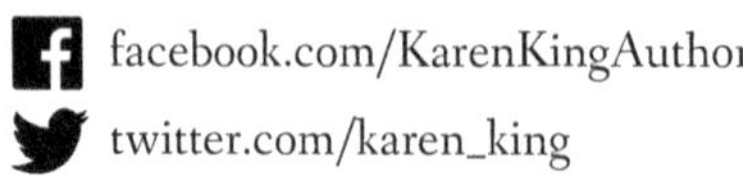

# ACKNOWLEDGEMENTS

There's a lot of things that go on in the background when writing a book, and a lot of people who help with the process. First and foremost, I'd like to thank my fantastic editor, Isobel Akenhead, and the Bookouture editing team of Alexandra Holmes, Dushi Horti and Becca Allen for all their hard work and constructive advice. A special thanks to Aaron Munday for creating yet another stunning cover. And to the fabulous Social Media team of Kim Nash, Noelle Holten and Sarah Hardy, who go above and beyond in supporting and promoting our work and making the Bookouture Author Lounge such a lovely place to be. You guys are amazing! Also to the other Bookouture authors who are always so willing to offer support, encouragement and advice. I'm so grateful to be part of such a lovely, supportive team.

Thanks also to all the bloggers and authors who support me, review my books and give me space on their blog tours. I am lucky to know so many incredible people in the book world and appreciate you all.

Massive thanks to my husband, Dave, for all the love and laughter you bring to my life, for being a sounding board for my ideas and for supplying the much-needed logic to some of them. Thanks also to my family and friends who all support me so much. I love you all.

Finally, a heartfelt thanks to you, my readers, for buying and reviewing my books, and for your lovely messages telling me how much you've enjoyed reading them. Without your support there would be no more books.

Thank you. xx